STUDIED DEATH

BOOKS BY BETSY STRUTHERS

The Rosalie Cairns Mystery Series:
Found: A Body. Toronto: Simon & Pierre, 1992
Grave Deeds. Toronto: Simon & Pierre, 1994

Poetry:
Running Out of Time. Toronto: Wolsak & Wynn, 1993
Saying So Out Loud. Oakville: Mosaic, 1988
Censored Letters. Oakville: Mosaic, 1984

A STUDIED DEATH

BETSY STRUTHERS

SIMON & PIERRE
Toronto, Canada

Copyright © 1995 by Betsy Struthers. All rights reserved.

No part of this publication may be reproduced, stored in a retrieval system, or transmitted in any form or by any means, electronic, mechanical, photocopying, recording, or otherwise (except brief passages for purposes of review) without the prior permission of Simon & Pierre Publishing Co. Ltd., a member of the Dundurn Group. Permission to photocopy should be requested from the Canadian Reprography Collective.

Editor: Tom Kluger
Cover Illustration: Steve Raetsen

Karen Connelly's poem, "Carefully, You Kill," can be found in her book *The Small Words in My Body* (Gutter Press/Kaleyard Books); Libby Scheier's "Dry Run" is in her book *The Larger Life* (Black Moss Press).

Printed and bound in Canada by Webcom.

The publication of this book was made possible by support from several sources. We would like to acknowledge the generous assistance and ongoing support of **The Canada Council** and **The Book Publishing Industry Development Program** of the **Department of Canadian Heritage.**

J. Kirk Howard, President

Simon & Pierre Publishing Co. Ltd., a member of the Dundurn Group

1 2 3 4 5 • 0 0 9 8 7 6

Canadian Cataloguing in Publication Data

Struthers, Betsy, 1951-
  A studied death

ISBN 0-88924-266-6

I. Title

PS8587.T67S78 1995   C813'.54   C95-931427-X
PR9199.3.S78S78 1995

Order from Simon & Pierre Publishing Co. Ltd.
2181 Queen Street East   73 Lime Walk   1823 Maryland Avenue
Suite 301   Headington, Oxford   P.O. Box 1000
Toronto, Canada   England   Niagara Falls, N.Y.
M4E 1E5   OX3 7AD   U.S.A. 14302-1000

*This one is for the Peterborough women writers for their support,
encouragement, and fellowship:*
*Jane Bow, Troon Harrison, Julie Johnston, Peggy Sample, Patricia Stone,
Florence Treadwell, Christl Verduyn.*

*My thanks also to Peter Callens and Joan Sangster
for their expert advice and assistance;
to the Ontario Arts Council for a Writer's Reserve Grant;
and always, Ned Struthers and Jim Struthers.*

so are set two reasons for the murder:

the lure of new experience,

political principle
— Libby Scheier, "Dry Run"

Carefully, lovingly, killing, an act

with its own science.
— Karen Connelly, "Carefully, You Kill"

ONE

For what felt like the hundredth time, I looked at my watch: 5:46 p.m. and now Sophia was over an hour late for her appointment. I checked the calendar posted on the bulletin board above my desk. Today was Thursday, October 14, and there was Sophia's name and "4:30 p.m." written in red ink so it couldn't be missed. Except by Sophia.

I picked up my phone and called the secretary whose office at the end of the hall acted as an unofficial waiting-room. Since the fall term began, I'd realized that posting office hours was a waste of time: students dropped in any time they were in the vicinity, and since the English Department offices were in the largest teaching building on campus – between the library and the largest residence, Jamieson Hall – they tended to drop in a lot. If the professor they'd come to see was busy, they'd hang around in Irene's cramped quarters, complaining to her while she tried to get on with her job in spite of them.

I let the phone ring six times before I hung up. Irene always left at 5:00 on the dot. I sighed, envying her her hours. Six short weeks ago, I'd been thrilled and enthusiastic at finally getting an academic posting – albeit a temporary one, an emergency sessional appointment to replace a faculty member who'd been unable to return from a year's sabbatical abroad. The official word was that he was ill and confined to bed for at least three months; the rumours said his illness was feigned, that he hadn't finished a book he was contracted to write and that he dared not come back until it was done. Whatever, his absence meant a job for me, in my home town no less.

"We're lucky to have you," the department chair, Lucy Easton, said when she called to offer me the job a week before classes began. They hadn't time to advertise the position, but Professor Easton knew my thesis supervisor at York and he had suggested she call me. I was almost finished writing my dissertation; I was back living at home with my husband, Will; I had no other commitments. Even a limited-term appointment was a foot in the academic door and would give me much-needed teaching experience. I was delighted to accept.

I had an office and two-fifths of a secretary's time, a computer and my own e-mail address. I also had to write and deliver three lectures a week to three different classes totalling 125 students. I met these same students in nine tutorial groups scattered throughout the week, including two evenings. I had to keep office hours open to deal with problems they might have and I had to attend the weekly department meetings as well as arrange meetings with the students for whom I was the academic supervisor.

Professor Easton had assured me that being an academic supervisor was a largely honorary role. I would be kept busy during registration week, helping first-year students arrange their timetables; after that, I might not see them again unless they were in my classes.

Sophia Demetris had been waiting at my office door on the first morning of registration week. She was so thin and stooped, she seemed a breathing shadow, her voice a whisper. At that first meeting and every time I'd seen her since, she was dressed in olive green overalls and a white T-shirt, both so big I thought she might have borrowed them from father or husband, although I soon learned she was living on her own. Her curly black hair was clipped close to the skull, but she usually kept it hidden under a black beret. She always had an armful of books she hugged as she plodded along, eyes on the floor, shoulder almost brushing the walls. In my office, she stood by the open door, ready to leave if the phone rang, if someone else came knocking. Even after six weeks, she wouldn't sit down.

In those six weeks, I'd learned to dread the quiet knock on the door, the hesitant approach in the cafeteria. She never said much and prefaced all her questions with the same muttered "I'm not bothering you, am I?" Her needs were multitudinous: how could she apply for a bursary, student loan, campus job? Could any of her community college credits from five years ago count towards a university degree? How could she balance a joint major in Media Studies and English? Could cross-listed courses be counted twice? Could she avoid taking the required first year course in Popular Culture and still get a degree in Media Studies? Could she avoid paying some of the student fees, especially those to support causes she didn't believe in, like the Sexual Assault Centre and the Aids Awareness Group? "When you make your bed, you have to lie in it," she frowned. "I don't care what those people do, but I don't see why I should have to pay for it." I thought she might be a member of one of the more conservative religions, but she also objected to having a levy exacted to support an ecumenical meeting on Sundays, a thin disguise for an evangelical group that had attained some power on the campus. She admitted that she had a learning disorder and needed arrangements for taping her lectures – did the university have taping facilities, how could she get the equipment, would she need the instructors' permission to tape their classes?

She seemed to have no friends; at least, every time I saw her on campus, she was alone. Against my own judgement and the advice of my colleagues in the department about fraternizing with students, I invited her to dinner a couple of times, but she always had excuses and never came. It was obvious that she wasn't eating well, or eating enough. Her face looked permanently bruised with exhaustion.

She would stand slumped against the bookshelves stuffed with my absent colleague's books while I made phone calls for her, tracking information through the various levels of bureaucratic and departmental procedures and regulations. I learned a little of the bare facts of her life: after dropping out of a community college fine arts course, she had worked in a flower shop for several years, living at home while she saved to come to university. Her father didn't approve of her ambition and her mother refused to support her, refused even to visit her in the one-bedroom apartment she'd found downtown. "They're old-fashioned," she said once. "They think I should live as if we were still in the Old Country, you know, at home until they find me a suitable husband. Although Mama says it's too late for that now."

"You're not that old," I protested. "You're not even thirty yet. Lots of women wait till they're in their thirties to get married. Or don't bother at all."

"It's not just age." She picked at a loose thread on the knee of her pants. "She says I'm too smart for my own good. Well, you know how it is."

The course content in the Media Studies program caused her — and, by extension, me — a lot of trouble. She was forthright about her reasons for coming to university as a mature student: she wanted a chance at a professional job, preferably in journalism, the field the Media Studies program trumpetted as part of the new emphasis on the career possibilities of an academic degree. All students in the program were required to take a course in Popular Culture. Sophia was appalled by the lecture topics which dealt with issues like feminism, pornography, gay rights, and abortion, among others. After the first few classes, her dismay was transformed into anger: the readings and direction of discussion, she informed me, were slanted to persuade students that *any* portrayal or practice of sexuality was not only acceptable but healthy. "It's wrong," she said flatly. "There's a lot more going on in the world than people fornicating. I don't know why we have to talk about *that* all the time."

I tried to arrrange to mediate an interview between Sophia and the course instructor, Frank Stanich, the new chair of Media Studies. Popular Culture was his baby; he'd designed and taught the course for years, "without interference from junior faculty," he roared the only time I managed to get hold of him. "If she doesn't like the course content, she shouldn't be in the program," he insisted before hanging up on me.

Matters came to a head when the class received its first assignment. Sophia edged into my office, the essay sheet in one hand, held by one corner as if contact with it would poison her.

"Look at this," she said. "It's disgusting." Her voice trembled on the edge of tears.

I looked over the short paragraph which set out guidelines for a 2,000-word essay in which the students were to describe their first encounter with sexuality and how that shaped their sexual identity.

"I said I wouldn't do this, and he," Sophia never mentioned

Stanich's name if she could help it, "said that if I didn't want to, I couldn't pass the course. It's prurient, that's all it is. No one has any business asking me such personal questions about my private life!"

The questions which provided an outline for the essay did seem intrusive, almost a primer for a what, where, when, why, and who of a tabloid article.

"Let me talk to him again."

"What's the use? You know he won't pay any attention to you. You're too junior. And a woman."

I raised my eyebrows. "Listen to you, Sophia. You're becoming a feminist in spite of yourself!"

"It's not feminism, it's just the way things are around here, and everywhere else, in my experience. But I refuse to be made a victim of one man's inflated opinion of his right to my personal life."

"What do the other kids in the class think?"

"Oh, them! They're all just out of high school and full of awe for their profs. They'll do anything if it means good marks. I'm sure some of the others aren't comfortable with this, but they won't do anything on their own." She fished a sheet of paper out of her backpack and handed it to me. "It's a petition requiring course changes on the grounds that the curriculum provokes a poisoned atmosphere for learning that could be considered harassment. If enough of the others will sign it, I'll take it to the Rights Committee and *make* Stanich revise the course or come up with an alternative required course. It's the only option I have."

"I see your point about this assignment; it does seem to be more intrusive than it needs to be. But let's talk …"

"Bull. You know as well as I do that Stanich will brush us off. He doesn't want to have to deal with this, but he'll soon find out I'm not a little girl about to cave in to him. I came to this university for an education, not to be jerked around by some pompous, opinionated, domineering man!"

She swept petition and essay guidelines off my desk and marched out of the office. I contemplated calling Frank Stanich and warning him, then thought again about the kinds of information the essay was designed to elicit. I didn't agree with Sophia's confrontational tactics and I felt that she had an overly sensitive regard to her privacy. But I could not deny that the questions verged on the indecent and did suggest an invasion into personal matters.

The petition certainly galvanized the student body. The college newspaper, *The Shield*, headlined an interview with Sophia in which she directed all her spleen against the program and its director, broadly hinting at harassment without any specific accusations. Unfortunately, she allowed herself to be sidetracked from the issue of the essay assignment into making sweeping condemnations of the course's emphasis on women's, gay, and various minority rights issues. The inevitable backlash erupted, with a spate of letters against her stand from the various spokespeople as well as from other students in the course. The real issue of invasion of privacy was lost in the debate over political correctness and free speech, a debate guaranteed to prod all the sacred cows into a stampede. Since the story and the furor broke, she hadn't been back to see me. That was why I was so surprised when she called me this morning, almost begging to meet me, and why I was so irritated now that she didn't bother to appear.

5:55 p.m. I spun my chair around and stared out the window at the fading light. My office was in the back corner of the fourth floor; my window a narrow rectangle that faced a blank concrete wall. If I got right up close to the glass and peered sideways along the length of the building, I could just catch a glimpse of the river which ran past the campus and into town. Alex Warren, whose office was next to mine, joked that we shared what used to be a washroom until space ran out and it had to be converted to house us. The room was much taller than it was long or wide; I barely had room to squeeze between my desk and the wallboard partition. Alex didn't seem to use his office much; he said he preferred to work at home. Once or twice, though, I'd heard him talking – well, to be honest, yelling – on the phone. He was writing a novel that he claimed would make him the Norman Mailer of Canada; he hadn't published anything in years and his tenure depended on the completion of this book. His ex-wife worked in Toronto as an executive in a bank and wasn't willing to move their children to what she called "the boondocks." In order to spend some time with his kids, he had managed to squeeze all his classes into the middle three days of the week. Except for weeks like this (the one preceding mid-term break was busy with essay deadlines and departmental meetings), he drove to the university early Tuesday mornings, spent two nights in a room he rented from another faculty member, and drove back to his apartment in the city on Thursday. This meant that he wasn't available for first-year advisees (or for department committee work, either, a sore point among some of my colleagues); and this meant that I had inherited Sophia Demetris from his roster of responsibilities.

6:00 p.m. and Will would be home, starting dinner. I rummaged through the papers stuffed in the basket on my desk and found the student directory. No telephone number for Sophia Demetris was listed. She must have forgotten our meeting, or been distracted. Yet she had been so insistent on seeing me today. She'd called twice to make sure I would be in my office at exactly 4:30. She wouldn't tell me what had upset her, but I could tell from the uncharacteristic animation in her voice that something had excited her, perhaps even frightened her.

I had a lecture to write. I had footnotes for my thesis to check. I didn't have time to babysit an adult, who should have learned by now to look after herself.

"Don't be so selfish," I said out loud. I made a face at my reflection in the dark mirror of the window pane. I didn't want to be responsible for Sophia Demetris, but I couldn't deny her my support. There, but for the accident of birthplace ...

Still, I'd waited long enough. I scribbled a note for her to call me at home. I'd leave it taped to my door and if she ever did show up, she could call me later. I yawned and heaved myself to my feet.

The phone rang. "Where've you been?" I snapped.

"Where are you?" a strange voice responded, a woman close to tears from the sound of it. In the background I could hear the chatter of TV cartoons.

"You must have the wrong number," I said, ready to put the phone down.

"Aren't you Rosalie Cairns?" she said. "The switchboard told me this was your number."

"Yes, that's me. How can I help you?" I sat down on the edge of my desk. I knew I had a couple of mature students in my first-year introductory literature course. This didn't sound like either of them, but I could be wrong.

"You can come and get this baby," she said. "She's supposed to have been picked up half-an-hour ago. I've got my own kids to get supper for, and my husband'll be home any minute. He'll have a fit if the kid's still here."

"Baby? What baby?"

"Look, I don't have time to fool around. Miss Demetris said you'd come to get Mara if she couldn't. If you're not here in fifteen minutes, I'll call Children's Aid, see how she likes that."

"Sophia Demetris? She has a baby?"

"As if you didn't know. I can't keep her here much longer. What's it going to be? You going to come get her, or do I call the cops?"

"Don't do that. I'll come right away. Where do you live?"

She gave me her address and hung up before I could ask her anything more. The street wasn't far away, just off the main road where the university bus ran. Luckily, I'd had an early class that morning and so had driven to work, rather than biking. I wondered how old the baby was, and if she needed a special car seat. Why would Sophia give the babysitter my name and then not tell me she'd done so? For that matter, how come she never told me she had a baby at all?

I quickly added the message that I'd gone to get her baby to the note before taping it to the door. I was waiting at the elevator when Alex burst through the doors to the stairwell. He stopped, panting, holding the door open for his companion, who stopped before entering the hall. I caught a glimpse of a tall, well-built man, his hair combed back from a broad tanned forehead. He wore a brown shirt, open at the neck, and matching pants. A huge bunch of keys swayed from a large ring on his belt.

"Beat you," Alex crowed. "Third time this week. You owe me a beer."

"Fair go." The two men shook hands. The stranger, seeing me, nodded in welcome, then turned to clatter back down the stairs. Alex leaned over the rail.

"You be careful," he shouted. "Man of your age could hurt himself."

The other snorted a laugh, but kept going.

"Who's that?" I asked.

"Bud Levin, head of security. Haven't you met him yet?" Alex bent slightly, panting to even his breath. "That's a lot of stairs."

"You ran all the way up?"

"Half-ran, half-walked. Bud and I have a bet on, see who can beat whom." He patted his stomach. "Great way to keep in shape."

"Great way to have a heart attack."

"It beats batting a little ball against the wall. It actually gets me somewhere."

"You don't have to be defensive. I wish I had time to play games." I sighed.

"Aren't you the cheerful one," he retorted. He glanced at my briefcase. "Working late?"

"I will be," I sighed. "I've been waiting for a student to turn up. Have you seen Sophia Demetris around today?"

"Sophia Demetris?" He paused. "Ah! The famous petition writer!"

"That's right. She was supposed to be *your* supervisee."

"Good thing she's not. I have enough trouble with good old Frank as it is."

"So you know what she looks like, then?"

"That's one student face that's etched on my brain. After the interview last week, more than a few people have pointed her out to me. I was co-opted into co-teaching that course, so I have to sit in on classes; she's missed so many of them I don't know where she gets the data to base her complaints on. I mean, the course outlines are pretty sketchy; you have to be in the room to understand the interpretations …"

"The essay assignment was very blunt," I disagreed. "I really do wonder how it could be excused as legitimate. You're on pretty shaky grounds if the petition does go forward."

"I know." He sighed. "After President Comaine rammed through that sexual harassment policy at the beginning of term, I've just been waiting for something like this to happen."

"Haven't you tried talking to Stanich?"

"Have you?"

I shook my head. "I've never even met him."

"There you go. Frank is not one to spend more time than he has to on campus. And he is not exactly tolerant of other viewpoints. Especially if they come from someone junior to him. I'm up for tenure this year, you know. I can't afford to have him on my bad side."

"So you just tolerate this sort of thing?"

"The other students aren't complaining. Maybe Ms. Demetris has some kind of problem about sex."

"Maybe Stanich does."

"Rosie, how very astute of you." He grinned, joking. "Besides, my experience has been that most of the kids lie; it becomes an exercise in creative imagining."

"That's no excuse and you know it."

"Look," Alex sighed. "People are supposed to come to university to expand their horizons, not to have their prejudices and small-mindedness confirmed."

"You just don't get it, do you?" I shook my head. "From the way I read the course outline, you can't pass the course if you don't hand in all the assignments, and if you don't pass the course, you can't get your degree in the field. And yet, you will agree that this requirement in particular appears to be almost deliberately offensive." I looked at my watch. "I don't have time for this now. We'll have to talk about it again. I've just got a call from her babysitter that I have to go and get her kid."

"I didn't know she had a kid."

"Makes two of us. But apparently she left my name as a contact."

"God, these students. Give them an inch and they'll take every advantage. That's why I told you not to get involved in her private life."

"She hasn't left me much choice. The babysitter's about to call Children's Aid if I don't turn up soon … If you see her, if she comes to my door, will you tell her to call me right away?"

"Sure thing. You better take the stairs, the elevator's stuck again on the third floor. And have fun with the kid." He began to whistle as he swung down the hall towards his office. I recognized the tune, one my mother used to sing, especially in spring: "Oh, What a Beautiful Morning."

"Yeah, right." I hurried off down the stairs, rooting through my briefcase for my keys, so distracted that I didn't see Irene Smith until I literally smashed into her. We grabbed each other to keep from falling and for a few precarious moments tottered on the edge of the step. Then I dropped my briefcase, spilling papers everywhere, and leaned back to catch hold of the stair railing. Irene regained her balance and immediately knelt to deal with the mess. I did too and managed to bump her head with my skull.

"Ouch," I shrieked, rubbing my forehead.

"Sorry, sorry," Irene spluttered.

"It's okay, it's my fault. I was in a hurry. Leave these, I'll pick them up. What are you doing here, anyway? I thought you always left on the hour?"

"I'm working for Professor Stanich in Media Studies, typing up his book. I only do it after office hours, in my time," Irene straightened, her hand balled in the small of her back.

"Did you hurt yourself?"

"Just cramps."

"Too bad." I shovelled the papers into the briefcase and snapped the lid shut. "You didn't see Sophia Demetris hanging about, did you?"

"No." She edged by me. For the first time since I'd started working on campus, she was not dressed in an "office outfit" – high-collared knit dress or tailored pant suit or starched blouse over a straight skirt accessorised by a neatly knotted silk scarf and matching polished low-heeled shoes – but was enveloped in an oversize sweatshirt worn over baggy corduroy pants and decidedly filthy runners. Her careful coiffure which tried to make the most of her shoulder-length mousy brown hair had come undone, her bangs hanging over her eyes. Her face was flushed; her lips bare of the pink gloss she normally affected. As her hand passed mine on the stair rail, I noticed that her nails were bitten to the quick.

"Are you sure you're all right?" I asked, impatient to be gone, but worried by the redness circling her eyes.

"Yes," she snapped. "Excuse me. If you don't mind, I've got work to do."

"If you see Sophia," I began, but Irene wasn't listening. She hurried down the hall, her hand still pressed to her spine. I'd had days like that, too. My keys were in my jacket pocket where I'd put them when I locked the car this morning. With briefcase under my arm, and keys in hand, I ran down the rest of the stairs.

The street I was looking for was in the area called the New North End, new because before World War II it had been farmer's fields. Returning soldiers needed homes for their new families, and whole neighbourhoods of small white wooden bungalows had been built to accommodate them. They all had the same plan: living room with a picture window at the front; two bedrooms at the back; kitchen, bathroom and minuscule dining room tucked in between. Some of the houses on this street had additions: a second floor looming high above the neighbours; a family room tacked on back or side; a garage or open car port attached to one side. The house I was looking for was one of these last. Its two-storey, two-car garage was larger than the original house and came so close to the lot line there didn't appear to be enough space for a person to walk between it and the next-door neighbour.

I parked on yellow leaves that carpeted the drive so thickly it was difficult to see where the lawn began. A couple of tricycles and a pink bike cluttered the lawn; a beach ball was wedged in the branches of a sprawling yew bush that hugged the foundation below the picture window. The drapes were closed. I opened the screen to knock on the door inside. The TV was still blaring, but the child I'd heard crying over the phone had settled down.

My knock was answered by a girl who looked about ten years old. She had long stringy hair and wore glasses whose bridge had been roughly mended with tape; chocolate circled her lips. The hem of her pink knit dress had come down and her once-white tights drooped about her knees.

"Hi!" I said brightly. "Is your Mom home?"

She turned away, yelling, "Ma. Some lady's here to see you."

I followed her into the house, but stopped in the doorway to the living room. It was spotlessly clean, the three-piece leather suite still covered in plastic. The girl plopped down on the floor in front of a giant TV set that took up most of one wall. It was flanked with shelves containing electronic sound and video equipment and an impressive library of tapes for both media. Two little boys were there already, staring raptly up at the screen. One small hand went back and forth from stainless steel bowl almost empty of popcorn to his mouth. The room smelled of candy and cigarettes. I heard the ping of a microwave and a wave of some sort of tomato sauce dish wafted through the room.

"Ma," the girl called again. "She's here."

The woman who came out of the kitchen was fat: not just overweight or heavy but hugely, magnificently fat. She wore what my mother always called a "muu-muu": a long, loose sleeveless shift made of vividly patterned cotton. Tendrils of black hair escaped from the tight knot that balanced precariously on the top of her head. Smoke from the cigarette stuck in the corner of bright red lips circled about her. Even outlined in blue shadow and thick mascara, the brows heavily lined, her eyes were almost invisible between the painted pillows of her cheeks.

I'm not very good at hiding my feelings. She flushed when she saw the look on my face, and one hand went up to touch the cigarette. She didn't remove it.

"It's about time you got here," she said. "I was just about to call the Children's Aid. I should've called them anyway. You're Professor Cairns, right? You look like a professor."

It was my turn to flush. I didn't think I looked any different than I ever looked: my hair long and too curly for a comb, but currently and at long last fashionable; wire-framed glasses; no make-up; a long black sweater worn over a tie-dyed skirt that reached to the top of the lace-up high-heeled boots I'd bought on a whim and then found surprisingly comfortable.

"I'm sorry it took me so long to find your house," I said. "I don't know this neighbourhood very well."

"That's as may be." She inhaled deeply. Some ash fell on the shelf of her bosom. She swept it away without looking. "I'm Joyce Holland, by the way. And I have to tell you, I'm real unhappy about this. I only took Mara 'cause Miss Demetris said it was an emergency. I told her I don't sit no more, I got enough to do looking after my own kids. She said she'd be here an hour ago. Good thing she left me your name. I was getting right frantic not knowing what to do with her."

"I don't know much about babies," I began.

She cut me off. "She's clean and she's fed. She'll probably sleep for a good long time. She doesn't fuss much, mostly naps. There's a couple extra diapers in the bag. You should be set for awhile anyway."

"Do you have Sophia's phone number or address?" I interrupted.

She squinted through the smoke. "You really don't know her well, do you? Funny she'd name you as next of kin. I always ask, you know, in case of problems like this."

"Next of kin! You're joking."

"That's what she said. Called you her sister. Well, how'm I supposed to know? I hadda take her word for it. Anyway, you gotta take the kid and get her out of here now. If my Gerry comes home and finds that baby here, he'll have a fit. He told me I wasn't to sit other people's kids any more, that we didn't need the money. It's hard to turn down the kind of money she offered though."

"She paid you a lot?"

"Well she'd have to, wouldn't she?" Joyce squinted at the stub of cigarette, then yelled behind her without looking. "Kevin, bring me an ashtray."

One of the little boys jumped up, grabbed a green porcelain bowl from the coffee table, and passed it to his mother, his eyes never leaving the screen.

"She paid you more than the usual rate?"

Joyce ground out the butt. "When I got a good look at the kid, I was sorry I took her cash."

"There's something wrong with the baby?" How would I cope with a sick baby, or one physically disabled in some way? I knew next to nothing about the care of infants.

"Oh there's nothing wrong with Mara. Not exactly. I don't hold with interfering in other people's business, calling in the law. Got enough trouble of my own to deal with. You just take that child back to her mother, and you tell her to look after her right. Christie, honey, go get the baby. She's in the back room."

"Oh, Mom, this is the best part."

"Christie," the woman's voice rose. "You do as you're told." She turned to me, sighing. "Kids these days, eh? I'll just go get that address for you."

I followed her into the kitchen. Three stools were lined up at the counter in front of three red plastic placemats, each set with dinner plates and cutlery. A bowl of spaghetti steamed on a hot plate by the microwave. On top of the refrigerator next to the wall phone was a pale blue basket filled with envelopes and various slips of paper. Joyce reached it down and pawed through it.

"Here you go," she said, handing me a slip of paper with an

address written in what I recognized as Sophia's handwriting.

I tried once more. "Can't you keep Sophia's child here until she shows up?" I asked. "I'll pay you extra."

"No, it's not possible." She turned and trundled back to the front hall. I had no choice but to go with her.

"But you agreed to sit this afternoon …"

"That was this afternoon. My kids are all in school in the afternoons and Gerry's not home."

I tried another tack. "What about Sophia's family? Couldn't you call them?"

"Yours is the name she gave me. I never met *Ms.* Demetris before."

"How come she left her baby with you then?"

She sighed. "I used to have a notice in the grocery store down the corner that I'd take care of kids, you know the kind of thing. I just forgot to take it down, I guess. And then she turns up right on the doorstep this afternoon. I should've known better, but I got a soft heart, that's my problem. And she said she'd pay double and in advance. It wasn't the money only, I could see she was desperate. So I took the baby, but I told her she had to pick her up before 5:00 p.m. I told her Gerry wouldn't like it."

"But if it's an emergency, wouldn't he understand? I'm sure Sophia's on her way right now. I live way over the other side of town; it's a long trip for her to come over there."

Joyce just shook her head. "I can't have that child in the house when Gerry gets home. He's funny that way, he don't like people coming into the house, not even little ones. And he wouldn't stand for it, the mother treating her like that, just leaving her with a stranger. He'd call Children's Aid right off, no question about it. I probably should've." She shook her head and glanced over her shoulder at her own children. "I know what it's like being stuck with a whining baby hour after hour. It ain't easy, specially if you're on your own. I felt sorry for the girl, I did, though she didn't want no pity, wouldn't sit down to a cup of tea. Just dumped the kid and left."

"Are you saying she's deserted her?"

"I don't know." Joyce busied herself lighting another cigarette. At the scratch of the match, one of the little boys looked up and stared pointedly at the glowing butt.

"When's Daddy coming home?" he asked. "You're not supposed to smoke in the house, you know. He said so."

"I want something to drink," the other added, without turning around, his hand still mechanically stuffing in the popcorn.

"Me, too."

"Well, go in the kitchen and get something. You're not helpless. There's soda in the fridge. And you don't need to tell your father what can't hurt him. Do you?" She glared at the child until he dropped his eyes. His brother shuffled out of the room, presumably searching for a drink.

Christie stomped back into the living room, carrying a blanket-wrapped bundle in both arms, a denim bag dangling over one shoulder. Joyce took the baby from her, unwinding the white knitted blanket as she did so. She gave the covering to Christie, who dropped it on the couch before returning to the cartoons.

Joyce caught the surprised look in my eyes. "It's my own blanket," she said. "My mother-in-law knit it for Christie before she was born and I've always kept it. Now this, this is Mara."

She handed the baby to me. Mara weighed next to nothing and put up with all the hauling around with very little fuss. She was dressed in yellow sleepers with an elephant embroidered on the chest. She seemed very thin to me, her cheeks hollow around the fist she'd stuffed in her mouth. Her skin was the colour of an unripe peach.

"She's got a lot of hair, I'll say that for her," Joyce said. She stroked the thick black downy curls that capped the little head, much like Sophia's own haircut. The baby blinked. "You should've seen my boys, bald as coots they were until they were nearly two years old."

"How old is she?" I asked. I shifted her from a prone position in my arms, to a more comfortable one, her head in the hollow of my neck, one of my arms supporting her bottom. Her little legs dangled. Her eyes were half-closed. She was so weightless, I was afraid that she might break.

"Ms. Demetris said six months, but it's hard to tell. She's right picky with her food." She picked up the denim bag. "There's a diaper in here, I washed the bottle and there's some formula. You know how to mix formula?"

"No."

"Well, the instructions are on the can." She held out the bag. I hitched it over my free shoulder. Mara murmured slightly, but didn't cry. Joyce noticed this, and smiled.

"She's a good baby. You won't have any trouble with her. Hardly makes a peep, 'cept when she has to be changed." Her face darkened. "You need to speak to that girl about mothering. She needs some lessons from somewheres. You tell her not to bring that baby back here, I won't be responsible for what happens."

"What do you mean?"

"Them as can't take care of babies, shouldn't have them."

"Lots of mothers work," I protested.

Joyce just shook her head. She opened the front door, shooing me out. "Oh good lord, Gerry's home. He'll come in through the kitchen, he always does. You hold Mara's head right close, he won't see her. He won't mind so much seeing you here. I can tell him you just dropped by, or something. Just don't let him get a good look at the baby."

"But ..." I was out the door. A black pickup truck was parked in the driveway, waiting on the slow rising of the automatic garage door.

Joyce glanced over at the truck, and waved, her face fixed in a smile. "Go on, go on, before he gets out, comes to see what's going on here. He's crazy about kids, he'll want to take a good look at her and if he does, lord only knows what he's likely to do. Get along now, I can't afford to risk no fuss."

"I don't have a car seat," I said, walking backwards down the walk.

"Just go," she said. "She'll be all right."

The truck disappeared inside the garage. With the ignition switched off, the roar from the TV welled out into the street. Joyce turned back into the house, slamming the door behind her. Across the street, a curtain in another bay window twitched.

TWO

I fumbled with keys, baby, and bag, all the time conscious of the house behind me, wondering what explanations Joyce was giving her husband for my presence.

We kept a blanket on the back seat to preserve the upholstery from our dog, a mixed-breed Labrador who constantly sheds hair. I hesitated for a moment but had no choice except to use it. I lay the baby on the passenger seat, while I folded the blanket into a little nest on the floor under the dash. She lay in it uncomplaining, although she was sucking so hard on her hand I could hear the little slurping noises she made. I wedged her in with her bag on one side, my briefcase on the other. I didn't know if she could roll or not, but I wasn't going to take the chance that she might somehow get wedged under the seat and hurt herself. It wasn't a very secure arrangement, but the best I could do. I hoped I'd be able to get home without any problems. It would be difficult to explain to anyone where this baby came from and why I didn't have a proper seat for her.

I started the car, switching on the headlights against the early dusk. I glanced down at Mara. She hadn't moved at all from the position I'd laid her in. I wondered if there was anything wrong with her. I thought babies were supposed to wriggle and squirm a lot. I wished I had more experience looking after one.

"Well, Mara, we're off on an adventure, aren't we?" I chirped, turning on the ignition.

The cough of the engine startled her into a squeak of fear. For a moment, her fist was out of her mouth, a small red "O" of shock. She squeezed her eyes tight and drew her legs up to her chest.

I put the car in gear and pulled away from the curb. The sooner I got home, the better. "It's all right," I soothed. "It's just the car noise." I thought for a moment and then began to sing. It surprised me slightly that I remembered not only the tune but all the words for "Rock-a-bye-Baby." It surprised me even more that Mara didn't scream, but simply shoved her fist back in her mouth and began chewing on it harder than ever. I hoped for her own sake that she didn't have teeth.

Between carrying Mara, her bag, and my briefcase, I had no free hand to unlock the back door. I resorted to kicking it with my foot, hoping to attract Will's attention. What I did attract was Sadie. Her deep bark ascended into a howling bay. I heard Will yelling at her to be quiet long before the door opened. Mara's face was buried in my shoulder, her little hands clutching so hard, I could feel the nails on my skin.

"It's okay," I said to her. "That's just how Sadie says hello. She makes a lot of noise, but she's really friendly."

"What have you got here?" Will asked. He took the bags and held the door open for me. I carried the baby into the living room. As soon as I sat down on the couch, Sadie was beside me, pushing her long nose into Mara's neck, trying to lick her cheek. The baby began to whimper.

"Sadie, behave," I ordered the dog. I stroked Mara's back. "It's okay, it's okay," I murmured. The fist was back in her mouth, stifling the cries.

"Who is this?" Will asked again.

I looked up at him. He dropped the bags on the floor by the corner bookshelves and leaned forward, peering through his glasses. In the last year, his beard had silvered completely, although his hair was still thick and dark. He'd changed from his workclothes into jeans and a sweatshirt with a baseball team logo on the front. There was an elastic bandage around one wrist.

"What did you do to yourself?" I asked.

"Oh, this." He waved the hand airily. "Sprained it trying to lift a kitchen counter into place by myself. Nearly dropped the fool thing. I'll have to be careful for a few weeks. It looks worse than it is. Anyway, who's the kid?"

"Mara Demetris," I said. "Her mother's one of my supervisees. Sophia Demetris, I'm sure I've told you about her. She was supposed to meet me this afternoon, but she never showed. I got a call instead from a babysitter that I was supposed to pick Mara up, so here we are."

"Where's this Sophia, then?"

"I don't know."

"Have you tried calling her?"

"She doesn't have a phone. As soon as the baby goes to sleep, I'll go over to her place and see if I can find out where she's got to." I stared down at Mara. She was so little, so helpless. How could her mother leave her with strangers? "The babysitter said she'd been fed and everything and should nap."

"And if she doesn't?"

Mara had settled into my lap, fist in mouth, eyes again half-shut. When I shifted my knee, she made a tiny mew of protest. Sadie thumped her tail on the floor.

"Sophia's bound to show up here sooner or later – after all, she told the babysitter to call me. And there's no point in taking the baby home, until we know where her mother is."

"Why did she tell the sitter to call you?"

I shrugged. "Beats me. I guess she was desperate to think of someone and, since she had set up a meeting with me anyway, she decided I'd take care of her baby for her. I didn't even know she had a child."

Will squatted down and spoke to the baby. "Hey, sweetheart, how you doing? Pretty confusing, isn't it?"

Mara shut her eyes completely.

"Friendly, isn't she?"

"She's just a baby," I nuzzled her head. "She's probably not used to men. Sophia doesn't have a partner, as far as I know."

"How do you get yourself into situations like this?" Will sighed.

"I can't help it if people think I'm reliable," I retorted. "What was I supposed to do, let the babysitter call the Children's Aid?"

"Maybe you should have. At least they'd know how to look after a baby."

"It's not that hard," I protested. "Besides, Sophia must have trusted that I'd look after Mara for her. I'm sure she'll turn up any minute. Oh dear."

"What?"

I held the baby away from me, looking down at the stain on my skirt. "She's wet."

"Oh, great," Will groaned.

"All babies get wet. Joyce said there were diapers in that bag. Get one for me, will you? And some dry clothes."

Will picked up the bag and rummaged through it. "You're in luck. Here's one of those disposable kind they advertise on TV all the time. Look at this, candy-stripe pink. How cute." He tossed the diaper over to me, along with a flannel sheet for a changing pad. I stood up, still holding Mara, and spread it on the couch.

"Come on, kiddo," I said. "You're going to have to help me here. I don't know how to do this very well." I untangled her fist from my hair and laid her down. She lay perfectly flat, but began to make a strange little sound, almost a yip that began to increase in volume as I unsnapped her sleeper. Sadie whined.

"There aren't any more pyjamas." Will picked out a pair of red corduroy overalls and a long-sleeved blue shirt printed with red and yellow ducks. "She can wear these for now." He held up a brown leather case. "Looks like your friend left her keys in here too."

With the sleeper off, I could see just how skinny Mara was. Her ribs were clearly visible under skin stretched almost to breaking while her little belly resembled a taut yellow balloon. When I ripped the tabs on her diaper, she began to cry in earnest.

"I don't like surprises," Will said. "I'll go and get dinner on the table and let you deal with it."

"Thanks a lot. Good thing we never did have babies. I can see who'd be doing all the changing."

"I'd get used to it if I had to do it all the time," Will defended himself. "It's just ... you know."

"Yeah, I know." I turned back to Mara. "You're really wet, aren't you, honey? Let's get out of these old clothes and put on something nice and dry."

I picked her legs up by the heels to ease the diaper off. Her bottom was covered with a red rash, some of the pimples crusted, others leaking into the folds of her skin. Her labia were so swollen and looked so sore that I felt a visceral tug of sympathetic pain.

"Will," I called. "I need some help here."

He came back into the living room, winced when I pointed out the rash.

"There must be some kind of ointment for this in the bag," I said.

Will dumped everything out. There was a plastic bag of clothes that must have been dirtied earlier in the day, a pink can of formula, an empty bottle and nipple, and one more diaper, but no medication of any kind.

"Maybe Joyce's daughter forgot the medicine," I suggested. "Sophia must have had something to deal with this. I wonder what we should put on it?"

"I've heard of diaper rash," Will said, "but I never imagined it would look that bad."

"I know. It's kind of like poison ivy, isn't it? Isn't powder what you're supposed to put on babies' bums? Maybe we could try some baking soda. It won't hurt her, at any rate."

Will brought the baking soda and I sprinkled some on. Mara whimpered, but lay perfectly still while I took care of her.

"What kind of mother would let a kid's rash get like that?" Will asked.

"I don't understand it." I fastened the clean diaper and sat Mara up. She screamed when I pulled the T-shirt over her head. I cuddled her again, rocking her back and forth until her cries descended into hiccups. Her fist was back in her mouth.

"You know," I said over her head, "Joyce Holland was talking about Children's Aid, too. She implied that she ought to have called, but didn't want anyone to get into trouble. And she kept talking about feeding her. She's awfully skinny."

We stared at each other.

"You think Sophia is abusing her?" Will asked.

"I don't like to think so." I paused. Mara's hair was a soft fuzz cushion against my cheek. "Maybe it's normal. All babies are different. How do I know if this one is particularly thin, or if that rash is particularly bad? Maybe I should call Karen."

"Karen Lewis? She doesn't have kids."

"She's always taking care of her nephew, and he's only a year old."

"How long do you think it'll be before this Sophia turns up?"

I shrugged, still rocking the baby. What secrets do you know? I asked her silently.

"What if she doesn't come back?" Will continued.

"Don't be ridiculous."

Mara yawned, her eyes drooping. They closed for a moment, then sprung wide again. I continued rocking, and spoke in a low sing-song. "Sophia's under a lot of pressure right now, coming to school, leaving home, moving. Maybe she needed some space, some time to herself."

"She could have asked you to babysit, instead of foisting the kid off on you like this."

"She might have been afraid I'd say no."

"And would you have?"

"I don't know." I watched the big brown eyes close and open, close and open. "There's one thing though …"

"What?"

"Well, Sophia has been going to classes and Joyce Holland said this was the only day she'd ever looked after Mara. So there must be someone else who's been babysitting. Maybe that's the person who hasn't been caring for her properly."

"And her own mother wouldn't notice that rash? I don't think so, Rosie. I think we should call the Children's Aid."

"I don't think that's fair until we hear her side of the story."

"Neglect isn't innocent."

"I know." I hugged Mara. "Let's talk to Sophia first, okay? Maybe she just doesn't realize." My voice trailed off.

Will was grim. "It doesn't take a medical genius to see that rash is causing a lot of pain."

"You know how it is, though. With abuse, it's like you're guilty until proven innocent. Once the law gets involved, she might lose her.

I think we have to give her the benefit of the doubt. If we don't believe what she tells us, then we'll call someone."

"I don't like it," Will said.

"I don't either. But what choice have we got?"

"We can't give the baby back to her, if she's the one who's been treating her like this."

"I know. But we should at least give her a chance to explain. She left her with us for a reason, after all."

"She's a baby, for heaven's sake," Will said. "She's not like a stray cat. Her mother can't just leave her with any old person and you just can't take her in."

"I'm not that old," I tried to joke.

"You know what I mean. It's not like she even knows you very well. For all she knew, you could have a history of abuse and violence. Or I could have."

"Don't be silly. She knows I'm not like that."

"How?"

I didn't have an answer for that question. "I wasn't talking about keeping the baby, I'm only suggesting we wait a couple of hours, maybe the night. I'll go over to Sophia's house as soon as Mara settles down and I'll find out where she is: she might even be there now, worried about what she's done."

"And what am I supposed to do while you're gone?"

"As long as she's asleep you don't have to do anything. But there's a bottle and formula; you could feed her. Sing her songs. If Sophia's home, I'll bring her right back. If she's not there – well, it's a good thing she did forget her keys. I'll need to get some more diapers and clothes."

"How long do you plan to keep this baby here?"

"She doesn't have anywhere else to go." Mara had given up the struggle. She lay so still that only the slight twitching of her eyelids and the faint pulse that throbbed visibly on her temples proved that she was only sleeping.

I gently laid her down, tucking the afghan around her, and surrounding her with cushions so she wouldn't roll off on to the floor.

"I'll go right away," I whispered. "I'll be back before she wakes up."

"I could go," Will offered.

"Sophia doesn't know you," I pointed out. "She might not believe you are who you say you are. She'll talk to me. And if she's not there – and I can't believe she'd leave Mara too long – I'll see if I can find something or someone to tell us where she is. I know she has family down in the city."

"You be careful," Will warned. "You have a habit of getting into things."

"Don't worry." I leaned over and kissed Mara's forehead. She twitched and moaned. I straightened abruptly, and headed for the stairs. The sooner I found Sophia and got Mara into proper care, the better it would be for all of us.

THREE

Will was reading the instructions on the can of formula when I came back downstairs, having changed into jeans and a heavy fisherman knit sweater Will's mother had made for him last Christmas. It was too small for him, but fit me perfectly. In the kitchen, bottle and nipple steamed in a pan of water on the stove. Will had settled in the rocking chair where he could watch Mara sleep.

"I'll be back as soon as possible," I said, pausing at the door. Sadie thought it was walk time. She sat expectant on the hall rug, her jaws open in a wide grin, her mouth hanging. I patted her. She realized she wasn't going anywhere. With a great sigh, she flopped down, head on her paws.

"No problem," Will said. "I want to meet this Sophia Demetris."

"You can always call Karen if you have any problems with the baby."

"I'll be okay. You be careful."

"If she's not there, I'll come right home."

Although the day had been unseasonably warm, there was a chill in the early darkness that announced that winter was not far away. Mist rose in the arcs of light under the streetlamps. Under the rustle of leaves falling from the maples that lined our street, I could hear the murmur of water rushing over the dam. I stood looking down through the darkness of the park towards the glint of the river. It was the same river that bisected the university campus farther upstream; the same river in which a woman jogger had accidentally drowned two months ago. I shivered. I myself had once found a body in the shallows; I didn't dream about it very much any more, but sometimes the cries of gulls brought back the vision of her corpse with a sickening immediacy. Geese clamoured overhead, racketing through the night as they followed the line of water south in faithful pairs. They made the journey twice a year, the sound of their passing the true knell of the season's change. I kicked through the drifts of leaves on the lawn. One of us would have to rake this weekend. If it didn't rain. Or snow.

Sophia lived in one of the two highrise apartment buildings that punctuated the downtown skyline. They had been built on the very edge of the shopping district, on a street facing two bars and the bus terminal. Their ground floors were given over to businesses: a health club, an all-night variety store, a flower shop, and a beauty salon. The lobbies were brightly lit aquariums lined with metal mail boxes. The area in front of each building was a bare concrete expanse that lapped right up to the display windows of the stores where a line of litter marked the tide of people passing by.

It was a late shopping night so I had a hard time finding a parking spot; all the guest spaces in front of Sophia's building were full and I had to circle the block three times before I could find a place to pull in. It wasn't just the extended shopping hours that had so many people downtown; Thursday night was a big night in the bars, when local bands warmed up the audiences for the travelling road shows that came in on Fridays and Saturdays. Still, for all the cars lined up at the curbs, there were few people on the street. Five high school boys in team jackets laughed as they crossed against the light on the corner, forcing a station wagon to a halt. One flipped his finger at the driver, a bald, business-suited man who glowered out his open window, but said nothing. He caught my eye and looked quickly away as he gunned the engine, wrenching his car into a right-hand turn. I locked my Honda and, with Sophia's keys in my hand, walked up to her building.

Inside the vestibule, I consulted the scrap of paper Joyce Holland had given me. Although the building had twelve floors, Sophia's apartment was in the basement. There were only three keys in the brown holder Will had found. One opened the security door. The interior lobby was tiny and stark: two elevators flanked a black plastic garbage pail centered beneath a sand-filled ashtray bolted to the wall. Fluorescent lights glared off the white-tiled floors and plain white walls. A red bulb blinked over a door whose tempered glass pane was scarred by some violent confrontation. I figured it led to the fire escape. The handle turned easily and opened onto a bleak stairwell made of unpainted concrete and metal steps. The door sighed shut behind me. The lighting in here was equally harsh. I took a deep breath, and started down.

The whole flight clanged with each footstep. I didn't know if I only imagined it swayed as well; at any rate, I kept close to the wall, hand on the iron tube railing although it was sticky with damp or something less healthy. The stairwell stank of air closed in too long, of concrete painted before it had had a chance to dry properly. I paused on the landing: had I heard the fire door swish open above me?

"Hello?" I called up the stairs. There was no answer, no footfall to set the steps singing. Get a grip, I said to myself.

The door at the bottom was equipped with a fire bar and a hand lettered sign: "Kip Close." I pushed the bar gingerly and stepped out into a hall even more depressing than the one above. Painted mushroom brown, it was ill lit by a series of recessed ceiling lamps, half of which seemed to have lost their bulbs. Another sign, this one printed on stiff grey cardboard, pointed towards storage lockers and utility rooms at the unlighted end of the corridor, to the janitor's suite and six numbered apartments at the other.

Sophia's apartment was in the middle of this inhabited stretch. I could hear music playing, some kind of modern classical piece with a lot of strings, chimes and rhythmic surf. However, when I knocked on the door, no one answered. I knocked louder, this time announcing myself. Perhaps I pushed against the door as well in my frustration; at any rate, it cracked open.

"Who're you?" demanded a male voice behind me. A hand clutched my shoulder.

I swung around, raising my fist, ready to fight.

"Okay, okay." He let go of me, raising both hands to shoulder height and stepping out of range of my feet or fists. Thin as a cadaver and not much taller than me, he wore a grey sweater over a white singlet and grey polyester pants held up by a string belt. What hair he had was long and slicked back from his forehead; the teeth revealed by his grimace of a smile were yellowed and broken. I could smell cigarette smoke and cheap red wine.

The door of the apartment across the hall was wide open. Eyes peered at me from the gloom within, a gloom lightened only by the blue flicker of a television playing without sound.

"I'm Tran," my assailant introduced himself. "Building manager. Who you looking for?"

"Sophia Demetris," I said. I nodded toward the door. "Is this her place?"

"She's not here."

Was this a question or statement? "The door's open," I protested.

He shook his head. "Not here," he repeated. "You come see about the baby?"

"That's right," I nodded. "Do you know where Ms. Demetris is?"

"Bout time someone came," the man grumbled. "I told her she didn't take care of that baby, I'd call up the law."

"I'm not ..." I began, but he continued without stopping, "All day, that music going on and on, and the baby crying. My wife said, she leaves the baby too much alone. I told her, one more day and I call the cops." He grinned at me.

"She didn't leave her alone," I protested.

Tran winked. "Yeah, yeah sure. You take the baby, I don't call no one." He turned to go back inside.

"Wait a minute. I'm looking for Ms. Demetris. Maybe you know where I can find her?"

He shrugged. "Inside, maybe. Upstairs, next building, laundry." The door of his apartment slammed shut behind him.

I turned back to Sophia's room. Calling her name, I pushed the door open further. There was no answer. I hesitated for a minute. Mara needed diapers, more formula. I stepped inside.

It was dark except for a red light blinking as the cassette turned in the deck perched high on a piece of furniture on the opposite side of the room from where I stood. I ran my hand along the wall to the right of the door, located the switch, and turned on a bare bulb hanging low over a table in the centre of the room. Sophia either didn't care to make her apartment more of a home, or was simply a terrible housekeeper. There were no pictures or posters to brighten up the walls whose cream paint had faded in yellow uneven streaks. Without shelves, books had been left in haphazard piles on the floor and the drawers of the dresser on which the tape deck sat were pulled half-way out, their contents a colourful jumble of nylon, cotton, and wool. I could see into the kitchen alcove on my left; the sink was piled with dishes and the cupboard doors were open revealing a jumble of boxes, cans, jars, and a stack of pots. On my right was another alcove, separated from the rest of the room by a long green velvet curtain that sagged from brass rings. The only window was high on the wall above the dresser; it was shrouded with a piece of the same heavy material, blocking out all light. The edges of the curtain had not been finished and various threads swayed in the draft from the open door.

"Sophia?" I called again. "It's me, Rosie Cairns."

With a whirr and click, the music ended and the tape turned over. A rush of tide and the calling of gulls filled the room. I crossed over to the bureau and turned it off. The machine was hot to the touch; it must have been playing for hours. I stared at the drapes which hid the alcove; with everything else in such disorder, why were they pulled shut?

I delayed looking behind them by examining the rest of the living room. It didn't take long: the only furniture besides the presswood dresser, whose pine veneer was beginning to peel, was a dinette suite, consisting of two chairs upholstered in yellow plastic and a table whose grey formica top was half-hidden under a blizzard of papers, some blank, some neatly typed. The typewriter itself was an old IBM Selectric; it sat square in the centre of the table, beside a pile of books bristling with tags of post-it notes. Wedged in the typewriter was half a piece of paper, roughly torn. I cranked it free and found that it was the bottom half of Joyce's ad; it had a brief description of amenities ("fenced yard"; "hot lunches"); strips with Joyce's phone number, several of them missing, ribboned the bottom. Sophia must have stuck it in the typewriter to save it, but why would she tear off the top half with the address?

The door next to the kitchen opened into the bathroom. The tub was half-filled with water in which diapers floated; the stench of ammonia stung my eyes. More diapers and some baby clothes hung over the shower curtain rail. The top of the toilet tank was off; a towel had been draped over it and the lidless seat. The narrow ledge of the pedestal sink was crowded with bottles of baby oil, shampoo, and various lotions. The grout along the edge of the tub and on the walls was black with age; the floor was buried under a layer of discarded towels, underwear, and more baby things.

I backed out of the room and shut the door against the smell. It was pervasive, joining with odours from the kitchen I didn't feel the need to investigate. Before I could think twice about what I was doing I crossed the room and pulled the velvet curtain aside, the brass rings carolling along the rail.

I didn't realize I was holding my breath so that the force of my sigh of relief at finding the alcove empty surprised me. A single bed, its sheets and blankets bunched at its foot, filled most of the space under a window covered again by the green velvet so that no light seeped through. Separated from the bed by a strip of floor so narrow one could stand or walk only sidewise between them, was a crib.

A cage was more like it. A piece of thick unpainted plywood lay across it, pushed half to one side for the moment, but the number of metal clamps laid on top testified to its use as a lid. One of those nursery activity centres had been screwed to the crib railings; an empty bottle lay on the sheeted mattress along with one stuffed toy – a blue rabbit. An odour of urine and old milk prevailed. Sickened, I let the curtain drop and turned away.

"Don't scream." A man had come into the apartment behind me. He held one hand to his lips, the other held in warning. "I'm not going to hurt you."

I backed up against the doorframe. "Who are you? What do you want?"

"You a friend of Sophia's?" He stepped further into the room, a big man, old, balding, a fringe of thick white hair combed back from a broad face that even in the bare light of the overhead bulb was ruddy with weather or high blood pressure. Gray eyebrows bristled over intense dark eyes. His nose was broad and squashed slightly to one side as though it had been broken in a fight long ago and left to heal improperly. His chin sagged in loose jowls away from pronounced cheekbones; either he hadn't shaved at all or was one of those men who needed constant recourse to a razor. He wore a long black leather coat over a dark suit and white shirt. He'd kept his gloves on.

"So," he repeated. "You a friend? I'm not going to hurt you or nothing like that. I'm her father: John Demetris."

The hand that had commanded my silence dropped, held out now in welcome.

"Thank goodness," I said, shaking it. "You're here for the baby? Where's Sophia?"

He ignored both questions. "How do you know her? You in school with her?"

"Not exactly. I'm her academic supervisor."

"What's that mean? You a professor, or something?"

"That's right. I help Sophia out with her courses. But she's left Mara with me …"

He interrupted, scowling. "You're one of them filling her head up with ideas, then, stuff she don't need to know. Look at this place," he waved his arm about. "A pigsty. Her mother'd have a fit, she could see this. She brought Sophia up right, though you'd never be able to tell it from this. That girl's been cleaning house since she was ten years old."

"Maybe that's why she let her own place go," I snapped.

"You approve of living like this?" he snorted, then wrinkled his nose. "God, it stinks."

I wasn't about to get into an argument over the state of the apartment. "Look, I'm only interested in finding Sophia and getting Mara looked after properly. Are you here to take her home?"

His face grew even darker. "I don't know nothing about Mara. I'm here for Sophia."

"But Mara's your granddaughter. Sophia's baby."

"And who else's? In my day, it took two to make babies, though god knows what damn fool stunt that girl's been up to. She used to be a good girl, did what she was told, listened to her father. Then she went and spoiled it all."

"How can you talk about your own daughter like that? Don't you care for her?"

He turned on me, his mouth twisted with rage. "Who are you to talk to me about Sophia? I love that girl, I would have done anything for her. I ask her to do this one thing ..."

"What thing?"

"Get rid of that brat," he spat out the words, then dropped his eyes.

"It's not the baby's fault," I said, "she couldn't help being born. And Sophia must have wanted her."

"Doesn't look like she's doing a very good job taking care of her," Demetris sneered. "You hear what that DP across the hall said about the crying going on for all hours? You see the cage she got rigged up for it? That girl was not cut out to look after a kid on her own. I told her. I told her there'd be trouble."

I looked back at the crib, heart sinking. How desperate Sophia must have been to leave her baby girl alone like this while she went out to work and school. How careful she had been to make sure Mara would not be harmed. Unless the building burned, a small voice whispered inside my head. Unless someone broke in.

I turned back to Mr. Demetris. "What do you mean, trouble?"

He shrugged. "Mother's sick. I come to take Sophia home to see her."

"You're not answering my question."

"I gotta go."

"Sophia left Mara with a babysitter with instructions that I be called if she couldn't pick her up on time. The baby's at my place right now until I can find your daughter."

"That's the new thing at colleges? Leaving infants on their own? Some kind of test to see if they can survive?"

"She's with my husband if you must know."

"Husband?" His eyebrows shot up. "I thought you must be one of those feminists, who won't have anything to do with a man."

"I beg your pardon?" I stared him down. He had the decency to drop his eyes, but his tone was still belligerent.

"Take her to an orphanage," he muttered. "It's where babies like that belong."

"She's your granddaughter. Your own flesh and blood."

"I told you that kid's nothing to do with me. I wash my hands of it. I wouldn't be here but the mother's taking on so, I hadda come get Sophia."

"And what was Sophia supposed to do with the baby if she went with you? Would you let her bring her along?"

"Of course not. She's none of my business. Or yours neither."

"It is my business," I insisted, almost shouting. "You can't just leave her with me."

"You tell Sophia her mother's sick." Demetris opened the door.

"Wait a minute ... the baby."

The door slammed shut behind him.

FOUR

I couldn't leave that apartment fast enough. I rifled through the papers on the table in the vain hope that there might be something there to indicate Sophia's whereabouts, but all I found were printouts from tapes of lectures, pages of notes, study plans, and a work schedule for shelving books at the library during the upcoming reading break. I helped her get that job. I glanced back at the bed alcove and shivered: did she really leave Mara caged in there while she worked and studied? There was a half-empty bag of paper diapers wedged in the corner by the dresser; I filled it with baby clothes, cans of formula, and a box of plastic liners and nipples. At the last minute, I took the tape that had been playing when I arrived. I remembered my friend Karen telling me that certain music soothed her nephew into sleep; if Sophia still hadn't turned up, we might need something familiar to quiet Mara.

"Will, how's the baby?" I called as soon as I opened the door, then bit my tongue with vexation as a wail answered me. "Is Sophia here?" I continued in a quieter voice. I dumped the diaper bag on the kitchen floor and went into the living room which was still in half-darkness, only the bookcase lamps lit.

The first thing I saw was Will, pacing back and forth, muttering softly to the baby in his arms. She'd already filled her mouth with her fist and clung to him, her little body shaking with suppressed cries.

"There, there," Will kept saying. "It's okay, nothing to worry about, little girl. Relax, relax. It's only Auntie Rosie. There, there." In the same soothing tone, he continued, "Rosie, meet Mara's grandma – she's come to take her home." With a nod of his head he indicated a woman half-hidden in the shadows of the front hall door.

"Mrs. Demetris?" I stepped forward, my hand out.

The woman who came forward to greet me was not ill, looked as if she'd never been ill a day in her life. She was tall, taller even than Will. "Statuesque" was the word for her, and "regal": she was perfectly coiffed, her silver hair cut short in curls that looked almost natural. Make-up accentuated her high cheekbones and brought out the vivid greenness of her eyes – so green, I wondered if she wore tinted contact lenses. A heavy bead necklace drew attention to her smooth, unwrinkled neck and echoed the pattern of the earrings that dangled from each ear. She wore a green business suit, the skirt fashionably cut just above the knees; her high heels may have been dyed to match. A cheery jingle of narrow gold bangles accompanied her movement as she reached forward to answer my greeting. She wore rings on every finger.

"Not Sophia's mother, no," she smiled. She nodded to Mara. "Her father was my boy, Martin. I've come to take the little one home."

Will picked up the baby's bottle from the cedar chest we used for a coffee table, and, still pacing, brought it close to her mouth. She reached out and batted towards it, her mouth opening in a round "O" of anticipation. We all watched her drink. After a few swallows, she let the nipple drop away, and lay back, a drool of milk slipping down her chin. Will wiped it away. "Every time I try to feed her, the same thing happens. She only takes a little bit and then stops."

"Did you mix the formula right?"

"I followed the instructions exactly."

"Maybe she's not hungry."

"Let me try," the grandmother said.

For some reason, I was reluctant to see her take the baby. Will must have felt the same way. He continued to rock her back and forth. "She's quiet for now," he spoke in an even, unhurried voice that seemed to soothe Mara. "Let's wait a minute and try again. Rosie, this is Barbara Lock; she arrived just before you did. And Mrs. Lock, this is my wife, Rosalie."

"Dr. Cairns." Her rings dug into my palm. "I'm so happy to make your acquaintance, so happy that you could be a help to Sophia." Her lipstick was very red.

"I'm not a doctor yet, " I said distractedly. "Won't you sit down for a minute? Do you want a drink? Tea? Coffee?"

She looked at her wrist. One of the bangles apparently was a watch, although it was no wider than any of the others. "It's getting late, now," she shook her head. "It's a long drive back to the city and it's been a long day for me and for Mara. I'll just take her few things and be on my way."

"Just a minute. I'm a bit confused here. You're Mara's father's mother?"

"That's right."

I turned to Will. "Have you heard anything from Sophia?"

He shook his head, his eyes on the baby. She was wriggling slightly, drawing her legs up and letting them relax. She'd begun to whimper again.

"Mrs. Lock," I began, but she interrupted me.

"Call me, Barbara, won't you? All my friends do."

"Barbara." I stopped for a deep breath. "Sophia asked me to take care of Mara."

"Yes, yes. I know all of that. I've just come from the babysitter, Mrs. Holland, that is. Her husband," and the fine nose sniffed in disdain, "was very rude. He tried to deny that Sophia had left the baby there, but I insisted on speaking to his wife. She told me you had her."

"You knew about Joyce Holland?"

"Mmmm."

"Sophia called you?"

Barbara looked at her watch again and then at Will. "She's alright now? She's asleep?"

"Not quite."

"How did you know about the babysitter?" I persisted. I thought of the poster torn from the typewriter, and the open door. Perhaps John Demetris had not been the only visitor to the apartment before me.

Barbara evaded the question. "I'm her grandmother. You have to give her to me. I have more rights to her than you do."

"Excuse me," I objected. "But Sophia left Mara in my care. I can't just hand her over to just anyone on their say so."

"That's right." Will spoke up so sharply that the baby let out a small cry.

I continued, "How do we know you are who you say you are? Sophia never mentioned your name to me."

"Or Mara's either," Will muttered.

Barbara picked up a handbag from the couch. Like her shoes, it was made of green leather, a large bag, halfway between a purse and a briefcase. The initials *BRL* were stamped in gold below the clasp. She unzipped a compartment along the side and withdrew a business card and a colour Polaroid. She handed me the card first.

"It's my own company," she said.

The card was embossed with the picture of a small green house under a big green tree. *Lock Realty*, it read. *Barbara Ruth Lock, Realtor*. The address was upscale, on Avenue Road in the north end of Toronto.

"My home address is underneath." Barbara pointed to the second address in very small print in the bottom left-hand corner. "That's in the Annex," she said. "Do you know the area?"

"I grew up there," I answered. I put the card down and took the Polaroid.

"You be careful with that. It's the one picture I have of Martin and Sophia together. Mara will want it when she's older." Barbara stroked the sleek surface with one long red nail. "The name itself is proof: Sophia named her after my boy: Martin, Mara – the connection's obvious."

I took the photograph and held it to the light. It was Sophia all right, smiling her familiar tight smile. Although the boy had his arm around her, she didn't look as if she enjoyed his embrace. Her arms were held at attention at her side, her body arched slightly away from him. Martin certainly took after his mother: he towered over the girl.

"And he isn't a basketball player," Barbara spoke as if I'd made some comment. "He takes after me, a studious boy. He could have gone into medicine at McGill, he had the marks for it and I would have helped out, even with the baby. He knows that. If he'd had a chance, he would have told Sophia that; she didn't have to run away."

"Where is he now?" I asked.

She didn't answer but busied herself with a crumpled handkerchief which she used to wipe her eyes. She did it carefully so the mascara wouldn't smudge.

I looked at the picture again. The two figures stood on a wooden wharf, behind them a vast blue expanse of lake and water, a ferry at dock to their left, a smudge which might be islands on the horizon. They were both dressed in jeans and sweatshirts. Sophia had a bicycle clip around one ankle, Martin dangled a yellow helmet in his free hand. The bikes were not in the frame.

"That was taken on Canada Day, two years ago," Barbara explained. "We went over to the Island for a picnic and to watch the fireworks over Ontario Place. We all were there: my husband, Walter, Martin and Sophia, my other boy Daniel, my daughters Marsha and Lisa, and Lisa's twins, and Daniel's friend's son and his girlfriend: the whole family. It was the last time we were all together."

"What happened?" Will was rocking Mara now, jogging her. She seemed to like it; at least, she didn't stop sucking at the bottle.

"I don't know." Barbara shook her head. "I guess Sophia must have found out she was pregnant and for some reason couldn't or wouldn't tell Martin. She just disappeared, left work, left home. Martin was frantic. He went to the house to talk to her father but the man threatened to shoot him if he didn't leave them alone."

"Why?" I peered at the young male face in the photograph. He was very ordinary looking, even attractive. A long lock of dark hair fell over his left eye and his chin was dimpled. His smile was open and infectious.

"John Demetris is a bitter man. And prejudiced. He treated Martin like trash. As if I couldn't buy and sell him twice over and not even notice. Just because we're not Catholic, or something. I don't know. How do you explain prejudice?" Barbara reached for the photograph. I handed it back. She sighed. "I should have realized there'd be trouble when Martin started going with her. We used to live next door and Sophia and my twins were best friends all through high school. The hours they spent on the phone! And never once was Sophia allowed to visit in our house or have the girls over to hers. Never once!"

"Where's Martin now?" I repeated. "Did he come here with you?"

She took a deep breath and squeezed her eyes shut. "What that girl did to my boy is hard for a mother to forgive. He was always a little wild, but after she left, he was uncontrollable. He got himself into trouble and left home."

"What sort of trouble?" Will asked.

She shook her head. "Walter says he won't have him back. Walter's in government, a *civil* servant, he can't afford to be always cleaning up the boy's messes." She caught her breath. "I don't care what anyone says Martin has done or what he's been up to. If he comes home and sees his little girl waiting for him, you can bet he'll straighten right up. So that's why I'm here, why I've come for the baby."

"So Sophia told you about her then?" I asked. "She's been in touch with you?"

Will put the bottle down and shifted Mara so that she lay now with her head buried in his neck, her fist in her mouth. He patted her on the back. "I sympathize with you," he said. "It must be hard not knowing where your son is. But surely you can see it from Sophia's point of view? We have to wait for her to tell us it's all right for you to take the baby."

"I've got the right," Barbara snapped. "I'm her blood kin. But if my word's not good enough for you ..."

This time she pulled a letter from her bag.

"Sophia wrote to you?" I reached for the note, scrawled on a piece of ordinary typing paper. It was Sophia's writing, for sure.

"I didn't want to have to show it to anyone. It doesn't reflect well on her."

I skimmed through, reading aloud certain phrases. "*I'm sorry to do this ... I'm desperate for money ... it's all Martin's fault. The baby is six months old now. I call her Mara. I thought I could do this on my own, but I just can't. I can't go to my parents, you're all the family I've got. Please send me $1000 ...*" The address she gave was a box number in the central post office in town.

"How did you find her?"

"She phoned me." Barbara twiddled with the clasp of her bag. "I wrote to her at that box number. I told her that Martin was gone, but asked her to come live with us, her and the baby. I told her I wouldn't send any money until I saw them both. So she phoned." Her voice trailed off.

"And?" I prompted.

"She said if I didn't send the money, I'd never see the baby, ever. Martin was my youngest, the light of my life. That baby is all I have left of him." Her voice trembled.

"Are you sure," Will said, "that she's your son's baby? Maybe Sophia …"

"That child is flesh of my flesh," Barbara snapped. "Sophia as good as told me so. Read the letter, see for yourself."

"If she didn't tell you her address, how did you find her?"

"I knew she was at the university, she always talked about getting a degree, bettering herself. She hated working in that flower shop, hated depending on her father. I guessed she'd enrol in the English Department, she always loved to read, so I visited the secretary there. We had a lovely chat." She smiled.

"You talked to Irene Smith?"

"I think that's the name. I told her I was the mother of Sophia's best friend in the city, not exactly a lie. And that I was trying to arrange a surprise party for my daughter, and, since Sophia had no phone and I had to be here on business, I thought I'd drop by and invite her. Well, the secretary was only too happy to give me the address."

"Just like that?"

"It was a long conversation. And," Barbara smoothed down the skirt of her suit, "I guess I looked respectable enough that she believed my story."

"She's not supposed to give out student addresses."

Barbara shrugged.

"So you went to her apartment and spoke to her?" I persisted. I wondered if this was the reason Sophia had been so anxious to see me this afternoon. "She told you you could take Mara? Where is she now?"

Barbara's tongue ran over her lips, tasting the gloss. She reached over and patted the baby. Will stepped back.

"I went to her place," Barbara admitted, "but she wasn't there. The caretaker let me in."

"That's why the door was left open," I said. "You didn't have the key for the deadbolt to lock it when you left."

"You've been there?"

"Just now."

"You saw what a mess it was? You saw that, that *cage* thing?"

I nodded, biting my lip.

"You wouldn't leave a dog in a place like that," Barbara shook her head. "It's not right. I don't know what's got into Sophia's head. I saw that notice about a babysitter. What kind of babysitter could it be, I asked myself, that a mother like this would leave her baby with? I determined right then and there to take that baby away with me no matter what, to give her a good home, bring her up in her daddy's place. Looks to me like Sophia will be well rid of the burden. She shouldn't have tried to carry it all alone, she should have let Martin be responsible, let me help." Her voice rose.

"I agree with you," I said, trying to keep calm to calm her down. "But I can't let you take her, not until Sophia has a chance to explain herself."

"I don't need your approval. I need you to do what's right by that child there."

"Sophia left her in my care this afternoon," I protested. "I'm responsible for her until she shows up."

"So you leave her with a man who doesn't know a thing about babies while you traipse off."

"Wait a minute," Will interjected. "I haven't had any problems with her. She likes me."

"I didn't *traipse* off," I objected. "I was looking for Sophia."

"Maybe she doesn't deserve to be found, a woman who'd abandon her baby."

"She didn't ..." I began, but Sadie's barking drowned my voice. Although Will had put her in the basement, probably when Barbara arrived, her deep bark was loud enough to waken Mara who began to wail in fright. The dog must have heard a car stop, its door open: above the cacophony of barks and baby, the doorbell chimed.

"Sophia," I said. "Thank god."

Barbara frowned, turning her back on me to stare hungrily at the baby Will was trying to shush. I yelled at Sadie to be quiet as I went to the front door, but the sound of the knob turning sent her into a frenzy of yaps as she complained bitterly about being stuck behind a door when all the excitement was happening upstairs.

"It's about time," I said, pulling open the door.

But it wasn't Sophia on my front porch. My heart sank. I recognized the man standing there, although he'd lost weight and a lot more hair since we first met a few years ago after Sadie and I discovered a body in the river near my house. His name was George Finlay, Detective Constable Finlay, and his job was investigating homicide.

FIVE

"How's it going, Mrs. Cairns?" Finlay smiled wearily, flapping his badge closed and shoving it into the inside pocket of his blue suit. "I hear you still got that big dog of yours. What was the name? Suzie?"

"Sadie ..." I began, but he interrupted me by nodding back over his shoulder to a young woman who stood behind him.

"This here's Constable Kathleen Quinn. We'd like to talk to you for a moment."

"Sure." I stepped back to allow them both indoors. Quinn smiled, a brief quirk of lips. She was a study in brown: brown hair cut short to frame a face tanned as a farmer's is by daily exposure to the elements; brown eyes behind thick gold-wire framed glasses, eyes that ranged around the living room, noting everything, filing it; tan pant suit worn over a chestnut-coloured turtleneck.

"You've got company," Finlay began, and then seeing what Will held, he grinned. "Hey, you've had a baby. Congratulations! Sure makes a difference in your lives, eh?"

"She's not ..." Will began, but I interrupted, anxious to know what the police were doing on my doorstep, fearing the answer I was about to hear. "How can we help you?" I asked.

Finlay ignored me and turned to our guest. "And you are?"

"Barbara Lock." She hesitated for a moment before holding out her hand.

He shook it, then introduced his colleague. Quinn smiled again without speaking. She tried to melt into the background, to be inconspicuous. I thought she'd overdone the camouflage. She was so colourless she demanded attention.

"You don't mind if I sit? I've been on my feet all day." Finlay sighed and eased himself into the rocking chair. Mara grizzled and Will rocked her gently. Quinn took her station in the arch of the hall door, leaning against the wall, a notebook in her hand.

Finlay cleared his throat. "I need your help, Mrs. Cairns. We got a body, female …"

I sank down on the couch. "Sophia?"

Barbara dropped down beside me, clutching my hand. "Oh my god," she muttered. "Oh, the poor motherless child."

"Sophia Demetris?" Quinn piped up. "Any reason you'd think it might be her?"

"She didn't keep an appointment with me this afternoon. I went to her apartment, but she's not there, either. And then, there's Mara." I nodded at the baby.

Finlay raised his eyebrow at Will.

"She's not ours," Will looked down at the wide eyes, the fist in the mouth. "She's Mara Demetris, Sophia's child."

"My grandchild," Barbara added. She stood up again, her hands kneading each other.

"Where's your phone?" Quinn asked me.

"In the hall."

Quinn was gone only a minute. "I called Jack Lansdown; he's with the CAS."

"I don't know why the CAS has to be involved. I'm her family!" Barbara declared.

Finlay held up his hand. "Wait a minute here. Let's get this straight. You're Sophia Demetris's mother?"

"No, I am not, and I'm more than thankful for that today. No daughter of mine would neglect her baby the way that young woman has treated this poor little thing. Mara's father was my boy, Martin."

"That's right? That's on the birth certificate?"

Barbara paused. "I don't know about that. She might have put it on ..."

"The father himself has to sign," Quinn interrupted. "It's the law."

"Well, he couldn't very well sign, could he? He didn't even know she was going to be born. She's all alone in the world, except for me. I've got the right to do what's best for her."

"And that's what we're trying to do, the best for everyone," Finlay countered. "What's the baby doing here, anyway?"

"Sophia told the babysitter to call me to pick her up," I said.

"Is that right? Nothing about Mrs. Lock? Or about young Mr. Lock?"

I shook my head.

"She's my boy's child. You can't take her away from me." Barbara turned to Will. "Let me hold her. Please?"

Will handed Mara over reluctantly.

Barbara hugged her, breathing deeply into the nest of curls that covered her head. Mara's whimpers turned into a grating cry. "I think she needs changing." Barbara felt the seat of the corduroy pants the baby was dressed in.

"There's a bag of diapers in the kitchen," I said.

"I'll show you." Will led the way into the kitchen where the baby's cries intensified into a full blown scream, before Barbara's croons and ministrations soothed her into a grumbling silence.

"My youngest was like that too, that age," Finlay remarked. "Hated to be changed. Now he's started dressing himself, I swear goes through a closetful of clothes a day."

"Tell me ..." I began, but was interrupted by Barbara. She marched back into the living room, her mouth pinched tight.

"You've seen this baby's backside?" she demanded. "How could you even think of giving her back to that woman? I don't believe in speaking ill of the dead, but no one, no one has the right to let this happen to an innocent creature who can't care for itself."

Quinn stepped forward. "What's the problem?"

"This baby needs antibiotics. She needs a doctor."

Quinn looked at me.

I grimaced. "I know she's got a rash."

"Rash! More like an infection. And she's so skinny. I haven't seen a baby this skinny except in news clips from Somalia, places like that. She's starving."

"I think you're exaggerating a little," I began, but Barbara shook her head.

"How can you say that? You can count her ribs, and she's obviously jaundiced. Don't you know anything about babies?"

I bridled, but before I could retort, Quinn tried to oil the waters.

"Jack will take her to the General when he gets here," she said.

"I can take her right now," Barbara answered. "We're wasting time, waiting. I've got a babyseat all ready in the car. You just tell me where to go."

"I'm sorry," Quinn shook her head. "Jack's the one who'll have to do that. He has to take charge of the baby until we get the paternity sorted out."

Barbara turned on Finlay, "How can you make us just sit here and wait when that baby needs attention right now?"

Before he could answer, Will returned, carrying Mara. "She threw up," he announced. "She's shaking like crazy. What are we going to do?"

"Poor baby." Barbara tried to peel one little fist free of its grip of Will's sweater, then the other away from her mouth. An odour of sour milk wafted through the room.

Sadie howled again, as more steps sounded on the front porch. Quinn let in a young man in a tweed jacket worn over blue jeans, a striped tie loosely knotted around his neck.

"Jack Lansdown, Children's Aid," he introduced himself quickly. "Hi, Finn, what have you got here?"

As Finlay explained, Lansdown took the baby from Will and cuddled her.

"She's been sick," Will told the social worker. "She won't eat and she's got a terrible rash. She started shaking like that just a few minutes ago."

"I'm taking her to the General, then." He considered Barbara who had collapsed on the couch. "You can come and see her there, if you want. They'll probably keep her for a few days. She looks malnourished to me, but I'm no doctor. You won't be able to take her home, though, until we get her condition stabilized and the paternity settled."

"There's no question of that," Barbara insisted. "It's in the letter, right here. Sophia says so."

Lansdown edged towards the door. "It's a bit more complicated than that. The courts will have to decide."

"Courts!" Barbara rose. "What do we need to go to law for? My husband works for the government in ComSoc; surely, you'll not deny we're a fit family."

"We have to have the baby's best interests in mind." Lansdown turned back to Will. "Did she come with clothes, toys, anything like that?"

"Here," I said suddenly. I reached into my jacket pocket and pulled out the tape. "This was playing in the apartment. I think it was for her."

"Thanks." He pocketed the tape and picked up the diaper bag of clothes with his free hand. "I'll be going then."

"I'm going with you," Barbara insisted. "I'm not letting that child out of my sight, now that I've found her."

Finlay and Quinn exchanged a look. Finlay nodded slightly.

"I'll go with you to the hospital," Quinn said. "We've got some questions for you, about the victim, how well you knew her."

"When did you get to town?" Finlay asked.

Barbara ignored him. "If you're coming, hurry up," she said to Quinn. "That man's getting ready to drive away. Do you think he's got a babyseat? I've brought my daughter's. We could take her to the hospital; he could meet us there."

"I'm sure he has a babyseat," Quinn soothed.

Barbara was already out the door, not bothering to say good-bye to any of us.

Quinn paused in the hall. "You'll come and pick me up, Finn, when you're through here?"

"Yeah." The big man smoothed a hand over his bald head. "Maybe the coroner will have something for us by then. I said we'd check in with him."

"I'll do that. What do you think? An hour?"

"Probably."

Outside a horn beeped impatiently. Quinn raised her hand in farewell.

Will slammed the door shut behind her. "I need a drink."

"Me too." I looked at Finlay. "And you?"

"Coffee, if it's ready. If not, a cola. I need the caffeine. It's been quite a day."

"You're telling me!"

He sighed. "We'd better get down to business: tell me what you know about this Sophia Demetris."

"She was one of my supervisees. She wasn't in any of my tutorials so I didn't know her very well."

"Well enough that she left her child with you."

"I still don't understand that. I didn't even know she had a baby until Joyce Holland phoned me."

"Joyce Holland?"

"The babysitter. She was anxious to get rid of Mara before her husband came home; apparently, he didn't like her taking stranger's babies into the house. She must have known how sick Mara was; she said he'd have a fit if he saw her and would insist on calling Children's Aid."

"Why didn't she?"

"Sophia paid her a lot of money to keep the baby there. I guess she felt she owed it to her not to say anything. She didn't even warn me what was wrong. She said Sophia had given her my name only when she insisted on having a contact. Sophia told her I was next-of-kin." I caught my breath. "I can't believe we're talking like this. I mean, it's just hitting me now that she's dead. How did it happen?"

"How about you let me ask the questions first?"

"That's not fair! Was it an accident?"

"Not this time."

"What do you mean, this time?" Will brought a tray of drinks into the living room and set it down on the cedar chest. He handed me a squat glass etched with a schooner in full sail, leaning into the breeze. I wished I was on board, free of responsibilities. The drink was amber, its scent sharp, bracing. I warmed the glass in my hands before taking a sip. Finlay downed his Coke in one long swallow, then wiped his mouth with the back of his hand before he took up his story.

"There's been three deaths on campus in the last four months. Since the university was built, we've had rapes and thefts and even a couple of clear suicides out there." He held up one hand and began to tick off the fingers: "In July, there was fatal hit-and-run in the parking lot by the science buildings. A graduate student struck full on and left for dead. No witnesses, no suspects. We had to let it go, specially as the powers-that-be were determined it was an accident. Said it was so dark the driver might have thought he hit a dog or something. First two-legged dog I ever saw! And the first time I ever heard of someone speeding by accident through a parking lot. Then about a month later, a woman drowned in the river."

I shivered. "I heard about that. It happened around the time I was hired. But she had no connection to the university. She was here for a conference or something, wasn't she?"

"That's right. She was out jogging. Looks like she slipped off the bank and the current took her. Her husband says she never learned to swim because she was terrified of going under; said she wouldn't even go to a pool or the beach. It doesn't make sense: if she was that afraid of water, what was she doing so close to the edge? She'd gone right down off the path."

"Suicide?" Will suggested.

"Same thing: why choose drowning, if that's what she was most afraid of? She had a nearly full bottle of sleeping pills in her room; they would have done the job much more pleasantly, if she wanted to die."

"You think someone killed them?"

"It's just a feeling." Finlay stroked his skull again. "This one, though. There's no doubt. Suicides don't stab themselves over and over again and then cover themselves up with a raincoat."

"How awful. Poor Sophia." I held the drink in my mouth a moment before swallowing. Tears pricked my eyes; I blinked them away.

"He's clever, whoever he is. No witnesses, no fingerprints. He just killed her and walked away."

"Where did you you find her? When?"

"Young couple thought they'd slip into the alley between the Arts Tower and Jamieson Hall for a little cuddle-and-squeeze on the way to dinner. I don't think either of them'll be eating anything tonight. Close as we can figure it, the last delivery was made to the residence at 4 p.m.; the body was found at quarter past six. Impossible to pin down completely, but I'm thinking 5, 5:30, in there somewhere."

"I left at 6, furious because she was late and had told the babysitter that I'd take care of her baby. I had to hurry because Joyce said that if I didn't get there fast she was going to call Children's Aid. I walked right by the alley on the way to the parking lot. Maybe if I'd used the fire door, or if I'd taken the time to look in the alley, I could have helped her …"

"Or we would have two victims, not one. He slashed her throat first, then it looks like he went into a frenzy with the knife."

"Please, Constable," I said.

"You wanted to know." He paused. "Anyway, the guy must have had some experience with killing before, or he'd done a lot of reading. He knew enough not to try for the heart right away, too much bone blocking it. And with her trachea cut, she wouldn't have been able to cry out, even if anyone had been passing by. She didn't struggle much, or he pinned her arms first somehow. She didn't have a chance to fight back: there was nothing under her nails."

"You keep saying *he*," Will interrupted. "How do you know it's a man?"

"He left his boots behind, size 13. Aren't too many women around with feet that big."

"But you said there was no evidence," I pointed out. "What about the boots?"

"Boots and a raincoat. Both utility brand names, available in at least ten stores just here in town alone. He might've bought them anywhere. No fingerprints of course. Gloves and a knife are a lot easier to get rid of than blood-stained clothing. He knew what he was doing. Laughing at us, he is."

"I still don't understand," I shook my head. "When I left it was just getting dark and there were still students in the building, coming from their last classes. Surely someone must have seen something?"

"We've put a bulletin on the radio, asking for witnesses to step forward. But he chose his spot, right at the blind end of the alley by the Arts Tower fire door. The residence loading dock sticks out a fair way, leaving that end shadowed. Plus there's a row of those big garbage bins lined up blocking what view there is. It's possible that someone passing by, even if they did look in, would see nothing. And some kids were partying in the residence, had a stereo still going full blast when we got there. If she'd had time to call out, no one could have heard her."

We sat silent for a minute. On the basement landing, Sadie groaned as she circled before flopping down to wait for us to let her upstairs. With only the bookcase lamps, the living room was still in the semi-dark that had soothed Mara. I leaned back and switched on a tri-light. The sudden radiance made me blink. I wiped the moisture from my eyes.

"So who sent you here?" I asked.

"There was quite a crowd, what with all the sirens and vehicles, ambulance and such," Finlay replied. "Someone said you'd been waiting for a student who never showed up." He consulted his notebook. "A Dr. Alex Warren. We found Ms. Demetris's backpack, her student card. But we need someone to identify the body."

"No," Will said. He squeezed my hand. "You can't make her do that."

"We can't find any trace of family. I could get that Mrs. Lock to do the identification, I suppose. She knew the girl and she's at the hospital. The body will be in the morgue by now."

"Her father's in town," I said. "He'd be the best person to make the identification, wouldn't he? And he'll have to be told."

"Her father?" Both men looked at me in amazement.

"I was going to tell you, but Barbara was here when I came in," I explained to Will before turning to Finlay. "I went over to Sophia's apartment to see if she was there. I'd just got back when you arrived. She wasn't there, obviously, but her father was: John Demetris. He was in a foul temper."

"He live in town?" Finlay's notebook was open again, a pen ready in his hand.

I shook my head. "Scarborough. At least, Sophia once said something about coming from *Scarberia*."

"You know why he was looking for her?"

"Apparently her mother's sick and wants Sophia to come home." I shivered. "He's furious with Sophia and won't have anything to do with her baby. I told him Mara was here and all he said was that she was nothing to him. Remember," I said to Will, "in the letter she told Barbara that she couldn't go to her parents for help."

"Where is this letter?" Finlay leaned forward.

I glanced over the magazines littering the top of the cedar chest we used for a coffee table. "Barbara must have taken it with her. She showed it to me. It was from Sophia all right, I recognized the handwriting. Sophia wrote to her for money, to help support Mara, I guess. I didn't read it too closely; I didn't have time."

"So Ms. Demetris names the Lock boy as the father?"

"She says it's his fault she's got the baby."

Finlay stretched his back and yawned. "Quinn will have it by now, I guess. Anything more you can tell me about the family? About the victim?"

"Not really. Look, I don't like talking gossip like this. I don't know any of these people."

"This is a murder investigation," Finlay replied. "You're obliged to tell me anything that might help find the killer." He opened his notebook again. "I've got to get over to the hospital, but I just got a couple quick questions first. Did you see Ms. Demetris at all today?"

"I told you, she didn't keep the appointment she'd made. She called me this morning and said she just had to talk to me. I thought it was about her Media Studies course; I guess you've heard about her petition against its content? The earliest I could meet with her was at 4:30, but she never showed up. I had a lecture to prepare so I worked on that until Joyce Holland called me. She sounded so urgent that I couldn't wait any longer. I left a note on my door for Sophia telling her to come here; it's probably still there."

"Did you see anyone hanging around? Anyone unfamiliar?"

"There are over 4,000 students on this campus. I barely recognize the kids in my classes, let alone the rest of them. But I didn't see anyone skulking around with a knife in his hand, if that's what you mean."

"How about when you left your office? On the way to the parking lot?"

"Well, I met Alex Warren in the hall. Oh, and I bumped into Irene Smith on the stairs."

Finlay raised an eyebrow. "Smith?"

"She's the department secretary. She's usually gone by 5, but she said she'd come back to do some extra work. A lot of the secretaries do that, typing papers for faculty after hours for overtime."

Finlay consulted his book. "She wasn't one of the bystanders. At least, I don't have her name here."

"Maybe she didn't come downstairs."

"With all that commotion? Wouldn't she be curious?"

"I don't know. Irene is one of those people who keeps very much to herself."

"Do you know where she lives? She might have seen something on her way into the building."

"You'd have to get her address from the administration. Or maybe the department chair knows it. Just a sec, I'll get you Professor Easton's phone number."

"That's alright. I already have it." He snapped the book shut and heaved himself to his feet. "I'll be going then. You can let that beast of yours upstairs."

Will spoke then. "What's going to happen to Mara?"

"Who?"

"The baby."

"The CAS will place her in foster care until we find her mother's killer. A judge will have to decide where she's to go then, whether to an adoptive home or to the birth grandmother – if Mrs. Lock is the birth grandmother. We'll have to try to find her son. It would be interesting to know if he's been around town."

"Wait a minute." I took off my glasses to rub my eyes. "So you think Martin Lock might have killed Sophia?"

"I have to consider every possibility," Finlay replied. He covered a yawn with one hand.

"Then why talk about those other deaths as if they're related?" Will demanded.

"Wasn't thinking straight," Finlay confessed. "I shouldn't have said anything, they probably are all coincidence. We'll have a talk with this Lock boy and go on from there."

I accompanied him to the door. He paused before descending the porch steps, one hand on the railing. "Listen, Mrs. Cairns, I don't have to tell you now, do I, to leave the investigation to us?"

"Don't worry."

"If you think of anything that might help, something Ms. Demetris might have told you one time or another, you get in touch right away, you hear?"

"Yes, Constable Finlay."

"If her father gets in touch with you, or Mrs. Lock ..."

"Yes, yes, I'll call. And you'll let me know what you find out?"

He shook his head. "When it's all over, maybe I'll come over, have a chat. You take care now."

He lumbered down the stairs. Behind me, Sadie greeted her release from the basement with excited yelps that triumphed over Will's repeated orders to her to pipe down. I stood on the porch for a moment, sniffing the sharp tang of dying leaves in the rain. In the darkness of the park below me, the river grumbled to itself as it carried its dark secrets over the dam.

SIX

Will was talking on the phone in the kitchen when I came back in. I went straight upstairs, suddenly so weary that I couldn't bear the thought of marking essays or checking my notes for the next day's classes. It seemed impossible to deal with such routine matters in the face of such a horrid, senseless murder.

I was snuggled deep in the duvet when Will came to bed. He undressed in the dark and sighed when he stretched out beside me. His feet were freezing so I rubbed warmth into them with my own.

"You're still awake?" he whispered.

"I keep thinking about Sophia. And wondering what will happen to Mara."

"That was Jack Lansdown I was talking to just now." Will shifted to face me, his face striped by the streetlight filtering in through the slats of the blind. "He says Mara's condition is pretty serious: malnutrition, dehydration, jaundice, a septic infection. She's way underweight and undersize for her age. They'll be keeping her in the hospital for at least a couple of weeks to clear up that infection and get her back to health."

"Poor baby."

"Yeah. She's suffering from neglect, abandonment – Jack's frustrated that there's no one to lay charges against. I mean, it's terrible that Sophia's dead, but to treat her baby like this!"

"I just don't understand it." I stared up at the shadows on the ceiling. "She was awfully quiet and intense, but she didn't seem the type to be so cruel. Do you think she hated her baby?"

"That, or she just couldn't figure out how to look after it. Jack was on his way to the apartment, but Barbara had already given him an earful about conditions there. She's hopping mad that they won't let her take Mara home. Apparently she told the doctor that there weren't any such diseases in Canada as malnutrition. It's a good thing Constable Quinn was with her; Jack thinks she's quite capable of grabbing the baby and taking off with her."

"Maybe Sophia resented having the baby so much, she took it out on her."

"She could have given the kid up for adoption. Or had an abortion."

"Perhaps she was simply overwhelmed – a new town, going to classes, a new baby. She was all on her own, with no one to help her. Her own family wouldn't have anything to do with her."

"Come on, Rosie, stop trying to find excuses for her. She was a grown-up, an intelligent woman, no teenager caught unexpectedly. If she was going to keep the baby, you'd think she would have the sense to read some books about childcare, or ask for help. She was on Mother's Allowance support, you know. Jack implied that she was using the baby to get the money to live on to go to school."

"That's awful."

We lay silent. Far off, a train whistle shrieked, a lonely wail that echoed the fear and despair of those lying awake in the small hours, their troubles gnawing away at them.

"Still," I said, "it was a terrible way to die. No one had the right to do that to her."

"I'm glad Finlay didn't persuade you to go look at her," Will traced the line of my forehead, nose, lips, chin. "It's not as if she was family, or anything."

"I can't get it out of my head that she left Mara to me. Why?"

"There was no one else. If she thought she wouldn't be able to pick the baby up, I doubt if she would have given Joyce Holland a real name. She wouldn't want you to find out how sick Mara was; you would have seen right away that there was something wrong."

"But she knew Barbara was coming to town. She could have called her and told her where to find the baby."

"Maybe Barbara's not the grandmother. Maybe Sophia had an affair with someone else and the baby's not Martin's. Maybe she thought if Barbara saw Mara and realized the truth, she wouldn't give her the money."

"What about the real father, then? Why wouldn't she go to him for help?"

I felt rather than saw Will's shrug. We both lay silent watching the lights from a car cruising around the park chase shadows across the ceiling.

"Do you think Sophia knew her killer?" I finally asked. "Finlay said there was no sign of struggle."

"Stop it, Rosie." Will lifted himself up on one elbow so that he could look down on me.

"Stop what?"

"I know what you're doing. You're thinking about getting involved in this. You heard what Finlay said: leave the investigation to him."

"I feel responsible," I protested. "If she hadn't been coming to my office, she might not even have been on campus."

"It's not your fault." Will flopped down again. "Maybe she did meet someone else first, one of the Locks or even her own father. She seemed to have a knack for making people angry."

"But the raincoat and boots indicate that the murder must have been planned. Barbara didn't know where or if she was going to find Sophia; her father said he hadn't seen her at all."

"He could have lied," Will pointed out. "And maybe Barbara was lying about her son. Maybe he's in town too."

"Those other two deaths that Finlay talked about," I began. "Do you think there could be a connection?"

"No way. And if there is, more reason for you to stay away from it all. Promise me you'll mind your own business?"

I didn't answer. I rolled over to fit myself against the curve of his body, stroking the fine hair that covered him like a pelt from the shoulders down. Sophia, mixed-up, confused, tormented and tormenting her child, was dead. But I was still here and lying naked next to a naked man, his heart beating under my hand, my own pulse hammering. Will pulled me over on top of him, hugging me tight. The first kiss banished murder and abandonment; the slow play of lips and limbs confirmed life.

The ringing phone woke me. I stumbled out of bed, grabbing my glasses from their perch on the dresser. We have to get a phone in the bedroom, I told myself for the hundredth time. I pushed open the study door just as the answering machine clicked in. I always forgot that Will had installed the machine to take care of business when he was out on a job. I could have let the damn thing ring and slept in longer. I listened to Will's voice as he recited the usual message about name and number after the beep.

"Come on, come on, wake up." It was Karen Lewis's voice. "Get out of bed, you two."

"Since when are you giving wake-up calls," I retorted, picking up the phone.

"It's past seven," she said. "Did you forget your alarm again?"

I looked out the study window at the grey, cheerless dawn. Leaves still left on the trees hung listlessly dripping rain. Fog from the river eddied under the big maples in the park. The streetlights had faded to a bilious yellow. Although I could hear a crow clearing its throat, there were no birds flitting about, no early morning joggers on the ring road.

"I hate it when the days start closing in," I replied. "And no, we didn't forget the alarm. It's just gone off. What are you calling so early for?"

"You're in the news."

I pulled the rocking chair over and sat down, still staring out the window. "Sophia?"

"That's right. She was one of your students, eh?"

"A supervisee. Have they caught the guy who did it?"

"Not yet. I just listened to the report. They're calling him the Kampus Killer."

"Oh god," I groaned. "The administration must be going nuts."

"Fill me in. What happened? And I had a message on my machine last night from Will, something about mixing baby formula?"

"It's a long story, Karen. I'm barely awake."

"Not fair. You have all the fun."

"Fun! It's not been much fun, thank you very much." Will came into the study with a bathrobe in his hand. I mouthed Karen's name. He shrugged, and draped it over me. I tucked it around me as best as I could. Until one of us went downstairs to let Sadie out and turn up the heat, the house was cold in the mornings.

"I'm sorry. I don't mean to be facetious. But a murder on campus! Who did it? A boyfriend? Who's the baby?"

I told Karen the whole story, beginning with the phone call from Joyce Holland. While I spoke, I listened to Will as he dressed and went downstairs. The furnace roared on as he turned up the thermostat, Sadie whined to go out, water sloshed into the kettle. Soon the smell of fresh coffee wafted upstairs. My stomach growled.

"So that's that," I concluded. "Finlay's in charge of the investigation and he made it plenty clear that I'm to stay out of it."

"I bet it's the boyfriend," Karen said. "I mean, his mother would say that he's out of the picture, to protect him. I bet she told him where Sophia was living and he came after her."

"Why would he kill her?"

"Jealousy."

"Of whom? Sophia didn't have any friends in town."

"How do you know that? I mean, she didn't even tell you she had a baby so you don't know what else she was keeping secret."

"That's true." I shivered. "I've got to go."

"You'll keep me up-to-date?"

"Sure thing."

"Dinner still on for tonight?"

"I guess so. See you."

Will had tuned the kitchen radio to the local AM station. He stood in the kitchen, cup of coffee in one hand, buttered toast in the other, listening to a very long jingle concerning a furniture sale. "News on in a minute," he grunted. I poured coffee for myself and pulled out the red kitchen stool to sit on.

The news reader relished the excitement of a murder; she usually only had car accidents and bar fights to report. She had very few details to add to what we already knew; she mentioned my name as the person Sophia was on her way to visit; she had a "no comment" quote from John Demetris as he left the police station earlier in the morning after questioning. Apparently he'd gone there voluntarily after hearing the first reports of his daughter's murder on a late-night newscast as he was driving back to the city. Finlay said that "the investigation was proceeding," gave a description of a young man that matched the photo I'd seen of Martin Lock, and requested that Lock contact him as soon as possible.

Following the interview with the police was a short announcement from the university president, Dr. Constance Comaine, her voice gravelly with interrupted sleep or uncharacteristic emotion. She had been appointed as acting president when her predecessor was felled with a heart attack. A number of people on campus hoped that the Board of Governors would confirm her in the position, making her one of the very few women university presidents in the country. However, as dean she had a reputation for procrastinating over important decisions while fussing over nonessential details. I'd never been able to figure out exactly what a university president did, other than go to meetings with bureaucrats and perform public relations services for the institution. And Dr. Comaine was certainly very good at the latter, projecting always an unruffled, carefully groomed exterior. This morning, she quickly side-stepped the issue of violence against women and downplayed the horror of a murder on the campus by suggesting obliquely that it was irregularities in Sophia's private life that were to blame for her death. The announcer concluded with the news that Mara and her putative grandmother were both at the General.

"I can see the newspaper headlines already," I groaned. "Single mother, child abuse. All the welfare-bashers in town will have a heyday, putting in a few good digs at the laxity and immorality of university life to boot."

Will switched to the other local stations, but all three were loud with country and western music interrupted by an appliance store's liquidation salespitch.

"Try the university station," I suggested.

" ... *one more vivid example of where violent pornography leads. The objectification of women's bodies* ... "The woman's voice was a monotonous nasal drone, devoid of emotion.

"She doesn't sound very upset," Will commented.

"She's probably never read anything over the air before. I bet she's just nervous."

A second girl had jumped in, her voice high-pitched and excited. *"... the vigil in the alley behind Jamieson Hall where Sophia Demetris, a sister student, fell victim to the random violence that stalks our campuses. We need to reclaim public space and not be afraid to go out on our own. The Sexual Assault Centre and the Aids Awareness Group are sponsoring a march on the administration office to demand better safety protection NOW!"*

"This is crazy." I reached over to turn down the volume. "None of these people even knew Sophia. They have no idea what she was like, how she despised the lot of them."

"If this university took violence against women seriously they would have cancelled classes today," the first speaker added. *"It's not enough to have harassment policies in print. We need action: better lighting, safety phones, security patrols. Sophia Demetris ..."*

The phone rang. Will turned the volume down and I answered, managing in the process to swallow a mouthful of coffee the wrong way.

"You're pretty choked up," joked my office neighbour, Alex Warren. "Going to join the march and boycott classes today?"

I cleared my throat. "Hi, Alex. What can I do for you?"

"I need some advice. It's my turn to lecture in Popular Culture this morning and, as we all know, the Demetris girl was in the class. What should I do? Cancel it? Try to carry on as if nothing happened? It's not as if she regularly attended, but there's all the fuss about the petition. If I cancel, do you think it will look like I've given into pressure?"

"I think it would look like respect. Listen, I heard you were at the scene last night."

"Couldn't miss it. Every cop car in town must have been there. Wait till the dean gets a look at the state of the lawn – they parked everywhere. I couldn't get my car out of the lot until nearly midnight."

"What were they doing?"

"You should know all that, shouldn't you?"

"What do you mean?"

"*The Semiotics of Murder.* Isn't that your thesis title?"

"That's got nothing to do with real life," I protested. "It's just literary theory. Listen, Alex, I'm in a rush. I don't know what to say about your class. Have you talked to the president? What's she decided to do?"

"Nothing so far."

"Well, why don't you give your class the opportunity to decide for themselves what they want to do?"

"Oh, my, aren't we radical this morning? I suppose I might as well cancel. I can't imagine how I'll keep their minds on censorship with all the gossip and rumours floating about. Say, did you hear …"

"Sorry, Alex, I've really got to go."

"About tonight," he said quickly. "Is it still on? Do I get to meet this fabulous friend of yours?"

"You could have met her weeks ago if you spent more time here rather than in the city."

"Guilty, as charged," he said. "But it's hard to stay away from the bright lights. Seriously, though, Rosie, I appreciate the invitation. I get sick of my own cooking. Although I'm a pretty good cook … Anyway, maybe after tonight I'll have more excuses to stay in town on the weekends."

"Right," I said. "I think I'm already regretting trying to get the two of you together." I put down the phone. "I forgot I'd asked Karen and Alex to dinner tonight."

"Match-maker, match-maker," Will half-sang, mocking me. I shook my head at him, but couldn't stop grinning.

"What are you talking about? They're two lonely people who might like each other. There's not many weekends when Alex stays over in town, so I thought it would be a good chance to introduce them. Alex is kind of strange though."

Will laughed. "So Karen will probably go crazy about him."

"Very funny." I balled up my napkin and threw it at him.

"Anyway, I thought you liked the guy?"

"He's a joker. Like you. But he can be rather full of himself. He claims to be writing the 'Great Canadian Novel,' and I'm not sure if he's not serious when he says so."

"Maybe we should call the dinner off? Do you really feel like entertaining?"

I twirled a curl around my finger, tighter and tighter, until the pull made me wince. I untangled the strand. "You're right. It's probably a bad idea."

"I'd like to go over to the General tonight and see how Mara's doing," Will said. "I can't help feeling a little responsible for her. And Jack told me it would be all right. Do you want to come with me?"

"Okay. Will you call Karen and tell her that dinner's cancelled? I'm sure to run into Alex on campus, so I'll explain to him. Maybe we can reschedule the dinner later, some time after this is all over. He might be willing to stay over a Thursday night sometime. Earlier in the week isn't any good for Karen; she's got too much class preparation to do. I swear she spends as much time preparing to teach six-year-olds as I do for my courses."

"If he's as interested in meeting her as you've persuaded her she is in meeting him …"

"Will!"

"Okay, okay. I'm sorry." He stared at me, then reached out to smooth the hair back from my eyes. "Do you have to go into your office today? You look exhausted."

"I'd better. I've got a huge pile of papers to mark. They're sitting on my desk waiting for me. And there'll be students wanting to talk, needing to talk. I imagine a lot of the kids living in Jamieson Hall will be pretty upset."

"Funny that the media hasn't connected this murder with those two deaths in the summer."

"I think the administration is fighting hard to keep them separate. Besides, it's just George Finlay's theory. A hit-and-run, a drowning, a stabbing – there's no pattern to it. I wonder if the victims knew each other?"

"Rosie," Will warned.

"What?" I rinsed my coffee cup and set it in the drainer.

"Don't play innocent. You said you would keep out of this."

"I don't see how I have any choice about getting involved. I probably knew Sophia better than anyone else on campus."

"Which isn't saying much. Look how much you didn't know: Mara, for instance."

"Who is exactly the reason I have to help as much as I can."

"Finlay's job is to do that."

We stared at each other.

"I'm afraid of something bad happening to you," Will finally admitted.

"I can take care of myself. I have for a long time."

"I know. But if there is a maniac out there, who's targetted the campus for women on their own …" He paused. "It's a long way from the parking lot to your office."

"I'll leave early. Besides, you can be sure there'll be security guards all over the place."

"Barring the stable door," Will muttered.

"Better late than never." I capped his maxim with one of my own, and, grinning, went up to decide on appropriate clothes in which to mourn my student and join the hunt for her killer.

SEVEN

The road that ringed the university buildings was crowded with cars parked illegally on either side and sightseers meandering across the lawns and walkways, ignoring intersections so that the cars trying to park were forced to stop and start indiscriminately. A security guard posted at the entrance to the parking lot demanded to see my faculty parking pass before letting me in.

"There's a lot of ghouls about today," he grunted. "We got to restrict parking spaces for those who paid for them."

"I've never seen anything like this," I said. "It doesn't get this packed even for convocation."

He shrugged. "Which building you going to?"

"The Arts Tower."

He shook his head. "It's even worse there." He rushed away to stop a yellow van from entering into the lot through the exit drive. "Wait a minute, you. Where you think you're going?"

I found a free space not too far from the path leading into the maze of buildings. I hadn't gone more than a few yards before I was stopped by a trio of girls dressed so alike they might have been in uniform: long black sweaters over black tights and black ankle boots. One had shaved her head, one had let her hair grow to her waist. The third hid hers under a black beret that reminded me of Sophia. Between them, they carried two long poles wrapped in a white sheet.

They hurried past me across the lawn which squelched under their boots. Ruts criss-crossed the grass, evidence of the police vehicles that Alex had told me about. A man paced the grass, head bent as he peered intently at the tracks. He had a pad of paper in one hand and appeared to be making notes. When I got closer I recognized Dean Albert Partridge. As always he was impeccably dressed in a blue pin-striped suit and a necktie tied with an elaborate knot that drew attention to the fact that he seemed to have no neck, his head set square on rounded shoulders. Like many short men, he tried to make up for his lack of height with an excess of dignity. He walked stiffly and even sat upright, his spine never coming into contact with a chair back. He bore a look of constant indignation, his pale eyes bulging between florid cheeks under eyebrows so thin they were almost invisible. His grey hair was still thick but he used a highly scented oil to keep it tamed flat across his skull. Today, the perfection of his appearance was marred by the galoshes that flopped around his ankles, allowing his pant legs to drag ever so slightly in the mud.

He peered at me as our paths crossed, his eyes squinting although the day, like yesterday, was overcast, a brisk wind threatening more rain.

"Professor Cairns, isn't it?" he inquired. His voice was high-pitched, the vowels drawled and flattened. He had gone to Harvard as an undergraduate forty years ago and adopted its speech inflections as a badge of distinction. He told me at the party held to welcome all new faculty that his family had emigrated to New England after the Napoleonic Wars. He collected Napoleonic memorabilia, decorating his office with busts of the little general, maps of his battles, even a framed letter signed by the emperor during his St. Helena exile. Before becoming dean – a promotion that owed as much to his longevity as one of the first faculty members at the university as to his ability to manage academic affairs – Partridge had taught European history. His lectures on Napoleon were famous for the tears he shed in describing the emperor's downfall.

"Have you lost something?" I paused to stare down at the ground.

"This lawn was pristine yesterday." Partridge turned over a loosened sod with the toe of one boot. "Look at the mess. Fall Convocation's only two weeks away; the lawn will never recover in time. I'm making a formal complaint to the police chief this afternoon. They had no business driving over the grass. There's plenty of room to park along the road."

"Not today."

Partridge glared at the cars. Another group of girls passed by, these carrying placards whose message I couldn't read. "Troublemakers," he hissed. "I told Dr. Comaine we should close the campus down entirely until this business has been satisfactorily dealt with. She hasn't decided what to do; look at the result: riffraff and sightseers everywhere. We should have posted guards at the gates and only let in those that belong here."

"It's a public institution," I protested.

"It's a nuisance." He made a mark in his notebook.

"It's not Sophia's fault she was killed here."

"Wasn't it?" His forehead wrinkled. "I believe she had some sort of paramour with whom she was not on good terms." His lips pursed as if he'd caught a bad odour in the air.

"I understood she was killed by whoever murdered those other two women."

"What are you talking about?" Partridge grabbed my sleeve, dropping his pad and pencil in the mud. "Look what you've made me do."

I picked them up and handed them back. "Before you start blaming the victim, perhaps you'd better find out what really happened."

"There's no connection. None. You're not to suggest that to anyone. Not anyone, do you understand? Do you realize what damage such a rumour could cause to the university? You're an employee here: you owe it to your colleagues to deny any such story." As he rushed on, his face flushed even redder, the veins in his temples beating visibly. He seemed to swell like a toad facing danger.

"Women are dying," I began.

"No, no, no. Accidents, regrettable I'm sure. People not staying away from the water, not taking care. Nothing to do with this."

"How can you know that?"

"As the dean of this institution, as your employer, I demand that you desist from making any such allegations. There is no proof of what you're claiming. If I see any such rumour in the media, you can be sure that your appointment will be scrutinized very carefully."

"Are you threatening me?"

He took a deep breath and swayed back on his heels, staring up into the sky. A gust of wind blew a shower of raindrops from the overgrown apple trees that lined the path.

"We have to be reasonable." His teeth were small, even, very white between the narrow bands of his pale, bitten lips. "We don't want to panic the parents of our students. We don't want any wild stories about a maniacal killer on the loose – just think of the consequences, Professor Cairns, the media circus! It's bad enough as it is without that." And again, he toed the broken sod.

"But you can see my point, that it's not fair to condemn Sophia until the truth is known,"

"The truth, that's it." He rocked back and forth, mud squishing up from his galoshes in a soft suck as he moved. "We all want the truth, now, don't we?"

"Without harming the reputations of those who can't help themselves," I insisted.

"She was one of yours, wasn't she?" Partridge squinted against the wind.

"My what?"

"Student supervisees. That's right, I was checking into all that this morning. I imagine you're a bit upset." He patted my arm. "People do say things they don't really mean when they're upset. But you want to be careful, my dear, not to harm the hand that feeds, so to speak."

I pulled away. "You seem to forget that a young woman is dead. On this campus. Doesn't that matter to you?"

"I wish it had been somewhere else," he muttered.

"Excuse me?" I couldn't believe what I'd heard.

"Too true," he sighed. "A great tragedy. We all, of course, hope her killer will be found without delay and that everyone will assist the authorities in their search for the perpetrator. But this unfortunate occurrence is no reason to disrupt the procedures or unduly blacken the reputation of this institution which has bent over backwards, it seems to me, to provide support and services for its students." He waved a hand in the direction of the parking lot where the security guard was haranguing a driver who'd tried to leave his car on the verge.

"It's a little late for that now," I retorted.

Partridge lifted his arm to look at his watch. The starched cuff of his shirt ringed his wrist so tightly the flesh was pinched into a thick white roll. "My goodness, it's getting late. I have a meeting with the president in a few minutes." He surveyed the lawn, his mouth pinched. "I shall certainly report on this flagrant abuse of property by our uniformed friends. But I shan't need to convey to her your fears about some sort of serial killer. You won't say anything untoward?"

"But if there's a danger that someone's out there …"

"Now, now, no need to jump to conclusions. We've brought in some extra security guards to patrol the grounds and we're going to insist that the residences lock all doors at dusk until this is all over. No expense spared. I'm sure the police will solve this soon. They seem to think it's a domestic affair." His voice trailed off as he concentrated again on the ruts in the grass.

"Is that what they've told you?"

"They haven't told me anything, but it's clearly self-evident. It'll be all over soon as they find the missing boyfriend, you mark my words. Messy situation. I believe there's a baby involved, of all things." He tut-tutted.

"You'll be late for your meeting," I reminded him. I wanted to get away from him back to my office. For the first time, I agreed with the rumours I'd heard about the insensitivity and self-importance of this odious little man.

"Yes, yes. Now, remember, mum's the word with the media." He placed a fat red finger against his lips and let one eyelid droop in what I took to be a wink.

"I won't say anything," I promised and added under my breath as I turned away towards the Arts Tower, "yet."

I rounded the corner of Jamieson Hall and stopped, staring at the crowd that swelled from the entrance of the service alley between the residence and the Arts Tower to fill the quadrangle bounded by those two buildings, the ring road, and a second residence. A police car filled the alley mouth; in front of it a number of vans were parked head to tail. I recognized the logos for two national television networks as well as the local station, a regional radio system, and three newspapers. The crowd consisted mostly of women, most of them young, but here and there men wielding large black cameras followed reporters as they tried to pick photogenic subjects to interview. A policewoman argued with several more male reporters – at least that's how I identified the perfectly coiffed men in blue suits who surrounded her. I edged my way through in the direction of the Arts Tower.

The crowd was mostly quiet, a sibilance of whispers and sobbing as one by one the girls stepped forward to lay their offerings of white roses and red carnations under the yellow crime scene ribbon that stretched between the two buildings across the alley mouth. A young man plucked soft blues from a guitar; a girl played a flute. The sheet I'd seen the girls carrying earlier was revealed now as a banner held on poles planted in the flowerbed that lined the road. *Stop Violence Against Women* it read in red uneven script. The placards I'd seen earlier were stacked on the curb; some were being used as temporary seats by people who'd found the ground too wet for comfort.

A knot of people huddled just inside the door of the Arts Tower. They stopped talking when I pushed open the door.

"Ah, Rosalie," Professor Easton stepped forward. "I'm sorry about this. Sophia was one of your supervisees, wasn't she?"

Lucy Easton had spent her whole life in schools of one kind or another, from nursery school to graduate school to teaching in the university. In many ways, she still looked like a student. She usually wore a denim skirt and one of a number of beautifully hand-knitted sweaters which I'd been told she made herself. Her thick red hair was cropped in a pudding-bowl cut that required little effort to keep tidy. She was only a year older than me, but she'd published two scholarly biographies since completing her dissertation more than a dozen years ago. On top of that, she was married (to a dentist) and had two children, both under ten. I'd met the youngest on the Saturday afternoon I was interviewed for this job; the older boy had gone to a birthday party and her husband had been called to an emergency root canal, so she had had to keep the little girl with her. While we discussed teaching loads and course outlines, the two-year-old drew pictures with thick bright crayons on the blank backs of old book lists. Professor Easton had always been welcoming, but had maintained a formal distance. I was surprised that she called me by my first name and even more shocked when she rushed over to hug me.

"It's just so awful," she said. "That poor girl."

"Have you seen Dean Partridge?" interrupted Lloyd Samuels, the university's public relations director. He looked as if he hadn't had much sleep since the news of the murder was made public. His eyes behind black-framed glasses were blood shot, his forehead creased with the frown that thinned his lips. He kept brushing one hand back over his curly black hair, trying to tame the rebellious duck tail that flipped back as soon as he left it alone. Under his Harris tweed jacket, his white shirt was wrinkled, the striped tie askew. He glanced from the silver disk of his digital sports watch up to the round white face of the clock above the information desk in the lobby. "He's late."

"He's checking the lawn on the other side of Jamieson Hall by the far parking lot." I slipped away from Professor Easton's encircling arm. "He's worried about the grass."

"The grass," Samuels snorted. "What a time to be worried about the state of the grass. What's the crowd like?"

"Growing. And there seems to be quite a few media people too, television as well as newspaper. They're interviewing everyone."

"That's it, then," Samuels blew out his breath in exasperation. "We can't wait any longer. What will it be, Dr. Comaine? You want me to summon the media to your office or will you go out and make a statement in front of the crowd?"

Everyone turned to face the president. As always, Constance Comaine was impeccably dressed in what my mother used to call "sensible" clothes: a grey wool suit over a navy blouse which tied with a neat bow at the throat. Her brown hair was artfully frosted and fluffed in careful curls; her make-up blended to complement the natural tones of her fair skin and to bring out the green in her eyes. Her earrings were pearl studs but she wore no other jewellery. Blue-rimmed half-glasses hung round her neck on a gold cord.

I recognized some of the others who waited to hear what she was going to do. The four men in suits were Giles Harding-Jervase, the registrar; Hugh Ascott, the vice-president of finances; Henry Ng, the dean of sciences; and Frank Stanich, the chair of Media Studies. The big woman in the black dress was Norma Ladurie, the principal of Jamieson Hall.

The fifth person stood back from the others in the shadow of the stairwell. He was the man I'd seen racing Alex up the stairs; Bud Levin, that was it, something to do with security. His shirt cuffs strained at the muscles of his crossed arms; there was some kind of patch on the shoulder of the tan shirt but I couldn't read it from where I stood. He grimaced as the silence was punctuated by a racket from outdoors.

"They've got a bullhorn," he announced. His voice was deep but rough with a smoker's catch. "I knew it was just a matter of time."

Henry Ng took off his glasses and wiped the lenses with the end of his tie. "Constance, you really must do something," he chided, his voice soft but insistent.

Norma Ladurie intervened. "Poor kids – they're so scared, they don't know what else to do but band together. They set up their own watch patrols in the halls last night and I had one after another come down to see me." She rubbed at her eyes, sighing. "I hope they catch the guy soon. Everyone's afraid of who's going to be next."

Dr. Comaine sighed. She looked down at the single sheet of print-out copy in her hand. The paper trembled; she crunched it in a sudden fist.

"I might as well go out and talk to them," she decided. "I won't have them saying I hid in here." She turned to me. "And we have to defuse this idea that there's a maniac on the loose out there. It seems the girl was a specific target; problems in her personal life."

"Is that true?" I asked.

She nodded. "Apparently it was a premeditated act. What was it that officer said, something about raincoats?" She shook her head. "You knew her: what can you tell me about her?"

"She was a very private person. She had a strong sense of what she believed was right," I avoided looking at Stanich. Alex had told me that when the chair first learned about the petition, through the student newspaper article, he'd thrown an ashtray at his office door, severely denting it. I wondered where he had been yesterday afternoon, what his alibi might be.

"She had a child out of wedlock," Norma commented, her voice soft. "It was reported on the news this morning. I didn't know that about her."

"It surprised me, too." I wondered how much I should tell Dr. Comaine, but reasoned that she had a right to as much information as possible before the media sprung the unpleasant truth they were sure to dig up. "I'm afraid that the baby's had to be admitted to hospital suffering from malnutrition and, I'm sorry to say, neglect."

Samuels groaned. "Great. Just great. Wait till the newspapers get hold of that one. *Trillium student victim abuses own baby.*"

"They can't say any such thing." For once, Dr. Comaine spoke decisively. I remembered that before beginning her climb up the administrative ladder her field had been child welfare law in the School of Public Policy. "It's a matter of the child's right to privacy. There won't be any mention of her at all, except her becoming a ward of Children's Aid. The newspapers won't be able to print a word otherwise."

"Unless they get into her apartment," I was unwise enough to add.

"What do you mean?" she snapped.

"The crib was turned into a kind of cage," I said. "And the superintendent of the building said that she used to leave the baby alone for hours."

"The police will have the apartment sealed until they solve the case." Dr. Comaine straightened the bow at her throat. "By then, hopefully, the papers will be busy with some other sensation. Please, Professor Cairns, what shall I say about Ms. Demetris?"

"She would hate the circus out there. She was an intensely private person."

Lucy Easton intervened. "You can say that she'd come to Trillium to make a better future for herself, that she believed in a woman's right to education for meaningful work. That's true enough, isn't it Rosalie? She was very insistent on taking courses that would lead to a job."

"Why was she studying Literature then?" Stanich muttered to Hugh Ascott who stifled a giggle in a poor parody of a cough.

"Sorry," he stuttered. "First cold of the season."

Dr. Comaine turned her back on the two of them. "Thank you, Lucy, for your help. I think I have sufficient information then, with this message to the university community that Lloyd drew up for me. Lloyd, you come with me." Stanich made a move as if to join them, but the president shook her head. "Not you, Frank. Not yet. Tempers will be a little high out there, and everyone knows about the petition against your course."

"That has nothing to do with this," Stanich glared.

She patted his arm. "I know, Frank. But I think it would be better if you kept a low profile until this thing is solved. Don't you, Bud?"

Levin nodded. Frank opened his mouth as if to protest, then shrugged.

Comaine stared at him for a moment, then accepted that he would not insist on coming. "Will you come with me, Lucy? I think a strong female contingent is in order." She checked the clock in the hall. "We'll convene in my office in one hour. The chief of police is bringing his crime team in to bring us up to date and give us some advice on what to do next. Bud, you'll be there for sure?"

"Yes Ma'am," Levin nodded.

Professor Ng opened the door, but Comaine paused before leaving.

"Do you know the family?" she asked me.

I shook my head. What was the point in describing my encounter with John Demetris and his angry condemnation of his daughter's lifestyle?

"Perhaps you'd be willing to talk to them? I tried calling earlier but the line was busy. And now I'll be tied up in meetings. I will, of course, be in touch soon, but I think someone should speak to them right away, and, as Ms. Demetris's supervisor, you were the closest faculty to her. I know they'll want to make their own arrangements, and of course, the university will be represented at the funeral. Which reminds me, Lloyd, " she turned to Samuels, "find out which mortuary is taking care of things and make sure a wreath is sent."

"Will do." He made a note in a small pad which he fished from his pocket.

"One of the things I'm announcing out there," Comaine inclined her head in the direction of the quadrangle, "is that we're going to establish a scholarship fund in her name, for other mature students. We'll make a formal announcement at a service we're going to hold in the chapel next week. We decided on Thursday, right?" The men around her nodded. "One week to the day. Hopefully, by then the police will have dealt with this situation. Professor Cairns, the family may wish to come to the service. Would you invite them? Would you give them our assurances that we are doing everything possible to assist the authorities in clearing up this matter? And if there's anything we can do … ?"

I nodded. She wasn't really asking me to call the family, but giving me orders. Besides, having such a commission from the administration gave me an excuse to call on the Demetrises at home. I was curious to meet the mother for myself and to hear from her why the family had abandoned their daughter and granddaughter.

"Lloyd, you have the address? Give it to Professor Cairns, will you? Let's get this over with."

Samuels ripped a page from his notebook and passed it to me as he hurried after the others.

Professor Easton squeezed my hand once more. "We should talk, later," she murmured. "Let me know what the family wants to do about the memorial."

Levin slipped out after her and followed, keeping well back from the official group. He was joined by one of the uniformed guards who appeared, from the excited waving of his hands, to be complaining about the camera cars blocking the road.

"God, I'm glad to be spared that," Stanich yawned and stretched. "Those dykes out there would eat me alive."

"For heaven's sake, Frank," Norma Ladurie glared at him. "You could at least show some respect for the dead. And those girls are not all dykes, and even if they were, you should be ashamed of yourself for talking like that."

"A man can't even make a joke among friends without being accused of being politically incorrect?"

"I wasn't aware that we were friends." Norma stalked out of the lobby. If the door had not been one of those designed for wheelchair access on a spring-loaded hinge, she would have slammed it behind her.

"Touchy, touchy," Stanich turned to the other men. "She needs to lighten up."

"It's difficult, don't you think," I said, "when a girl has been murdered behind your home and you're responsible for all the kids still living there? She's probably worried sick. And I agree with her, your remark was not only inappropriate but offensive."

"Ah, Professor Cairns," Stanich looked me up and down, slowly. I stared back, but could feel the flush rising in my cheeks. He let the silence stretch too long before speaking. "We meet at last. You're the one who's been after me about my Popular Culture course? You've been naughty," he wagged his finger at me. "That girl was a pain in the neck with her foolish petition. Not that it would do her any good. The other students have never objected to my teaching methods or to the curriculum. I doubt any of them would have signed it."

"Sophia was very uncomfortable ..."

"We're not here to make people comfortable, but to make them think." Ascott and Ng nodded in agreement.

"By offending them deliberately? Anyway, that's no excuse for you refusing to answer my calls."

He shrugged. "What's there to say? The department decided on the qualifications for degrees and approved the curriculum. If she didn't like it, she could always change her major. I mean, we weren't forcing her to take the course. It was her choice."

"But she wanted to study journalism," I pointed out. "She couldn't take any of those courses without your required course."

"If she was so thin-skinned she couldn't stand a little controversy, she certainly was not the right person for a media career," Stanich spoke back over his shoulder. "She was in the wrong place at the wrong time in more than one instance, it looks like to me. Come on, fellas, let's get a coffee before Comaine comes back, foaming for action." He set off down the hall with Hugh Ascott and Henry Ng in his wake. One of them made a joke; their laughter echoed.

I jabbed at the elevator button, imagining my target was Stanich's self-satisfied smirk.

"I know he's a little hard to take," Giles Harding-Jervase said. He picked at the brush of hair on his upper lip. The registrar was a man in his middle fifties who carried himself with an almost military bearing. His eyebrows made a solid line across his wide brow, his salt-and-pepper hair was trimmed close to his skull. His nose was long and sharp, his face pitted with old acne scars, his chin punctuated with a large obtrusive mole. His three-piece navy blue suit fit him so well I wondered if he still patronized a tailor. On the lapel was pinned a loop of white ribbon. "I can't stand him myself."

I smiled back at him. Last spring, Will had worked on extensive renovations of a cottage that Harding-Jervase and his partner had bought up at Rock Lake, just outside town. I had accompanied Will to the party celebrating the completion of the job. Harding-Jervase had had us in stitches with his gossip about various members of the academic community.

"How can a person like that still teach in a university?" I asked him now.

"Tenure." Harding-Jervase grinned. "It's the last stand of the dinosaurs."

"But he's such a pig. I can't believe he's chair of a department."

"Now there's a story. Media Studies, as you may have heard, is not one of our more collegial programs. It's partly a problem of the kinds of courses they offer, partly theoretical and partly practical, business administration-type things, the kind your student wanted to take. Then within those two major divisions are the Marxist faction, and the deconstructionists, and the neo-conservatives, and so on. You can imagine what departmental elections are like. Last time, the old chair left after some sort of brouhaha about admission standards for the program. Each faction put forth one candidate, then that got whittled down to two, let's call them a right- and left-wing division, though it was more complicated then that."

"And Stanich was the right-winger and won?"

"Would that it were so simple. No one much likes Frank. He was hired back in the days when the university was desperate for anyone with a semblance of a graduate degree; he has an M.Phil. And he isn't a man to make friends easily, although women used to find him quite attractive. Rumour has it he's slept with every willing wife on campus."

"Oh, come on."

"S'truth." He crossed his heart. "Oh, in the old days, it was quite a lively place, let me tell you. Back in the sixties, I'm talking about. All-night parties with faculty and students. Musical bedrooms, we called it. Like the kid's game, only spiced up with a lot of bad wine and not a few drugs."

"You're joking!"

"Hard to believe nowadays, isn't it? Frank came here with one wife and he's had two since, both of them his students, and the relationships did not necessarily begin after he taught them, if you know what I mean." He winked.

"I don't think you should be telling me this." I pushed at the elevator button again. Perhaps I should take the stairs. Like Alex, I could do with the exercise.

"Wait a minute. Let me tell you about the election. One of the groups, I won't say which one, decided to finesse the election by throwing in a lame-dog candidate who would draw enough of the middle-of-the-road vote that their opponent would lose. Frank didn't realize this, of course. He was chuffed that they came to him and asked him to stand. And then, lo and behold, what happens? So many people couldn't commit themselves to either of the two serious candidates that Frank wins on the first ballot and now they're stuck with him for five years!"

"That's terrible," I said, trying not to laugh. "Couldn't they have another election?"

"Democratic process, my dear," Harding-Jervase wiped his eyes. "There's nothing quite like academics indulging in political action. The theory's all there, but the practice ..." He chuckled.

"What about the students? Don't they find him offensive?"

"Well, he's not in the classroom much any more. *Administrative duties*, you know. And he's very careful when he's not around those he thinks of as his own kind. Especially since Dr. Comaine approved the sexual harassment policy at the beginning of term. He's a clever fellow, our Frank, but not a nice one. Oh no. He's not a man to forget or forgive."

"Are you trying to tell me something?"

"A friendly word." The elevator at last arrived. Harding-Jervase waited while I stepped inside, then held the doors open to finish what he had to say. "I know you were doing your best for your student, trying to find a substitute for that required course. And I'm sure you advised her against that petition."

"I tried. She was so angry, she wouldn't listen to me."

"That course is Frank's baby. It's true he managed to finesse Alex Warren into sharing the teaching load, but he kept control of the content. He was furious when he heard that some student was trying to start a petition against it and incensed when he heard that you were asking questions. He doesn't like criticism. He doesn't like junior faculty complaining about his curriculum to the higher-ups."

"But I didn't have anything to do with Sophia's petition. It was all her idea."

"Not according to Irene Smith."

"What's Irene got to do with it?"

"She used to be Frank's secretary until he managed to have her transferred. It was supposed to be a promotion for her, *administrative assistant* to Lucy Easton. But the real story is that Frank was tired of her and she's still carrying a torch for him. He wanted her out of the way, but not too far: she types all his academic papers for him. Not that there's that many of them."

"That's why she was here last night," I remembered. "She said she was doing some work for him."

"She's very loyal. She took it personally that Ms. Demetris was slandering the course."

"It wasn't slander. Have you seen the course outline? The essay topic she objected to?"

"Well, no."

"I wouldn't want to answer such leading questions about my relationships, neither in a paper nor in front of a class. I sympathized with her anger, though not the way she was dealing with it."

"That's as may be," Harding-Jervase wagged his head. "It doesn't matter much now anyway. I'm just telling you to be careful."

I stepped into the elevator and pushed the fourth floor button. I'd noticed how Irene's attitude to me had hardened in the past few weeks. Perhaps her conviction that I was in complicity with Sophia over the petition was the reason.

Harding-Jervase held the doors open. "Keep out of his road and he'll leave you alone. Be careful what you say in memos you route through Miss Smith. And by the way," he raised his voice as he disappeared behind the door, "I am sorry about Ms. Demetris. It's a tragedy, no matter what."

With a groaning clank and the rattle of cables, the elevator began to crawl upward. Its walls were papered with printed posters advertising various campus activities but the back of the doors had been liberally covered with graffiti I tried not to interpret. I was angry enough already and didn't need evidence of the puerile misogynism that characterized most such writing to exacerbate my mood. I thought of the registrar's story of the Media Studies election and allowed myself to grin as I imagined the faces of the conspirators when they learned how badly their plot had misfired. Still, having Frank in a position of power to influence the careers of young people was too high a price to pay for their machinations. I wondered which side of the action Alex had been on. And, considering Alex's tiny office stuck at the end of the hall with the English Department and the fact that all he had been given to teach were first-year introductory courses, I thought it quite likely that it had been the wrong one in the new chair's view.

EIGHT

The door to Irene's office was open, but, for once, there was no line-up of students waiting for her attention. I peeked in. Irene sat with her back to her computer screen, staring out her window. Her view was better than mine: she could see across the quadrangle to the light glinting on the windows of the library. If she looked down, she would also be able to see the crowd around the alley, although she wouldn't be able to hear whatever was being said down there. None of the windows in the Arts Tower could be opened, in order, it was said, to conserve heating costs in winter and keep in the air conditioned coolness in summer. The circulation system, however, suffered from as many faults as the elevator and too often the result was a moist, heavy airflow that neither cooled nor warmed, but left one feeling slightly sticky and out of breath. Most faculty spent as little time as possible in their offices and tried to get lecture and seminar room space in one of the older buildings on campus where the air was at least natural, if not controlled. Poor Irene had no such option; she seemed to be constantly battling head colds. She kept two boxes of tissues on her desk and seemed to empty one a day.

"How are you feeling?" I asked her.

She jumped, her chair sliding backwards into the desk. The computer beeped in protest at the jar.

"Sorry," I added, "I didn't mean to scare you."

Irene clutched a sodden mass of tissue in one hand. Her face was red and swollen with either a terrible cold or tears, it was difficult to tell. She was dressed today in one of her usual office ensembles: a black sweater over a white blouse and red tartan skirt.

She glared at me. "You could knock and warn a body."

"The door was open. Are you sure you should be here today? You don't look well at all."

"And that's with being up half the night with the police, thanks to you. Why couldn't you mind your own business?"

"They asked me who I'd seen on campus when I left," I defended myself.

"And now Professor Easton will hear about it and I'll be in trouble for moonlighting."

"Don't be silly. Everyone knows you do extra work at night; as long as it's on your own time, why should she care?"

"You don't understand." Irene picked another tissue from the box and blew her nose loudly. She tossed it into her wastepaper basket which was already nearly full. "If you don't mind, I have work to do. Department work."

"Did Sophia ever talk to you about herself?" I asked. "She seemed to hang around my office a lot and I wondered if she ever came in to chat with you."

"I don't chat. I work."

"I just wondered."

"I don't have time for conversations with students," Irene stared at the words scrolling across the computer screen. "I tell them what time to expect you faculty – when you bother to let me know when you'll be in – and I take messages. That's all. They have their lives, I have mine."

She began to type, glancing down at a handwritten sheet of paper on the desk beside the keyboard.

I gave up. Irene had always been polite to me until Sophia had begun circulating her petition. She'd cornered me in her office one morning and lectured me about my duty, as a junior faculty member, to defend my senior colleagues and to dissuade my supervisee from stirring up trouble, especially such malicious trouble. She would not believe that I had no influence with Sophia and came close to accusing me of aiding and abetting what she saw as a crime against the Media Studies chair. Since then, she had become increasingly acerbic, if not downright unfriendly to me. Since there was little I could do to change her mind about me, I tried to stay out of her way as much as possible.

One corner of her office was devoted to the department mailboxes and bulletin board. I picked up my mail: two literary journals I subscribed to, a university affairs newsletter, a notice that the regular department meeting for that afternoon had been cancelled.

I flipped through one of the journals as I walked down the hall. The quiet was unnerving, more like a Sunday afternoon of a long weekend than a Friday morning. I unlocked my office door and flicked on the light, sighing. Another day, another dollar. My calendar was still open at yesterday's date, Sophia's name written in red. I shivered, and turned the page before hanging my jacket on the hook behind the door. I plunked my briefcase down on my desk and fell into my chair, swivelling as usual to look out up at the sky. What I could see of it was grey and cheerless.

Which is how I felt about my day. I could grade essays, work on the footnotes to my thesis, check the e-mail for memos. Perhaps there would be something about Sophia and the new security measures, taken too late of course, but nonetheless welcome. I reached to switch on my computer, and stopped.

Lying across the keyboard was a single long-stemmed red rose. I picked it up and sniffed the faintly medicinal odour of a hot-house flower. There was no card, no note. I looked at the office door: yes, it had been locked. Irene had a master key to the offices; perhaps she had opened the door for someone. She certainly hadn't acted as if there was a surprise waiting for me. Maybe Will had sent it to cheer me up? Unlikely. In all the years of our marriage, he'd only brought me flowers on Valentine's Day and once or twice when I was too sick to get out of bed.

Flower in one hand, mug in the other, I wandered back down the hall to the water fountain by the elevators and Irene's office. I filled the mug, then looked in on her. She was busy typing, a long cord dangling from the ear plug that connected her to the dictaphone. I waved the flower, but she ignored me. I went right up to her desk. She had no choice but to look up. Heaving a giant sigh, she lifted her fingers from the keyboard.

"What?"

"Sorry to bother you, but I was wondering if you might have some scissors so I can cut the stem to fit in the mug."

She yanked open a drawer, and thrust a pair of scissors at me. I held the stem over her wastepaper basket as I snipped.

"Who brought it to me?" I asked.

"How should I know?" She made a correction on the screen.

"It was on my desk. I assumed you must have unlocked the door."

"No."

"No?" I repeated. "But then how did it get in there?"

She moved the cursor to another word and deleted it.

I tried again. "No one asked you to open my door for them?"

"I don't do that," she said. "If someone wants to leave something for a faculty member, I tell them to put it in their box. I've been told that some faculty don't like students poking around in their offices when they're not there, that some faculty have important documents to keep private. I do what I'm told. I didn't open any doors for anyone."

"I'm not accusing you of anything. I just wondered where this came from."

She didn't respond, but typed in a few words at the end of a paragraph. I gave up. I stuck the rose in the mug and returned to my own office. Perhaps in my hurry to leave yesterday I'd forgotten to lock the door behind me, and someone, knowing that I had been trying to help Sophia, had brought me the flower in condolence. And then locked the door to make sure no one else came in and took it? This didn't make a lot of sense but was the only solution I could come up with for the mystery.

It was hard to get down to work. I phoned the hospital but they wouldn't give me any information about Mara. I tried calling Jack Lansdown, but his shift didn't begin until late afternoon and no one else at the CAS would discuss the Demetris case with me. George Finlay was not in his office; neither was Constable Quinn. I thought for a moment about going back downstairs and joining the vigil in the alley to see if I could pick up any news. The pile of essays on my desk dissuaded me. I had work to do.

"Who's the secret admirer?" Alex lounged in the doorway.

"What? Oh, the rose. I don't know. You didn't see anyone in my office earlier today, did you?"

"I just got here. Good thing I didn't cancel the lecture, the hall was packed. Not that anyone paid much attention to me until I started talking about the media impact on murder investigations. Boy, that sure perked them up!"

"Alex, how could you?"

"A learning opportunity," he said. "It's a natural. The class can use this as a case study; I've assigned study groups to look at each aspect of the media coverage, and I've got a couple of real go-getters who are anxious to interview the cops on the case." He picked up the rose and stroked the silky petals.

"I can't believe you can be so crass. Sophia was one of the students in that class."

"More reason to use her as an example. Besides, it'll distract the others from thinking about her as a person to thinking about her as an object of media manipulation. And I can use their results for my research. I thought you might help as well."

"What research?"

His answer was interrupted by a loud knock on the door.

"Professor Cairns? Can we speak to you? In private?" Three of the women standing in the door were the trio I'd seen carrying the banner from the parking lot. The other was Ani Lyons, the editor of the student newspaper, *The Shield*. I recognized her from my fourth-year poetry course. Although she was only auditing it for her own interest, she was vocal in her criticism of the lack of female and Canadian authors in the curriculum designed by Isaac Pleasant, the man whom I'd been called in to replace. I agreed with her, but other than assigning essay topics, I had no time or freedom to redesign the course to reflect more contemporary interests. All four were dressed in identical black outfits: black tights, black T-shirts, loose black jackets. If it wasn't for the fact that I'd never seen Ani in any other colour, I would have thought they were in mourning.

"Ani," Alex smiled. "Sorry I missed you yesterday. I got hung up on the squash court. I did try calling, but you must have left already. Did you wait long?"

"Not really. I left the essays I marked with your secretary. I guess that's all right?" As she answered him, I noticed the other girls exchanging looks behind her back, a matter of grimaces and raised eyebrows.

Alex must have noted their silent exchange as well. He stood up slowly, his eyes on Ani. She couldn't look away from him. He smiled. "Ani's my teaching assistant this year," he explained to me. "As well as my one grad student. Her research field and mine are very similar."

"What's that?" I asked.

"Murder," he grinned.

"It's not a funny subject," the long-haired girl snapped. "Especially today."

"I apologize. I didn't think."

"Evidently," she muttered.

"Lisa," Ani warned. "There's no need to be nasty. Alex apologized. And he's right, it is our field: the exploitation of murder and its victims by the mass media."

The other girl shrugged, but didn't reply.

Alex's lips quirked in an awkward grin. "I'm on my way then, Rosie, to give you some space for your meeting. And Ani, I'll see you later. Weren't you supposed to have an outline of your thesis ready for me to look at?"

She sighed. "It's going to be a little late."

He wagged a finger at her. "The slippery slope, my girl. You've got to respect the deadlines I set or you'll end up wasting your year."

"But I've promised to get this memorial organized. For the girl who was murdered."

"Your work is also important." He noted the droop of her shoulders, and relented. "All right, I'll give you till Monday, 9:30 a.m. on the dot."

"Thanks, Alex."

He waved a hand in farewell and slipped out the door. It had barely closed behind him when the girl called Lisa hissed at Ani, "I don't know how you can stand to be in the same room with him."

"He's not that bad."

"He's one of Stanich's boys. He even lectured today on the murder, didn't even have the decency to cancel his class. He's callous, he'll use anybody or anything for his own purposes. Can't you see that yet?"

"This isn't the time or place ..." Ani protested.

"So when's it going to be a good time for you to face up to how he's using you?" The girl tossed her head, her long hair falling about her shoulders in a blonde shower.

"He's not using me," Ani nearly shouted. She took a deep breath, reining in her temper. "How many times do we have to go over this? The man is my thesis supervisor. I work as his teaching assistant. That's it. Period. I'm insulted that you suggest anything different. I mean, it is possible for men and women to work together without getting involved. Don't you agree, Professor Cairns?"

Caught off-balance by her sudden appeal, I merely nodded my head.

"Look," the girl with the shaved head intervened. "We're not here to talk about Ani and Professor Warren. That's their business. We want to talk to you about Sophia Demetris."

The fourth girl nodded, the beads on her tight rows of braided hair jingling as she did so. "It's this memorial we're organizing for her?" Her voice rose at the end so that I wasn't sure whether she was asking me a question or not.

"The administration," I began, but Ani interrupted me.

"You don't know these people, do you?" she asked me. "This is Lisa McKenzie of the Aids Awareness Group, and Sandra Withers and Dawn Starr from the Sexual Assault Centre."

Dawn Starr was the girl with the shaved head. She was thin enough to be the disaster victim depicted by the state of her clothes: tights torn at the knee and shirt hem shredded. McKenzie was the long-haired girl; Withers the one with corn-row braids. Ani's hair was a thick black brushcut, stiff with gel.

"They won't get it right?" Withers voice rose again, plaintive. I realized it was her way of speaking. "They'll take too long to get it scheduled and they'll ask all the wrong people?"

"They'll make it into a ceremony," Starr continued, her voice thin, hurried. "They'll wait until they hope we've forgotten all the details of what happened, and they won't say *murder*, of course, they'll say stuff like *tragic loss of young life*, just like in church, and we're supposed to sit quietly in rows while they go on about her being a good student, but how would they know that, she was only in first year and no one knew her. Except for the story in the paper." She finally ran out of breath and stopped.

"We don't want to wait," McKenzie took up the thread. "We've got to demand some action now."

"Action? I thought you were talking about a memorial?" I sat on the edge of my desk, pushing aside the mug with the rose in it to do so.

"It's the same thing," McKenzie continued. I recognized her voice now; she'd been one of the announcers I'd heard on the student radio this morning. "Sophia Demetris died because this administration didn't pay attention to our concerns about lighting and safety on campus. It could have been any of us."

"Don't," Starr whispered. Her eyes filled with tears which she brushed away with an impatient hand. "I'm sorry, I promised I wouldn't cry, but every time I think about it! I mean, I live in Jamieson Hall, I go to the library almost every evening. And it could be anyone who did it, he might still be on campus, waiting." Her voice trembled.

"Stop it," Ani commanded. She stared at the other girl who sniffed back insipient sobs. "Sorry, Professor Cairns," she turned back to me. "I'll get right to the point. We want you to speak for Sophia at the memorial. You were her supervisor so you probably knew her better than anyone else on campus."

"As it turns out, I didn't know her well at all," I said. "But what are you planning to do? And when?"

"Tomorrow at dusk," McKenzie replied. "At the very time she was killed. We'll meet in front of the alley and have a few speeches – yours, if you will too, please – and then march on the administration offices to force them to live up to their promises. And we need a picture of Sophia, if you've got one."

I shook my head. "No, I don't have one. Couldn't you use the one that was in *The Shield* article?"

"Well," Ani hesitated. "We don't really want to remind people about that article, if we can. I mean, Sophia said some things there she didn't really mean, in the heat of discussion, you know?"

"I don't know." I looked at them all in turn; they wouldn't meet my gaze. "Sophia had some pretty decided ideas about women and education and about raising student fees to support what she called non-essential services, like the Sexual Assault Centre, Aids Awareness, the proposed walk-home program. How are you going to deal with all that?"

"We're not," McKenzie answered. "It's obvious how wrong she was. If she'd just listened to us, paid attention to what's really going on, women being killed right here on our campus."

"Women?" I questioned. "Plural?"

"A friend of mine, Ariane Ramos, was killed in a hit-and-run in the far parking lot last summer."

"And that social worker who drowned?" Withers added.

McKenzie continued, "They say they were accidents, but we think differently. We've asked and asked for better lighting and emergency phones. All the administration has done is implement that totally useless human rights policy, as if anyone," and she glared at Ani, "would have the guts to complain about behaviour. I mean, words on paper don't cost money, lights and phones do. How many of us have to die before they'll spend those few precious dollars ..." Her anger choked her.

The awkward silence that followed this speech was broken by Starr's whisper. "If we had a picture of Sophia, we could use it for the poster. If you had one, that is."

"We're going to mobilize everybody?" Withers continued. "We're going to march and sit-in if we have to? We're going to make them listen to us this time?"

Ani said, "We've got a whole set of proposals worked out. I tried calling the president's office to arrange a meeting, but she's not available, according to her secretary. Probably trying to arrange damage control, defuse the situation. It's too late for that. It's not just campus safety we're after any more. We want mandatory classes in self-defence for women and awareness training for men. We want the student levy raised to support more funding and space for the Assault Centre. We want ..."

"Wait a minute," I interrupted her speech. "What does all this have to do with Sophia?"

They looked at me, astonished. "She's been murdered," McKenzie said. "What more evidence do you need that this campus is unsafe, that we are all in danger?"

I shook my head. "Granted, you're right about the lack of safety measures on campus, it's too soon to assume that Sophia was the victim of a random killing. She had a life, a rather complicated one. Her death could have been related to that. Perhaps you should wait until the police finish their investigation before you make her into a symbol for the cause."

"How long is the investigation going to take?" Withers demanded.

McKenzie snorted, "We all know the police don't treat domestic violence seriously. If it was her boyfriend who killed her, I mean. They'll probably say she brought it on herself."

"I think you're a little out-of-date on police sensitivity towards this kind of crime. I know the detective in charge of the case. I can assure you he takes it very seriously. You should be more careful about what you say. You can get yourself in a lot of hot water."

"I'm not afraid to speak the truth." McKenzie tossed her head again.

"So you're going to tell the whole truth about Sophia then? That she didn't agree with anything that the rest of you stand for? That she was circulating a petition against course contents that included discussion of sexuality? That she resented and fought against every dollar added to her student fees for causes she didn't believe in, that she felt passionately were outside the ambit of education?"

"But that's not the point," McKenzie said. "What she thought is irrelevant. What counts is how we can use her to save other women from the same fate whether or not they believe in what we're doing for them."

"So the end justifies the means?"

"You just don't understand!" Withers shouted.

"I'm trying. I want you to understand, before you get into this too deeply, exactly what you're doing. What do you know about Sophia's personal life? Did any of you ever talk to her, outside of Ani's interview?"

They looked at one another uneasily.

"She had a baby," Starr said. "It was reported on the news this morning. She's in the hospital, but they didn't say why."

"Because she's a ward of Children's Aid now."

"What about Sophia's family?" McKenzie was still angry. "What right does the government have to step in and take a baby away from its family? It's just one more example of interference. Now they'll probably have to go to court to fight for it."

"They don't want her," I said. "I met Sophia's father last night and he refused to have anything to do with her child. But that's not all: the baby's in hospital because Sophia neglected her, perhaps abused her. She's in intensive care, suffering from malnutrition, dehydration, septic infection – the result of long-term neglect."

"So you're blaming the victim," McKenzie crowed. She turned to the others. "We're wasting time here. Let's go."

"I'm trying to identify all the victims," I objected. "And all the victimizers. People can't be simply labelled; they're a lot more complex than that. Sophia was a person with a lot of trouble in her life. You have to acknowledge her life, as well as her death, if you truly want to remember her. And you can't avoid the fact that she did some very cruel things to her own baby."

"It's the government's fault," McKenzie insisted. "They reneged on their promises for daycare, and with all the welfare and student loan cutbacks, it's not surprising that a single mother would have trouble coping. We've tried for years to get a childcare centre on campus with subsidies for students like Sophia so that she could leave her baby safely while she went to classes."

"She never told anyone here about Mara," I said. "If I'd known, I could have got her some counselling on childcare and some support for babysitting. But all the 'could haves' and 'should haves' mean nothing. I've been trying to come to terms with this myself, that she neglected that baby on purpose."

"Are you saying she deserved to be murdered?" Starr whispered.

"No, of course not. No one deserves that. But she was not the kind of person you would ever seriously consider a feminist hero if you'd actually known her."

"That's not the point," Withers repeated.

"But it is the point," I insisted. "Why do you want me to talk about Sophia? Because you cared about her? Or because her death gives you more leverage to get the kind of publicity you want? Don't you see that you're acting just as cynically as you claim the administration is?"

"It's no use," McKenzie opened the door. "Sorry to waste your time."

"Wait a minute." I held up my hand to stop them. "If you want to make Sophia the symbol for your outrage, you'd better make sure you're ready to accept everything about her. Otherwise, you're making a mistake that's going to end up costing you a lot of credibility."

"We'll think about it," Ani edged towards the door, shooing the others before her. The door closed behind them with a bang, but not before I heard McKenzie's exasperated cry: "Of all the reactionary ..."

"Thank you, Sophia," I said to the air and then flushed, ashamed of myself. It was easy to give lectures about judging character and using real people for symbolic means and yet I was as guilty of this myself. I couldn't get past the fact of Sophia's mistreatment of Mara. Everything I thought about her was coloured by the memory of the baby's condition. What could have led such an intelligent person as Sophia had appeared to be, to treat her baby so badly?

I picked up the first essay from the pile of first-year topics: a handwritten twenty-four-page opus on the significance of flowers in Shakespeare's comedies. I dropped it, sighing. How could I possibly deal with these papers when all I could think about were Sophia and Mara? I didn't dare question George Finlay about the investigation; he'd already warned me off that. But there was nothing to stop me from looking into Sophia's past. In fact, it would be completely understandable for me to visit her family, to give my condolences to her mother, and perhaps get a clue from her as to why Sophia had behaved as she did. Perhaps Mrs. Demetris might have some proof of the baby's fatherhood, some evidence that would help Barbara Lock gain custody. Mara should have a chance at a loving, caring home to make up for the squalor of her beginnings. And just perhaps, in finding out why Sophia had been so cruel, I just might stumble on the identity of her murderer.

NINE

A sharp prick on my index finger reminded me that I was still holding the rose. I leaned over and picked up the phone, hoping Will would still be in his workshop. He answered on the first ring.

"So how'd you do it?" I asked.

"Do what?"

"Get the rose into my office. It was sweet of you to think of me, but I want to know how you got through a locked door without Irene noticing."

"I don't know what you're talking about. What rose?"

I put the flower back in the mug. "You didn't leave a rose here for me this morning?"

"No."

"I found one on my desk. The door was locked and no one seems to know how it got here. I thought maybe you'd brought it by on your way to work this morning and persuaded a cleaner to open the door."

"Wasn't me, but I wish it was. It's probably something to do with Sophia; someone who knew you were her supervisor. Or maybe you have a secret admirer."

"That's what Alex said. I don't like the idea of people getting into my office when I'm not here."

"Anything missing?"

"Not as far as I can tell."

"Maybe you forgot to lock up last night."

"Maybe."

"If nothing's missing, I wouldn't worry about it."

"I guess. Listen, let me tell you," I recounted the story of the meeting with the four girls. "I just can't concentrate on marking," I concluded. "All I can think of is Sophia and Mara."

"Finlay warned you against getting involved with the investigation."

"That's not what I had in mind," I shivered. "I know better than to go looking for trouble. No, it was Sophia's mother I was thinking about. This will be a terrible shock to her, especially since she's so ill. I thought I'd go see her in person to give my condolences and see what the family plans to do about Mara."

"You should talk to Jack Lansdown first."

"I tried, but he doesn't come to work until late this afternoon. If I leave now, I can be in Scarborough shortly after noon and still get back early this evening."

"Why don't you just phone?"

"I'm not sure she'll talk to me. If I'm right there on the doorstep, it may be harder for her to send me away. And I'm hoping her husband won't be home. He scares me."

"He may have taken the day off work," Will pointed out. "Wouldn't you if your daughter had been found murdered?"

"I still think I should go. Besides, Dr. Comaine asked me to contact the family. A visit will be better than a phone call from a stranger."

"Want me to come with you?"

"No need. Listen, did you call Karen?"

"Rats, I knew there was something I was forgetting. Just a second." He put the phone down and I listened to the indistinct roar of voices shouting over the whine of a circular saw. A moment later, he came back on the line. "Sorry. One of the guys didn't realize I was on the phone. We're in a rush around here. As usual."

"Don't forget to call her. I'll be back around seven or so. Do you want to go straight to the hospital when I get there?"

"Yeah. Then we'll go out and get a pizza or something."

"That's what I love about you – you're so romantic."

"And I love you too. Drive carefully."

"I always do."

Now that I'd made up my mind to go, I was in a hurry to get on the road. I stuffed the essays into my briefcase, scrawled a note that I'd be back on Monday for office hours, and taped it to my door. I double-checked that the lock had engaged before heading off. The elevator at the end of the hall stood open. Thanking my luck, I raced for it, slipping into the empty chamber just as the doors wheezed shut.

I stepped out of the Arts Tower into a fine mist of rain. Around the corner, the crowd had considerably thinned, the musicians were gone, and the banner drooped disconsolately from its poles, the red paint running. The mass of flowers laid under the yellow tape were already sodden, their white petals muddied. The scent of their rotting followed me along the footpath. I nodded at the policeman sitting in the cruiser parked at the alley mouth. He stared right past me, watching the small group of girls who kept vigil under the uncertain shelter of a large piece of plastic they held over their heads. I recognized Ani and Dawn Starr, but neither Withers nor McKenzie appeared to be there. They were probably busy making posters in the student paper printroom, or back on the radio with their call to arms. *Rosie, Rosie,* I chided myself. *Don't be nasty. They mean well, they're young, and they're scared. They don't know what else to do.*

The address Lloyd Samuels had given me was for a house on Victoria Park Avenue, one of the major north-south routes in the east end of Toronto, in the suburb of Scarborough. That made finding it easy: I could stay on the 401 until I reached the Victoria Park exit, then head south until I found the right number. It was only just past 10 a.m.; with luck and light traffic, I'd be in the city by noon.

I was out of town and on the highway heading west when I remembered I'd forgotten to tell Alex Warren that dinner that night was cancelled. I could stop at a service station and call him. I glanced at the fuel gauge; the tank was nearly full. I could call him from the city or, for that matter, wait until I got home. I'd invited the two of them to come for dinner early, about 7 or so; given the situation with Sophia's murder, I was sure Alex probably expected and wouldn't be surprised to hear that the date was off. I fished out my wallet and looked to see if I had any change: pennies and loonies. That decided it.

I didn't want to waste time buying something I didn't need just to get some quarters; besides, by now, Alex probably wouldn't be in his office, anyway. I would call him at the house where he boarded when I got home, and hope that he wouldn't mind the late cancellation. After all, I told myself, there's no reason that he and Karen couldn't go ahead and see each other without Will and me. That matchmaker crack of his still rankled.

Mid-morning and the highway was almost deserted. I revved into fifth gear and drifted, my eyes wandering from the road in front to the mirrors and back again, my fingers tapping along with the music from the tape I'd pushed into the deck without looking. As I neared the turn-off to the 401, I took hold of myself, feeling my heart begin to pound, my fists clench on the wheel. I hated the highway, the tension of the high-speed race to the towers of the city. Transport trucks roared by, their tailwinds buffeting my little car. I manoeuvred into the middle of the three lanes and kept up a steady pace, ignoring as much as possible the antics of other drivers who seemed to feel that switching lanes at high speeds without signalling was not only the acceptable but the only way to get ahead faster. The traffic bunched and thinned as it passed through Oshawa and Pickering, and built to a steady stream as the expressway widened into twelve lanes.

I paid little attention to the tape until I was forced to slow down as the traffic began its stop-and-start dance at the Kingston Road exit. With the idling of the engine, the music swelled to fill the car. It was the Crash Test Dummies' song, "The Ghosts That Haunt Me," an appropriate, if depressing, lyric. I jabbed the eject button to stop the tape, my eyes stinging with tears. I knew that song well, and the following lines repeated themselves in my head without need for accompaniment. A car horn behind me blared. I shoved into first gear and followed the truck in front of me over into the collector lanes. I gradually picked up speed as cars peeled off one by one onto the various feeder roads. My exit was coming up. I sniffed back tears and fiddled with the radio dial until I found a classical music station: a Chopin *Nocturne*. The weather and the air waves were conspiring to reduce me to melancholy. I switched the radio off and drove along in the whir of tires on asphalt, the rush of passing trucks. Negotiating the exit and adjusting to the slower speed on Victoria Park Avenue took my mind off thoughts of death. The street was lined with little box houses, squatting behind narrow strips of brown lawn. The numbers were far too high; the Demetris house must be all the way down near the lake.

I couldn't stand the pressure of silence, heavy with thoughts of the interview to come. I didn't keep many tapes in the car, but luckily I hadn't cleaned out the dash since our last trip up to the cottage. There was a Bonnie Raitt tape there, along with Leonard Cohen. I chose the blues, Bonnie's raunch over Leonard's cool. Singing, I passed blocks of bungalows, neatly uniform, their driveways empty, and then the long stretch of strip plazas and fast food drive-aways. I wasn't hungry, although it was past noon. The stink of meat fried in old grease pervaded the car at every stoplight, and there were many of those. The road dipped past a small golf course, deserted in the rain. A bus making a left turn into the subway station held up traffic for a few minutes. Then the street narrowed to two lanes from four, the sidewalks shaded by tall trees which dropped yellow leaves onto the wet pavement. The houses were mostly pre-war brick semi-detacheds, with here and there a four-plex or a sixties bungalow with its bay window a jungle of plants. I slowed, looking for the number. It was on the right, two houses from a corner, one of the red-brick duplexes. I turned the corner and found a parking spot almost immediately. Luck was with me still. I doubted how much longer it could last.

Instead of the usual wooden verandah that linked the two halves of the house, this building had two separate staircases made of precast concrete blocks roofed with aluminum awnings held up on black wrought-iron poles. The Demetris yard was enclosed in a five-foot chain-link fence; the gate was unlatched and wedged open with an old brick. The lawn had been scraped clear of leaves and the flowerbeds on either side of the steps had been heaped with mulch for the winter. A shrub at the outside corner of the building was shrouded in grey burlap. Although the day was grey and cheerless, no lights shone in the house and no one answered when I rang the bell.

I should have phoned, I cursed myself. Just because Barbara Lock said the mother was sick, I should not have assumed she'd be at home. Perhaps she was in a hospital. Perhaps I'd wasted my time with this drive.

For good measure, I knocked loudly on the glass fan-light of the front door. This time I heard footsteps. The door was wrenched open by a woman who might have been Sophia's opposite image: she was almost as wide as she was tall, her hips flaring under the rolled-over elastic waist of a long, black skirt, her breasts straining at the buttons of a long-sleeved black silk shirt. A long braid of black hair hung over one shoulder. Her face was blotched, her eyes red-rimmed, her lips chapped.

"What do you want?" she said. Her voice was a low growl, husky with too many cigarettes or tears. "We're not talking to reporters." She began to close the door.

"I'm not a reporter. I'm from Trillium University." I stuck out my hand. "I'm Rosalie Cairns, Professor Cairns. Sophia was one of my students."

The woman looked me up and down, then blew out her breath in a long, exasperated sigh. "You'd better come in." She looked over my shoulder up and down the street before slamming the door shut. "Ghouls," she muttered.

"Excuse me?" I bent down to take off my shoes, damp from the walk round the corner from the car.

"Don't worry about the floors," she said, pointing. A strip of plastic covered the broadloom. "So many people have been in and out since we got the news, there's no point in trying to keep it clean."

"I'm sorry if you think my visit's ghoulish," I began.

Her lips quirked in a half-smile, one hand stroking down the length of her braid. "Not you. I was talking about the neighbours. Old Mrs. Benson across the street hasn't moved from her front window since the police called here last night. Nosy old bat. I'm Rita Petrie, by the way. Sophia's cousin." She bit her lip on the word. A small drop of blood swelled and was sucked away.

"I'm terribly sorry about Sophia," I said. "It must be a great shock to the family."

"Yes, it is. Look, come in and sit down. I guess you've come to see Uncle John and Aunt Mary-Ellen? He's at the funeral home trying to make arrangements. The police won't release her body yet and he's raising the roof about that. Well, you can imagine."

"I met him, briefly, last night. Before the news."

Rita looked me up and down again. "Aunt Mary-Ellen's resting. She'll be getting up soon. Would you like to wait?"

"If it wouldn't be any trouble. I drove down to give her my sympathies and to tell her about the memorial service the university is planning."

"Oh, she won't go to *that*," Rita shook her head. "I mean, it's good of you to come and all, but she's blaming the university, you see, for Sophia's death. If Sophia hadn't been accepted into the program there, she would still be at home. At least, that's what Aunt Mary-Ellen thinks."

"And do you agree with her?"

"She'd always lived at home until last year. I don't know why she moved out, or how she could afford to; she certainly wasn't making a lot of money at that flower shop she worked in. Next thing we hear, she's left town. We didn't even know she'd gone to university until last night. My Mom tried to find out where she was, but Aunt Mary-Ellen wouldn't tell her. Still won't. We're talking here about a family big on secrets."

"So I've found out."

"Did you know her well?" Rita wouldn't look at me as she asked the question.

"Not really. I was her academic supervisor, helped set up her course load and apply for bursaries. Things like that. She didn't seem to have many friends on campus."

"That's Sophia, all right. We were close when we were kids, but once we grew up, she changed. Then I got married." Rita shrugged. Head tilted towards the steep stairs that filled most of the tiny hall in which we stood, she listened for a moment as if a sound had alerted her and warned her into silence. She put her finger on her lips and nodded to a door in the shadows under the staircase. "I was just making some tea. Will you have a cup with me in the kitchen? The living room's kind of crowded, ready for the wake." She gestured at a doorway on the left.

I peeked into the narrow living room, darkened by pulled blinds and musty with the odour of the vases of flowers perched on several small tables which were pushed against the wall and lined up across the front window. A brocaded chesterfield suite was backed against the wall facing me; centred over it was a framed oil painting of a white village perched on a cliff over a gently heaving sea. The paint and the colours had been applied with a very heavy hand. At right angles to the chesterfield and marching through a rounded arch into what must be the dining room were rows of folding chairs. They faced a table draped in white lace and pushed flush against the back window, whose blinds were also drawn. The only light came from two tall candles in silver holders on either side of a framed portrait of Sophia.

"That was her graduation picture from high school," Rita followed my glance. "It's the most recent one they had." Her lips tightened.

Even ten years ago, Sophia's face was closed, frowning, her eyes glancing away from the camera. Her hair had been long then, gathered back from her forehead with a wide black ribbon and lying loosely over the shoulders of the academic gown she was posed in. The photographer had added some tint so that her lips and cheeks glowed unnaturally bright. The candlelight reflecting in the glass made her eyes flicker, as if she were about to look up right at me. A kettle whistled and broke the spell.

"This way." Rita led me through a swinging door into the real heart of the house: a kitchen bright with fresh yellow paint and lit by fluorescent lights in the ceiling and under the glass-fronted cupboards. Red lace curtains were looped to either side of a wide window above a gleaming white porcelain sink. The back door was open, letting in the sound of rain pattering on the aluminum roof of a patio overhang. The kitchen was spotless, the dishes and cans in the cupboards stacked in neat rows, the appliances lined up against the white tile wall above a wide countertop crowded with boxes, tins, and bowls. Rita saw my look of bemusement.

"Everyone keeps bringing food," she explained. She lifted the kettle from a burner and at the same time opened the oven door. The air was redolent with the smell of baking.

"Hand me that mitt, will you?" she asked.

A red formica table in the middle of the room was flanked by chairs upholstered with naugahyde in the same deep colour. On the table were a pair of oven mitts in the shape of roosters. She slipped one on and pulled out a pan of muffins. While these cooled, she warmed a squat brown teapot with hot water, dropped in a handful of loose leaves, and filled it. The tea cosy was another rooster, its quilted head pulled back in a silent crow. Rita centred the teapot on a trivet of black iron, arranged the warm muffins on a plate, and laid cups, saucers, bread-and-butter plates, knives, and spoons on the two cork mats she first placed on the table, one across from the other. Still without speaking, she fetched a small pitcher of milk from the fridge and added a matching bowl of sugar.

"Sit," she commanded. However, before sitting down herself, she went to the door and pushed it open. The hinges squeaked and she breathed out a quiet curse. For a moment she stood there, listening, head cocked towards the stairs. She let the door swing shut and joined me at the table.

"I bake when I've got nothing else to do," she said. "Not that Aunt Mary-Ellen needs any more sweets in the house."

"Do you live here with your aunt and uncle?" I asked.

"God, no. I've been married for ten years. I've got four kids, all boys. Do you have children?"

"No."

"You don't know how lucky you are. Somedays, I just wish I could drown them all, like kittens, you know?" She grimaced. "Not really, I can't imagine what life would be like without them. They're sweet, but boys will be boys! I swear they eat socks. And grow. You wouldn't believe what I have to spend on shoes. It's a good thing Paul – that's my husband – is in steady work. He's a plumber. But you don't want to hear about me. Sometimes I just don't know when to stop talking. My Mom and I have been taking turns sitting with Aunt Mary-Ellen. She's in a bad way."

"I heard she was ill."

"Sophia told you? I didn't think she knew. Uncle John went up there to find her and bring her home."

"I know. I met him at her apartment when I was looking for her too. She'd left Mara for me to look after."

"Mara? Who's that?"

"Her baby."

"Baby?" Rita sat quite still. Then she removed the cosy from the pot and poured tea into two cups, one of which she handed across to me. The cup rattled in its saucer before I lifted it from her hands and set it down on the table.

"I didn't know anything about a baby," she said.

"She seems to have kept quite the secret." I savoured the aroma steaming from the cup, a blend of lemon and mint.

"She was always full of secrets," Rita replied. She swallowed. "I can't believe Aunt Mary-Ellen hasn't told me about the baby. I wonder if she even knows about it?"

"Your uncle does. And he's quite adamant that he wants nothing to do with the poor little thing."

"How old is she?"

"About six months."

Rita screwed up her forehead, counting. "That's why Sophia didn't come to Christmas dinner at Grandmother's last year. She would have been showing by then. So she had a lover. Who'da thunk it? Who is he? Did they get married? Was he the one who did it? Killed her, I mean."

"The police haven't found the killer yet."

"Where's the baby now? A baby!" She shook her head. "Of all the people I know, Sophia is the very last I would ever imagine having a baby without being married properly in a church with bridesmaids and ushers and the whole shebang. She's Uncle John's and Aunt Mary-Ellen's only daughter. She was embroidering towels for her hope chest when she was in kindergarten!"

"Apparently your uncle didn't approve of her boyfriend."

"Who is he? Has he got the baby? What's her name again?"

"She's called Mara. And I hate to tell you this, but she's in intensive care in the hospital."

"Oh, God, whoever killed Sophia tried to kill the baby too? This is awful." Tears slipped down Rita's face. She wiped them away with a rough swipe of the oven mitt.

"No, it wasn't the killer." I paused, trying to think of some way I could tell the truth without being too harshly critical of her cousin. "She – Sophia, I mean – didn't take very good care of the baby. Mara's sick. The doctors think she'll recover all right, but she's pretty thin and weak."

Rita held up her hand. "Wait a minute. You're telling me that Sophia abused her own baby?"

"They're calling it neglect." I described Mara's condition and the way she'd been kept imprisoned in the apartment. Rita listened with her face buried in her hands. Before I'd done, she jumped up and went to stand with her back to me, staring out the window.

"I'm sorry to tell you all this." I faltered to a stop.

Rita turned around, leaning back against the sink. The oven mitt was twisted in her hand.

"So where is the father? Why isn't he helping out? Maybe he's the one who made Sophia treat the baby so badly."

I shook my head. "She was living alone. The father's mother only found out where Sophia and the baby were living yesterday. She wants to adopt Mara."

"Who is she? I mean, he, the father?"

"Martin Lock."

Rita began to giggle. She doubled up, her hands on the sink, heaving with laughter that struggled and finally succumbed into tears. She began to choke. I jumped up and thumped her hard between the shoulder blades. She caught her breath and straightened up, ran some cold water into the sink, and splashed her face clean. She dried it with a dish towel she lifted from a hook under the counter.

"I'm sorry. You must think I'm crazy. That the whole family is crazy."

I shook my head, while secretly agreeing with her. "You know Martin Lock, obviously? What's so funny about him?"

"You met his mother? We used to call her *Lady Lock*."

I nodded. That would be a good name for her.

"The Locks lived next door for years when we were all kids; my parents' house is around the corner. Sophia and I were best friends with the twins, Lisa and Marsha. Uncle John of course didn't want us to have anything to do with them. He's a lot older than my Dad and was a lot more influenced by my grandfather's prejudices, stuff from way back, before the family ever came over here. According to him, the Locks were not our kind."

"So?"

"Well, it didn't matter much to us kids, we all went to the same school and everything. But Uncle John was furious when he found out who lived in the house after he'd bought it. He insisted on tearing down the verandah and putting in the fence. They put up with him for years. I'll say one thing for Mrs. Lock: she never held his behaviour against Sophia and me. She always welcomed us to her house, would give us cookies and stuff. My parents didn't care where I visited, but Sophia had to sneak in. We would tell Aunt Mary-Ellen that she was coming over to my place, then creep in through the back yard. The twins had great toys, a stereo system, their own colour TV in their room. We had such a time." She sighed and rubbed at a spot on the counter. "Then Mrs. Lock inherited a real estate company from her father and they moved. That was right at the end of high school. The twins went to university. I still see Lisa sometimes; her son and my youngest are in the same day care. But Sophia wouldn't have anything more to do with them after they moved. She said they got all stuck-up, but I think she was just jealous because Uncle John refused to let her go to university herself. He got really possessive when she started growing up, wouldn't let her go on dates until she was eighteen, stuff like that. I mean, I wasn't really surprised when she left home, just amazed that it took her so long to get up the nerve to do it. Even Aunt Mary-Ellen seemed happy that she was finally getting on with her own life, but Uncle John was furious. He almost accused me to my face of hiding her somewhere when she disappeared. Like I told you, I didn't even know where she was until the police came last night."

She paused, looking down at her hand, adjusting her engagement ring to show off the diamond. "You'd think coming over here to look after Aunt Mary-Ellen would be paradise after the bedlam I'm used to living in, but I don't mind telling you this house gives me the creeps. Always has."

She pushed aside a couple of cake tins to lay the oven mitt on the counter, trying to iron out the creases with the flat of her hand.

"Marty Lock!" she repeated. "You know, that's quite impossible. Sophia couldn't stand him. None of us could. He was a spoiled little brat, a mama's boy, always getting his own way."

"But Barbara Lock said he was the father. And she had a letter from Sophia that pretty well said the same thing."

Rita tossed her head, her braid swinging like a metronome. "I don't believe it. Sophia had as little to do with him as possible, just like the rest of us. He made matters worse with Uncle John, all the trouble he got up to and his mother making excuses and trying to cover up for him. She was convinced that the love of a good woman – or any woman, for that matter – would "cure" him. She has no idea, none at all, what a little shit he really is. His own sisters won't have anything to do with him. He was working for his brother for a while until Dan found out he was forging company cheques and fired him. Now his mother won't speak to him." She glanced over at a calendar. "Marty couldn't have killed her anyway. Even if he was capable of something that would require so much effort."

"How do you know?"

"He won't be out of jail for another six weeks. He got caught embezzling from the car dealership where his mother got him a job as a salesman. They weren't as forgiving as his brother had been. His father has a really good position with Community and Social Services, some kind of manager. The whole family is embarrassed by him. I could tell you stories …"

"Who's this?"

We both jumped and turned to face the door. A small woman stood there, holding herself upright with the aid of a gnarled black stick. Her white hair was loosely gathered in a bun from which strands had escaped to frame the wreckage of a face: eyes sunk into black hollows, their lids drooping and inflamed, skin sagging from the high cheekbones into jowls that wobbled when she moved her thin lips. Her voice was a cracked whisper.

"You were told to keep strangers away. Reporters." She spat the word.

Rita rushed over and put her arm around the older woman's shoulders urging her into the room. I stood up. Mrs. Demetris shuffled across the floor, her feet slipping in backless sandals. She had a white crocheted shawl tightly knotted around her throat. The dress whose hem dragged at her ankles was black.

"This is Professor Cairns. She's one of Sophia's teachers at the university."

Mrs. Demetris glared at me. "I want to sit."

Rita pulled up a chair and the old woman fell into it. She picked up one of the muffins and sniffed at it. "Chocolate?"

"Chocolate chip oatmeal. The boys love them."

"Chocolate is for cake, not muffins." Mrs. Demetris replaced it and shoved the plate away. "So, what do you want here?" She barked at me.

Behind her back, Rita grimaced, mouthing an apology.

"I wanted to say how sorry I was."

"So, you've said it. You can go."

I forged on. "And to tell you that Mara is being well taken care of. The Children's Aid Society have her in custody until the father is found."

The intensity of her stare silenced me.

"Have a cup of tea, Aunt Mary-Ellen?" Rita fluttered around the table, jiggling cups and saucers.

"Mara," Mrs. Demetris tried the word on her tongue. "That's what she called the baby?"

Rita dropped a cup, but caught it before it hit the floor. She placed it on the table. "You knew about the baby?"

"No business of yours," her aunt snapped.

"She was my cousin. The baby is cousin to my boys."

The old woman ignored her. "You said what you come to say. You caused your trouble. Now you can leave us to take care of it as we can."

I felt the anger rise like a red tide in my cheeks. With a mother like this, no wonder Sophia was so hopeless at looking after Mara. "I guess it's just bad luck on the baby that her mother was killed and she has no father to look after her."

"I don't want to talk to you any more. You aren't welcome here." Mrs. Demetris stood, pointing her stick at the door. She could barely hold it up off the linoleum.

"Mara's in the hospital, Aunt," Rita said. She had her arm around the old woman again and gently pressed her back down into the chair. "This lady was telling me Sophia treated her very badly. She's very sick and it's all Sophia's fault."

Mrs. Demetris huddled over, her hands in her face. When it became obvious that she wasn't going to speak, I moved towards the door. Rita came after me, and stopped me with a hand on her arm.

"About Mrs. Lock," she whispered. "Will she get custody?"

"Not on her own say-so," I answered in a similarly low tone. "Look, I'm sorry for what I said to her. I lost my temper. No-one in this family seems to care about Sophia's baby. Her own granddaughter," I added in a slightly louder voice. The form in the chair shuddered.

Rita sighed. "I care. I'd like to come and see her when this is all over." Her glance swept over her aunt and back to me. "What's going to happen to her?"

"She'll be in hospital for a few more days, at least. If Mrs. Lock admits that her son's in jail, he'll be asked to submit to a paternity test, if he wants to claim the baby. If he isn't the father, I guess she'll be put up for adoption."

"I've always wanted a little girl," Rita's voice was wistful.

"No." Mrs. Demetris struggled to her feet. "That is a child of sin. She cannot come into this family."

"But she belongs with us," Rita protested.

"Never. Not while I still breathe."

The two women stared hard at each other. Mrs. Demetris crumpled first, almost falling back into her chair. Rita knelt down beside her, taking her hand and stroking the prominent blue veins. Her voice was a soft insistent singsong.

"Tell me, auntie, what does it matter now to God or anyone how the baby was born. She's helpless and innocent and all we have left of Sophia."

At her daughter's name, the old woman began to cry, her voice rising in a piercing wail while she rocked back and forth, her arms wrapped around herself, hugging the stick to her body.

Rita patted her back, murmuring comfort the old woman would not hear.

I couldn't take it any longer. I should never have come. Let Dr. Comaine write a letter of condolence and stand by the coffin at the funeral. I had had enough. Even as I reached to push open the swing door, Rita stood.

"You'd better go," she said. She lifted one hand and let it drop, helpless.

There was a pad of paper on a small shelf below the wall telephone by the door. I picked up the pencil, scribbled my phone number and handed it to her.

"Call me," I said. "I'll talk to the CAS worker and tell him you want to visit Mara."

"Thanks." She folded the paper into tiny squares and shoved it into the side pocket of her skirt. She glanced back at her aunt, then quickly wrote her own address and phone number down. "Take this. I'm generally home suppertime if you need to contact me."

"Okay. I'll see my own way out."

"Bye, then. And thanks for coming after all. It helps to talk." She nodded towards her aunt. "She'll be better after the burial. It's always better then."

"If she tells you anything at all that might help us find Mara's father, will you call me?"

"Sure. You bet."

Mrs. Demetris looked up again and hissed, "You. Get out of my house. And you, Rita, if you have no better sense than to talk with that one there, you can go too. Go, all of you, leave me." She dropped her head again, shaking with sobs.

"Go, go, before she starts up again." Rita propelled me through the door.

Outside, the rain was coming down harder, the passing cars spraying the sidewalks as they swished through puddles. I walked back to the car with my head uncovered, letting the water wash away the sediment of despair that had settled on me the moment I entered that sad house. I had no appetite for anything but going home.

TEN

The drive back took nearly two hours. The 401 was already clogged by commuters, slowed to a crawl through the suburbs and satellite cities by the pouring rain. For most of the trip I was hemmed in by transport trucks, my windshield wipers battling to clear the screen after each one flooded my little car as it passed. It was a relief to turn on to the highway north. I found a radio station that played continuously songs from the sixties and distracted myself from thinking about Sophia and her family by trying to remember words to every verse and where I was when I first heard the song.

Sadie greeted me as though I'd been gone a month by taking my wrist in her jaws and lovingly tonguing it. In a lull in the rain, I took her up to the park for a vigorous game of fetch. She wasn't very good at it: she'd catch the stick all right and bring it back to me, but for her the fun came when I tried to take it away from her to throw it again. When she had enough, she lay down and chewed the branch to slivers. I realized how short her games now were. At ten years, she had become an old dog, her muzzle silvered and her gait slowed to a walk. When we returned to the house, she drank a whole bowl of water before flopping down in her favourite spot beneath the dining room table. Seconds later, I was treated to the second old-dog symptom: the smell of her flatulence drove me upstairs.

My head ached, a spike searing through my left eye into my skull. I lay down on the bed with a cold cloth over my eyes. After a minute, I loosened my clothes and pulled the duvet up around me. The rain pattered against the sloping ceiling as the day faded.

"Rosie! Rosie!"

I was trapped in the dark. Someone was coming up the stairs and I could not escape. My jaws ached with the need to hold in my cries; if I made a noise, I would be in great trouble. If I lay still, still as stone, perhaps whoever it was would not see me ...

Why was Sadie not barking?

At the moment this thought jolted me into opening my eyes, a hand shook my shoulder. I leaped up, lashing out with both fists, the duvet tumbling on the floor.

"Watch it!" Will stepped back from the bed, rubbing his chest where one of my punches had connected.

"Sorry." I rubbed my eyes. "I must have fallen asleep. I had a terrible dream."

"How was the visit to the family? Never mind, I can tell just by the way you look – pretty grim, eh?"

"Yeah. And the drive back was endless. Is it still raining?"

"Stopped about an hour ago. Listen, how about going to the hospital now? Jack Lansdown said he'd be there around 6; if we hurry we can just make it."

I squinted at the alarm clock on the bedside table; it was nearly 6 now. "I need a shower first. Give me about fifteen minutes, okay?"

I stood under water as hot as I could bear, then towelled and dressed quickly. Will put down the paper when I came into the living room.

"There's a picture of the demonstration on the front page," he said.

"Is there anything new about the investigation?"

"Just that the police are following up leads. Do you think they've found Martin Lock yet?"

"If they check their computers they will. He's in jail."

I told Will the substance of my conversations with Sophia's cousin and mother. He shook his head when I finished. "If the father's not Martin Lock, then what did Sophia mean in the letter about Mara being his fault?"

"The letter wasn't very coherent. Maybe she meant that going away was his fault. Maybe he found out who the true father was – or maybe he told her parents she was pregnant before she was ready to break the news to them."

"Or maybe he was blackmailing her."

I thought about this idea while we drove over to the hospital. It was an old red brick building that had sprouted various additions in various materials from all sides so that it resembled a child's building block construction. The parking lots were situated at the bottom of the hill, long flights of wide stairs leading up through flower gardens and past a helicopter landing pad to the front entrance, formal under a pillared portico. A number of people, some in white uniforms, others wearing jackets over their bathrobes, stood under its dubious shelter smoking cigarettes. The pall of smoke was a blue cloud in the harsh glow of the floodlights that were trained on the building's facade. No one was talking; each smoker stood alone, back turned away from the others. As we pushed open the entrance doors, a chorus of coughs signalled that the cigarette break was coming to an end.

The lobby was busy with families visiting relatives in the various wards. Pediatrics was on the fifth floor. We shared the elevator with a man and his three children on the way to visit their new baby sister. "But why can't we call her Bunny?" a child who seemed to be about four was insisting. "I like the name Bunny."

"It's a stupid name for a person," her older brother snapped. He was carrying a large pink helium balloon that he released to bump against the elevator ceiling. "How come we can't see Mom?" he asked his father.

The man looked as if he hadn't slept for a week. "She's sleeping," he said. "It took a long time for your little sister to be born. I told you. Your Mom had to have an operation; she'll be all right, but she's very tired."

The doors slid open on the fourth floor. The family trooped out into a chorus of wails from the nursery whose glass windows faced the hallway.

Will shivered. "Hearing that kind of stuff makes me glad that you didn't have to go through any of that."

I didn't answer. A couple of orderlies got on, one pushing a mop and bucket on wheels. The elevator lurched upwards.

The walls of the Pediatrics Ward waiting room were bright with Disney cartoon cut-outs. On the rag rug, which centred a collection of chairs and couches upholstered in orange plastic, were scattered a number of yellow trucks and wooden animals. Magazines which, from their cover art, appeared to be concerned with parenting and childcare, littered the top of a black plastic table. Barbara Lock was thumbing through one of them. She was wearing the same green suit, but her hair had lost some of its careful curl and hung in tendrils around her neck. In the harsh overhead lights, she looked grey and ill. When Will went to the nursing station to inquire about Lansdown and Mara, I crossed over to sit down beside her.

"Have you been here since last night?" I asked.

"I'm not leaving without that baby." Her voice was weary, as if she had repeated this line many, many times. She turned another page.

"I went to Scarborough today. I talked with Rita Petrie."

"Who?" She stared down at the picture of a fat baby sitting in the middle of a rubber tire.

"Sophia's cousin. Rita Demetris before she was married."

"Oh, Rita. Lisa's friend."

"That's right. She told me about your son. About Martin."

The magazine trembled but didn't close. She said nothing.

"I know he couldn't have killed Sophia," I pressed on. "He's got an alibi, doesn't he? Have you told the police where he is?"

She looked up at me, her eyes ringed with weariness and tears. "You are not to say another word about him," she hissed.

"But don't you see it lets him off? Besides, all the police have to do is put his name through their computers – if they haven't done it yet. They probably know he's in jail."

The elevator doors sighed open. Constable Quinn stepped through, followed by a grey-haired, grey-suited man. He saw us and immediately rushed across the room.

"Barb," he snapped. "What are you doing here? Why didn't you call? I've been worried sick."

She just looked up at him, then turned her attention back to the article. When she spoke, her voice was the same repetitive monotone. "I'm not leaving without that baby."

Constable Quinn ignored her. "Good evening, Professor Cairns," she said. "This is Ken Lock, Mrs. Lock's husband. He's come to take her home."

That got Barbara's attention. She slapped the magazine closed. "I'm going nowhere without my granddaughter. I've made that perfectly clear to everyone involved. If I have to sit here a month, here I'll sit and no one," she glared at her husband, "no one can make me leave."

"I talked to Marty today," Ken Lock put a hand on her shoulder, then pulled it back as if stung as she shook it off. "He didn't do it, Barbara."

"Of course he didn't kill her. The very idea." She drew herself upright, still managing to avoid looking anyone in the eyes. "My boy would never do such a thing."

"He didn't father the baby." Lock's voice was gentle, persuasive.

Barbara shook her head violently. "Of course that's what he'd tell you. He was always afraid of you, of what you'd say if he admitted to even the tiniest mistake. If you'd left him alone."

Lock sighed and sank down in a chair at right angles to his wife. He reached over and tried to grab hold of one of her hands. She tucked them under her arms and leaned away from him.

"Let's not start this again," he said. "Whatever I did or you did, would make no difference. Dr. Simcoe explained all that when we went for counselling. Marty is the way he is and he's the only one who can help himself. We did everything for that boy ..."

"We? You were at the office."

Lock drew a deep breath. "I'm not going to argue with you about this here and now, Barbara. Get your coat on. I'm taking you home."

"You can't make me." Her voice was that of a petulant child. "I told you and I've told everyone I won't go without Mara. My granddaughter."

"She's not your granddaughter." Lock stood up so abruptly his chair slid backwards, squeaking on the linoleum.

"I've got a letter to prove it." Barbara pulled the envelope out of her purse.

"It's not proof," Lock began but she interrupted him.

"She says right here that we're all the family she has. Explain that any other way you can."

"You know what John Demetris is like. He probably kicked her out of the house when she got pregnant. Marsha was her best friend for years; of course, she'd think of us as family."

"And what about this: 'it's all Martin's fault.' What more does she need to say?"

Lock sighed. He glanced at Quinn, who nodded slightly. Then he squatted down in front of his wife, taking hold of her hands. She tried to pull away from him, but he would not let go. "When I talked to Marty, he didn't just deny the baby. He confessed that he, that he … that he tried to blackmail Sophia."

"Blackmail Sophia?" I exclaimed. "But she didn't have any money."

Lock grimaced, answering me without looking at his wife. "He suggested to her that she call his mother. He knew I wouldn't let Barbara throw away any more money on him so he thought he'd get the money through Sophia instead. Using the baby."

"So it is his baby!" Barbara crowed, triumphant. "I just knew it was."

Lock shook his head. "It's not his. He met Sophia coming out of Dr. Simcoe's office one day and managed to get a peek at her file on his desk when the good doctor left the room for a moment. You know what that boy is like, always prying into things that don't concern him. He saw enough to guess at the truth, but he didn't do anything until he needed money for his appeal. He saw Sophia one day here in town when he was out on a day pass. He followed her to her apartment and told her that unless she came up with the money he needed, he'd tell her father where to find her."

"I don't believe it," Barbara said. "Martin would never …"

"It's true, Mrs. Lock," Constable Quinn put in. "I was at Warkworth with Mr. Lock while he was talking to your son. Martin was out on a day pass on Thursday; when he realized we suspected him of murder, he told the truth to clear himself. He had no motive for killing Sophia: she was cash in his pocket as long as no one found out the truth. Now we're looking to talk to John Demetris again."

"Why him?" Will asked.

Lock and the constable exchanged glances. Then Lock drew a deep breath and said, "John Demetris is the father."

"Sophia's father is Mara's father?" Even as I said it I realized how this explained why both Mr. and Mrs. Demetris were so determined not to acknowledge Mara. She was the symbol of his guilt and her failure at protecting her daughter. And Sophia — had she kept the baby to punish herself for what her father had done to her and then found a certain sadistic pleasure in punishing Mara because of how she had been conceived? I shuddered.

Barbara kneaded the letter into a ball of paper. "But the baby ... She said on the phone it was Marty's baby."

"She lied," Lock said. He straightened up with a small groan. A bone in his knee cracked. "From what the constable here has told me, it looks like she didn't care much for the child. No wonder. The man must have forced himself on her. Poor girl."

Barbara's lips trembled. "And what will happen to her now? Mara, I mean?"

"She's being well taken care of," Will said. "When she's better, Jack has several clients who've been waiting for a baby for a long time. He'll place her with one of them."

"What about us? Couldn't we have her anyway?" Tears began to seep down her cheeks.

Her husband pulled her to her feet, wrapped her coat around her. "It's time to go home, Barbara. We'll talk about this later."

She shrugged off his arm. "I want to know now. Can we apply to adopt her?"

"But why?" Lock shook his head. "She's nothing to us. We've had our own children; we've got grandchildren, for heaven's sake. I'm retiring in two years, I don't need a baby in the house. It's over, Barbara. It's time to go home."

For a moment, she seemed about to fight him, her back rigid, her eyes blazing in spite of the tears. From down the hall came the screams of a toddler in a tantrum. We all flinched. Barbara's shoulders sagged. She dropped the letter on the floor and, without a word to anyone, stalked off towards the elevator. Her husband hurried after her. Quinn followed.

"Well." I picked up the letter. "That's one for the books, all right."

"Poor girl," Will sighed.

"Which one?"

"Both of them. Families: what they do to each other in the name of love!"

"Hey, Will, Professor Cairns," Jack Lansdown called out to us. He looked relieved when he saw that Barbara had gone.

"Come to see Mara?" he said. "She's doing well. A little scrapper, that one."

He led us down the hall to a private room. Inside, Mara slept in an incubator, tubes running into her nose and the veins of her tiny arms, held down with wide white bands so that she could not loosen them.

"I don't care what John Demetris did to Sophia," I said, swallowing back tears. "She had no right to do this to her baby."

"Poor little thing," Will whispered. He laid one hand against the glass of the incubator. Mara stirred, but didn't waken.

I left the room, stood with my back against the wall of the corridor, gulping in deep breaths as though I were the one needing oxygen. A boy shuffled down the wall towards me, pushing an i.v. stand along beside him. He carried a movie cassette in his free hand and was whistling tunelessly in spite of the tube taped to his cheek and disappearing into his nose. He grinned at me and held up the film. "Who you gonna call?" he sang and then shouted the answer, "Ghost Busters!"

"Robert Mackintosh, you stop that noise," a young nurse stuck her head around the corner. "You get back to your room and let the little ones sleep."

"Yes ma'am." He sketched a salute at her and winked at me. "Isn't she something?" he said. "I'm going to miss her when I gotta go home."

He continued down the hall, the i.v. a patient dog trundling at his heels.

Jack Lansdown joined me. "Are you all right?"

"I just can't stand seeing such a tiny creature in so much pain."

"She'll recover, and she's young enough, she won't actually remember what went on and if we can get her into a family soon, she may not suffer too much from loss of affection. It's hard to tell with these little ones."

"Will said you had a family for her?"

Jack nodded. "That's right. We couldn't do anything until this thing with Mrs. Lock and her son was resolved. I mean, if he was the father, he could claim certain rights here. But he says he's not. And if John Demetris is – well, incest is against the law in this country. And I imagine if he knew where she lived, he might have followed her out to campus. Maybe they had a fight and he killed her."

"I don't think so. When I met him, he honestly didn't know where she was. But no wonder he was so angry about the baby and the way she'd been kept. He must have been scared that someone would find out and start asking questions and that Sophia might end up having to tell the truth about him. He was angry and rude, but I don't think he would have been so calm if he'd just come from killing her."

"Police business," Will said. He closed the door gently behind him. "Not ours. So, where will Mara go to live?"

Jack yawned. "Sorry, I've had a couple of rough days. And I can't tell you, you know that. I will say that there's two families I'm considering. One's got two boys, five and three. She'd be going into a nice family environment there, stable, secure, siblings in place, nice big farm. The other's a couple with one other adopted child, a little girl that must be nearly eight by now. They've been waiting for a sister for her for a long time. But she's not ready to leave here yet, and her mother's situation has to be clarified before we do anything."

"Sophia's cousin, her best friend, knew nothing about the baby," I said. "She joked that it was a family that kept secrets but also that things changed when Sophia became a teenager, that her father didn't like her going out ... She wants to come and see the baby, Jack. Can she?" I handed him the scrap of paper with Rita's address on it.

He pocketed it. "I'll talk to her, sure. As for coming up here – she might change her mind when she hears who the father was. People are funny that way, not wanting to acknowledge the sins of the fathers, as it were."

I laughed, a little shakily. "That's what Mrs. Demetris called Mara: a child of sin."

"Then she must have known."

I nodded, sobered. "You're right. What a guilt to live with. No wonder she's so sick."

A blare of music echoed down the hall. The young nurse dashed round the corner and brushed by us. "Excuse me," she muttered. "I've just about had it with that young man. I'll tan his hide if he wakes up the Potts kid again …"

"He's only doing it to get your attention," Jack joked.

She rolled her eyes. "They get younger every year. I'm old enough to be his mother."

"Not quite," Jack grinned. "Still on for coffee?" He looked at his watch.

"Let me tame the restless horror," she said. "I'll be with you in a minute."

Jack watched her walk swiftly away from us. "If there's nothing else?"

Will took my hand. "We'll be off, then. You'll let us know if there's any change in Mara's condition? Or if there's a problem with the families? Now that you can tell them about her father. They might not like that."

"Sure thing." Jack fidgetted. The soundtrack noise was smothered, but a small child began to wail. "Listen, that's the Potts boy: what a temper that child has. She'll be hopping mad." He frowned as he saw his date with the nurse evaporate. "Maybe I can get him settled down. See you." He hurried off to the source of commotion, meeting the nurse at the door of the room and standing back to let her enter before him.

"True love," Will murmured.

"It seems Mara will be all right." I wanted reassurance that my responsibility towards her had ended.

Will put his arm around me. "She'll be fine. Much better off. Let's go home."

"I thought you wanted to go out to eat?"

"Let's get a pizza. I want to be at home. I can't face a crowd tonight."

"Okay."

We rode the elevator back to the ground floor and left the building, threading through a new group of smokers on the stoop. Will drove home. I leaned back against the head rest, eyes closed, the blanket I'd used to tuck Mara under the dash a warm weight in my lap.

"Did you ever ..." Will began.

"I wonder ..." I said, then stopped, laughing. "You first."

"It's just: Sophia leaving Mara with you like that. Did you ever think about keeping her?"

"For a bit," I admitted. "When Barbara Lock wanted to take her away. I was ready to fight her tooth and nail. Funny, isn't it?"

"The old maternal instinct."

"And paternal. You were the one taking care of her."

"Yeah." He pulled into the garage and we sat for a moment gazing into the reflection of the headlights on the woodpile against the back wall. "Jack will make sure she gets into a good home."

"Like a kitten, remember you said that? That Sophia couldn't just dump a baby like a stray cat on strangers."

"Don't cry, Rosie." Will hugged me.

"Maybe we made a mistake not trying for an adoption when we knew for sure we couldn't have babies of our own," I sniffled.

"It's all right," Will said. "All that's behind us. I love you; you're enough family for me."

I put my arms around him and held him tight, feeling the solid block of him, reassuringly there, beside me.

Someone knocked lightly on the windshield. We looked up, startled. Alex Warren grinned and waved. Behind him was Karen Lewis.

"Didn't you call to tell them the dinner was off?" I asked Will.

"I thought you did."

I wiped my eyes with the cuff of my jacket and turned to open the door. "We'll just have to order a second pizza."

Will switched off the engines and the lights died.

ELEVEN

"I hope that's a tape you've got in there to scare off burglars and not a real dog," Alex said. He watched Will unlock the back door and stoop to grab Sadie's collar before she could run out to greet us all. "My god, it's so big!"

"She's very friendly," Will said. "A lot of bark but never any biting."

Alex hung back. "I'm not too keen on dogs. In fact, I'm allergic. Is there anywhere you could put her away from me?"

Behind his back, Karen rolled her eyes.

"I'll put her out for a bit," Will said. "But you don't need to be afraid of her. She's a real marshmallow."

"It's not a question of fear." Alex still hung back waiting for Sadie to be banished to the backyard. "What kind is she, anyway? She's awfully big," he repeated.

Sadie thrust her muzzle into my hand, her head leaning heavily against my thigh as she waited for the back gate to be opened.

"She's part Lab and part who-knows," I said. "She was supposed to be part spaniel, but if so, it's so far back in the gene pool the only thing left of spaniel is the eyes." I ruffled her ears and her jaws dropped in pleasure, the pink slab of her tongue lolling. Behind me, Alex stifled a startled curse. He's really afraid of dogs, I thought. Will pushed the gate open and I led Sadie into the yard, then followed our guests into the house.

"So, where've you been?" Karen demanded. She stopped me from going into the living room after Will and Alex. In a lower voice, acid with sarcasm, she hissed, "That Alex is a real peach, Rosie."

"What do you mean?"

"I biked over and he was already here, sitting in his car. We talked for a bit on the front porch, but even though it's turned so cold, he wouldn't ask me to wait in the car. I practically had to beg. He said his heater was broken, but at least it was out of the wind. Then he made a big production about having to move files and stuff into the back seat to make room for me to sit. I was ready to leave when you turned up. At last."

"You know he commutes to the city every week. Maybe the car's like a second office to him."

"Yeah, well, I'm still freezing." She rubbed her arms. "Besides, I think he has a crush on you."

"What are you talking about?"

"All he could do was talk about you, how nice it was working next to you, questions about your thesis, how it was getting along. Questions about Will and how long you'd been married. How long we'd known each other. It was a real interrogation."

"You're exaggerating. I'm the only person you two know in common. He was probably just trying to make conversation."

"I tried to change the subject by talking about movies. I figured we'd at least have that in common, with him being in Media Studies and me such a buff. But oh no, he only wanted to talk about you. It's a sure sign, Rosie. He's in love."

"Don't be ridiculous."

"I have a lot more experience than you," Karen continued. "You've been married too long, you don't see the signs. I do."

"Don't be so high school." I marched into the living room. Will was thumbing through the directory, looking for the pizza delivery number. Alex hovered by the bookshelves.

He turned and smiled at me. "Listen, I can see this is bad timing, that you're bummed out from visiting the hospital. Maybe we should do this another time. Lunch, or something."

Behind his back, Karen winked at me. I frowned at her, then quickly yawned to cover up any confusing signals Alex might be receiving. He was staring at me rather intently. And he'd dressed up in a loosely woven white cotton sweater over black jeans. His exercise on the stairs had certainly paid off: he looked fit and strong. I would really have to consider following his example and quit using the elevator.

"Don't you like pizza?" Will looked up. "We could order Chinese."

"I just thought Rosie might be tired," Alex explained. "I mean, going all the way to the city and back: you should have asked me to come along. I could have shared the driving."

"I wouldn't want to bother you."

"No bother. She was my student too. Besides, I would have liked to have seen her home, talk to her mother. Background, you know."

"For what?" Karen thumped down on the couch. Sadie whined at the back door to be let in. She hated missing any party.

"Alex is using the murder investigation for a class project." I couldn't keep the disapproval out of my tone.

He flushed. "It's not just for the class. It's research for my novel. I'm interested in the victim's homelife, the parents' reaction to the crime, that sort of thing."

"You're writing a murder story?" Karen asked.

"Sort of," he said. "I don't really like talking about it. Afraid to jinx it. You know what writers are like." He laughed apologetically.

"Not really," Karen grinned. "I always thought they were starving in a garret somewhere, waiting to hit the big time. Daydreaming on a settee, bottle of wine in one hand, quill pen in the other."

"If only," he sighed. "No, writing is very hard work. Especially when you're really reaching for psychological truth."

"So why don't you write about life at university?" Will asked.

"Been done. And the only way to make it work is to be satirical like Robertson Davies. I'm afraid I don't have that kind of voice."

"Where's the story set?" I asked. "Small town, small-time murder sort of thing?"

"A cosy, you mean? No way. It wouldn't sell, and my only reason for dabbling in genre fiction is to come up with a bestseller, a John Grisham, Stephen King kind of thing."

"What about art?" Karen struck a pose. "Literature and all that."

He shrugged, "Well of course it'll be well written, better than their books probably. I've only been teaching popular culture for years, there's no reason I can't write it. Except that I'm having trouble getting the details set."

"So where is it set?" I asked.

"New York."

"Oh, you know the city well?" Karen perked up. "I've always wanted to go, but haven't the faintest idea how to begin. I mean, have you seen the number of hotels listed for Manhattan alone? I'd love some tips."

"I'm afraid I can't help you much. I hate to admit it, but I haven't been there in years."

"So why doesn't your story happen here, or in Toronto?"

"A New York publisher won't be interested in Canadian stuff. The book has to be relevant to the market. I'm using a street map and a couple of tourist guides to make sure I get it right. But it's not place so much as character development that's the problem."

"But isn't character formed by place?" Will objected. "I wasn't the same person when I worked for the government in the city as I am now that I'm working for myself here."

Karen agreed. "I think place is everything. I mean, if Trillium had been a big downtown campus, you can bet that Sophia would never have gone down that alley. She would have had the street smarts to realize there might be danger. Whereas here," she shrugged, "part of the shock of her death is that it happened here at all. We just don't expect it, which makes it even worse."

"That's as may be," Alex said, "but the reasons for her death would be the same anywhere. Isn't there a jealous boyfriend in the picture? The father of the child she left to go to university. That's what I've heard …" He looked at me.

"Not exactly." I paused, debating whether I should tell what I had learned that day. They were friends, after all. I described my conversation with Rita Petrie at the Demetris house and with the Locks in the hospital.

Alex rubbed his hands together. "Better and better. You could go two ways with this one."

"What do you mean?" Karen asked.

"Well, we've got two people with good motives and better opportunity. First, there's the father, the *double* father, so to speak. He finds out Sophia's up here, comes after her demanding that she return to him, she refuses, and *voilà*: he kills her."

"The police have questioned him already and let him go," Will pointed out. "He didn't have the time to do it. Apparently, he left work about the time she was killed and met Rosie in the apartment when they both still thought she was simply missing. And he let the police search his car; they didn't find any weapon or other evidence that would implicate him. The guy's a bastard for what he did to his daughter, but he's no murderer."

"Okay, it's a bit of a cliché, anyway. The incest thing's overdone."

"How can you be so dismissive?" I demanded. "It's a tragedy and a crime whenever and wherever it happens. I hope he goes to jail for what he's done. You should see that poor baby in the hospital. I believe Sophia treated her so badly because she couldn't stand the proof of what her own father had done to her."

"Why wouldn't she abort or give it up, then?" Karen asked the question that had been haunting me since Mara came into my life.

"There's a lot of reasons she didn't have an abortion: religion, or maybe she realized too late that she was pregnant, or maybe she just believed that every fetus has a chance at life …"

"But she tried to kill the baby!" Will said.

"Neglected it," I answered. "It's not quite the same thing. And I want to believe that she was coming to see me about Mara, that that's why she left her in my care. Maybe hearing that Barbara Lock was coming to see her woke her up to what she was doing: after all, she didn't leave the baby alone that day, she took her to a babysitter. She must have known that either the babysitter or I would insist on getting medical care for the baby. She must have been on the verge of giving her up."

"But why wouldn't she do that from the beginning?" Karen repeated. "That's what I don't understand."

"The only thing I can think of to answer that is that she kept Mara to punish herself, by living with the evidence of what had happened to her. She had very decided views about sexual behaviour; she said more than once that people should lie in the beds they'd made for themselves and stop whining for help. She was very intolerant of the rights of victims of abuse. Her own mother called Mara "a child of sin": with that attitude towards her own granddaughter, you can imagine how rigidly she brought up Sophia, and so Sophia would feel guilty, probably believing that she had caused her own father to abuse her."

"Whatever, whatever," Alex waved away our discussion. "You're forgetting there's a second suspect: Barbara Lock."

"What?" We all three stared at him.

"It makes perfect sense. She thinks the baby is her precious son's child because of the ambiguities in the letter Sophia sent her. Sophia meant that it's Martin's fault that she's short of money because Martin's blackmailing her, but Barbara thinks it's because he's the father. She discovers Sophia's address and comes up to offer to adopt the baby or, at least, to welcome both mother and daughter into her family. She discovers evidence of abuse: the caged crib and so on. She tracks Sophia down on campus, they have an argument – well, it's the same scenario as the first, only with different players."

"There's no way that the woman who came to this house looking for Mara had just murdered someone," Will stated. "She was perfectly calm and in control until she realized she wasn't going to be able to take the baby away with her. I don't believe that, if she had just killed someone, she would have been able to hide it so well. She wasn't acting shock when Finlay announced Sophia's death. She was definitely shaken. Don't you agree, Rosie?"

"Absolutely."

"But it's got to be one of them," Karen protested. "What about the Lock boy? He was on a day pass, right? What if he ran into Sophia and she refused to pay? He might have been angry enough to kill her."

"Not possible," Will shook his head. "The police are convinced by his alibi."

"Okay," Alex said. He stood silent for a moment, chin in hand, eyes closed. "Follow along with me on this one, then. They're a bit more farfetched, but I've got two more suspects: my esteemed chair, Frank Stanich and his loyal secretary, Irene Smith."

"This isn't fun any more," I said. "We shouldn't be playing a game like this over someone's death, and accusing perfectly innocent people of murder. It's not decent."

"Come on, Rosie," Alex pleaded. "Just let me show you the motives."

"You're going to talk about the petition. I just don't believe that would anger either Stanich or Irene enough to kill over it. That's ridiculous. These things happen all the time."

"But Frank is angling for Partridge's job as soon as Partridge retires. A scandal like this over the course he designed and has taught for years would undermine his credibility, especially with the more politically correct among the faculty. And Irene will do anything he says. We've all seen that."

"So Mara is a red herring?" Karen suggested.

Alex grinned. "Exactly. Gets everyone distracted into looking for the weapon and the opportunity for one of the people close to Sophia to kill her. They just have to wait for enough time to go by; with no evidence turning up, the whole episode will be filed away."

"I don't buy it," I shook my head.

"Why not? It's perfectly logical. Frank is such a rigid personality, can't you see that any threat to his vision of himself as an authority would tip him over the edge?"

"I think he'd wait to see the results of the petition. He seemed very sure that not many in his class would sign it, especially after Sophia revealed herself as such a reactionary in that newspaper interview."

"Well then, how about a student? Maybe one of the people in one of the groups she offended decided to take matters into their own hands."

"Students talk a lot, but they don't usually act," I said. "And I can't see any of them acting with such violence. Nasty letters about her in the paper, an exposé of her personal circumstances in *The Shield*: that I could accept. But not killing her. That's stretching things too far."

"So you won't grant me any suspects at all?" Alex mimed a pout, but seemed seriously upset that we could refute all his theories.

Karen frowned. "So what are you saying, Rosie? That it's the proverbial mysterious stranger who killed her after all?"

"I'm saying that we're making wild and irresponsible guesses," I answered. "We don't know what evidence the police have found or what clues they're following. For all we know, they might already have somebody under arrest."

Before the others could reply, Will interjected, "Let's not forget the other two deaths."

"What deaths?" Karen and Alex spoke together.

"What was it, Rosie, a hit-and-run and a drowning?"

"What connection could they have?" Alex demanded. "Just because they both occurred on or near the campus doesn't mean anything. They were both accidents."

"The detective on the case ..."

I interrupted Will. "Come on, guys, it's been a long day. I've had enough. Let's order a pizza and eat and talk about something more cheerful. Not the weather." I nodded towards the rain speckling the window. "We're going to have to let Sadie in, Alex. We can put her in the basement."

"I won't stay, if you don't mind," he said. He smiled at Karen. "Maybe we could go to a film, the four of us? When this is over?"

"Right," she answered, her lips mimicking a smile.

"You're welcome to stay." I covered a yawn with one hand.

"No, no. This conversation's given me a lot to think about." He shook Will's hand. "Nice to meet you, at last, Will. I've heard so much about you from Rosie here." He turned to Karen. "You won't mind if I don't offer to drive you home? I couldn't possibly fit your bike in my car."

"I might as well stay and eat pizza," she said. "I'm pretty hungry."

"Goodnight then, one and all."

I opened the front door and watched as Alex raced through the rain to his car.

"What a dork," Karen said behind me. "He even locks his car on a street like this. He must think he's in New York. This is absolutely the last time, Rosie, that I agree to let you set me up with anyone."

"I wasn't trying to set you up."

"Especially someone who's got a thing for you."

"Oh, shut up." I slammed the door. Sadie bounded in from the kitchen and jumped up to greet both Karen and me, her big paws leaving wet prints on our clothes.

TWELVE

Saturday morning it was still raining. I lay snuggled into the duvet in the grey light, listening to the small noises of Will downstairs making coffee. Karen had stayed to watch a video with us while we ate the pizza. After driving her home, I'd immediately gone to bed. Now I longed to luxuriate in warm comfort, sleeping in until noon as I used to when I was a teenager. The front door slammed shut as Will took Sadie out for her morning walk. They wouldn't be long: for a part-Lab, Sadie had an unnatural aversion to water. She wouldn't swim and hated rain.

I rolled over and looked at the clock. Nine-thirty. If I got up and went out to campus, I could have all the rest of the essays marked by suppertime. That would leave the rest of the study break free for me to finish the conclusion of my thesis. My supervisor at York was anxious to see the completed dissertation and to schedule my exams. And Lucy Easton had hinted that if I got my degree before the academic year was out, I'd have a good shot at a tenure-track job for next fall. If the university got an increase in its operating grant ... if the dean approved another appointment ... if, as was rumoured, Isaac Pleasant did not come back ...

A lot of ifs, and they depended in part on my ability to get the thesis finished. I groaned and rolled out of bed. I'd just stepped under the shower when I heard Will and Sadie return, Will's laughing curse as she shook herself in the hall before he had a chance to towel her dry. A moment later the bathroom door opened.

"How's the water?" Will asked.

"Lovely." I stood directly under the spray with my face raised and eyes closed.

The curtain swished back, letting in a blast of cold air.

"What?" I turned around.

Will stepped into the bath. "I'm freezing; it's bloody cold out there. You can feel snow coming. You've got room for me here, haven't you?"

He put his arms around me, one hand cupping a breast. I leaned back. His mouth found mine. We let the steam rise around us for another couple of minutes before surrendering to the heat. The bed was still warm when we tumbled back into it.

It was easier getting up the second time: we were both starving. I made a brunch of eggs benedict and coffee while Will ran down to the corner for the weekend papers from the city. I couldn't concentrate on the news, not even on the highly lurid accounts of Sophia's death that the media, for want of any hard news, indulged in. One reporter had interviewed Tran, the apartment building supervisor. Although it lacked specific detail, her article suggested child abuse and bolstered this with a flat statement that Mara was in hospital pending clarification of her paternity. The same reporter had spoken to neighbours of both the Demetris family and the Locks, and had concocted two possible scenarios for murder. In the first, the old-fashioned father avenged his family's honour by destroying the wayward daughter. In the second, a grandmother, driven to extremes in her neurotic desire to replace her own criminal son with the child she thought was his, killed the young woman who not only refused to give the baby up but to confirm its parentage. None of the papers had attributed any importance to Sophia's petition, nor to her interview in *The Shield*. And none had linked her death with the other two that occurred earlier in the summer.

All I could think about was the pile of essays waiting on my desk to be marked. I drained my mug and stared out the back window at the rain. "I really should go to the office and finish that marking," I said.

Will rustled through the pile of newsprint for the Travel section. "I thought you were on some sort of break this week. What about the easy life of the academic I've always heard about: all those holidays, hardly any classes? You're keeping longer hours that I am, and I've got a business to run."

"Goes to show. Jobs always look easier on the outside. I've got to get those grades in before I can get back to the thesis. And without the thesis, I don't have a chance of stretching this job into a career." I stretched. "It's a miserable day, anyway. What were you planning to do?"

"Food shopping. Library. World Series finals at three ..."

"Sounds like I won't be missing anything then." I checked the time. "I'll go work till suppertime; maybe we could go out?"

"There's a recipe I've been wanting to try for awhile: Singapore noodles. Why don't I get some wine and a couple of videos, escapist stuff. We'll have a night to ourselves without one word about murder."

"It's a deal."

The Saturday campus was more deserted than usual as the combination of the murder and reading break had encouraged most of the residents to either go home to their parents or to find some safer and sunnier milieu to study in. The sodden pile of flowers and posters at the alley mouth lent a further air of desolation to the scene. The yellow tape still drooped across the passage, but the police car and its attendant officer had gone.

I unlocked the Arts Tower door and trudged up the stairs, unwilling to trust that the elevator would not stall and leave me stranded with no help to be found. Other than the buzz of the fluorescent fixtures, the halls were silent. As usual on weekends, the air circulation system had been turned down or off: the building smelled stale with the ghosts of too many bodies breathing within its walls, too many feet scuffling down its corridors. I wondered what had happened to all the security guards President Comaine had claimed would be on patrol. Perhaps with the exodus of students, the need for them seemed less important than saving the extra costs.

The air in my office was close and cloying with the browning of the rose I'd left in the coffee mug on the window sill. How I wished those windows had not been sealed shut in the interests of heat efficiency. I left the door slightly ajar and hung my jacket on the hook already burdened with a cardigan, a canvas bag from the bookstore, a forgotten umbrella. The lights flickered into a steady glow. I plunked myself down in my chair, swivelled around to face the essays on my desk.

On top of the pile were two more roses, tied together with a white ribbon. I poked at them. Three petals fell off, bloody tears curling on the green blotter. Who could have left them? Karen's teasing comment – *he's got a crush on you* – came back to me. I glared at the wall between my office and Alex's, leaned over and thumped on it with my fist. All I got for my effort was a bruise. I swept the flowers into my garbage pail, adding the one from the window for good measure. That should give whoever was leaving them a clear hint that such attention was unwelcome. I nudged the pail with my foot around the corner of the desk out of my sight. The scent lingered.

"God damn it to hell!"

The shout so startled me that my hand slipped and sketched a long red slash across the page I was rereading for the fourth time. I recognized Frank Stanich's voice.

"I'm sorry." That wailing cry was Irene Smith. They must be in her office at the end of the hall.

I eyed my door, wondering if I should go and close it. I didn't want to eavesdrop, but I also didn't want to draw their attention to my presence. Their voices dropped. I started again at the top of the page trying to make sense of a paragraph without punctuation, one twelve-line string of subordinate clauses leading, as far as I could tell, to no subject or conclusion.

"I didn't ask you to interfere." Frank shouted again. "Why can't you ever mind your own business?"

"I was only trying to help." Irene must be crying, her voice a nasal whine.

"When I want your help I'll ask for it. Who told you to give my course outlines to the president's office? You had no right to do that without my permission."

"But the girl's dead …"

"And people are saying it's because of that bloody petition."

"That's not true, Frank, you know that's not true. No one could ever imagine that you would ever do such a thing."

He talked over her protests. "I had to stand there and listen to Comaine tear my outline to shreds – *my* outline. I tried to explain that it has to be taken in context. Everyone's forgetting the context: that girl, that Cairns woman, now the president. It's those women activists that've got her going, all this human rights stuff. Life writing is a legitimate tool of exploration."

"You're right, Frank. I'm sure it's just that the president is upset, all this fuss and bother. It's all that girl's fault, that Sophia. She was trouble from the moment she came in the door, I could tell."

"And what makes you such a sterling judge of human behaviour? You're a secretary; you should be following orders and not giving out information that doesn't belong to you. If anyone's caused trouble around here, it's you. It's always you."

"Oh, Frank, don't say such things."

"I've had it. Had it up to here." A squeaking groan signalled the opening of the stairwell door. "Don't bother finishing that paper I gave you. I've made some changes in it. My new secretary over in the department office will do it. *She* does what she's told." He stamped out.

Irene's sobs rose and diminished as she closed herself in her office. I debated whether I should go and speak to her, try to give her some comfort. She would know then that I'd overheard their conversation – how would we ever be able to face each other again? It sounded as if she had, in all innocence, dumped Frank in hot water with the senior administration. Served him right, in my opinion.

I had my hand on my door handle on my way down the hall, when I heard the elevator open and the shuffle of feet. I peeked out in time to see Irene, dressed again in the sloppy sweats I'd seen her in on Thursday night, get in to the car. She leaned against the wall, head down, shoulders bowed, a picture of despair and misery. I was sorry that I'd delayed going to her at once. The doors slid shut. I went back to the essays.

The second interruption was a tentative knock on my door. "Professor Cairns?" It was Ani Lyons, *The Shield* editor. "Can I talk to you for a minute?"

"Sure." I reached over and picked up the pile of library books off the one extra chair my office had room for. The date slip stuck between the pages of the top volume reminded me that I had to return them soon. At one time the faculty could keep books out of the university library as long as they needed them. Now, to raise revenue to supplement the meagre acquisitions budget, the library charged overdue fees to everyone regardless of position. I'd had these three books for a week and hadn't had time to open the cover of even one of them.

Ani settled into the chair. She leaned over to place her knapsack of books on the floor. Her indrawn breath was a hiss of shock.

"What's the matter?" I leaned over to see what had surprised her.

"Nothing," She straightened up. "It's just – how come you're throwing out your flowers?"

"Do you know anything about them? How they got in here?"

She shook her head, eyes wide. "No. Didn't you bring them? I noticed you had one the other day."

I wasn't sure I entirely believed her denial. "Someone keeps sneaking in here and leaving them on my desk. I don't like it. If you know who it is, perhaps you could ask them to stop."

"I don't know anything about them," Ani declared. "I was just surprised, that's all."

I frowned at her. She looked past at the window and then around the room.

"This still looks like Professor Pleasant's room," she changed the subject.

"He's supposed to be coming back. There's not much sense in bringing all my gear out here just to truck it all home again at the end of term."

"That must be hard, not knowing how long your job will last. Alex is always talking about *publish or perish* but it must be even worse for you. It's why I've decided against an academic career: not enough opportunity. I want to really make something of myself."

Thanks a lot, I said to myself. Aloud I asked, "So what can I help you with? You still want me to make a speech?"

She waved a hand in dismissal. "Oh that. We're still discussing what to do about that. The vigil's over, you might have noticed. No one wants to stay out in the cold and dark until the murderer's been found, and it's been so wet." She looked down in her lap. "I know it makes us seem pretty wishy-washy after we were all so fired up yesterday. It's partly that the shock is wearing off a bit. Dawn and Sandra are concerned about the effect of the news of her neglect of the baby, that it will make us look like we're supporting child abuse. Lisa thinks we can incorporate that into a general indictment of the system, but we think we should wait a bit. It might be better not to tie in our demands for a safer campus to one person, if you know what I mean."

"Will you all be coming to the university service for her on Thursday?"

"Don't know." She fingered the hem of her sweater. "It depends." Her voice trailed off, then brightened. "Anyway, what I've come to see you about: I'd like the Demetris's address, if you've got it. I want to go and interview them."

"Since when is *The Shield* going out of town for stories?"

"It's not for the paper; it's for my thesis. I've been having a lot of trouble with my topic. It's a study of murderers and the media, a kind of Ann Rule thing. Alex suggested it. I've been doing a lot of archival work, reading old interviews and stuff, but it's all so static. It would be a great help to talk to some people who are directly concerned about the effects of a murder on the family, what kind of approaches from the media they've had, how they feel about it."

"Alex suggested you go to see them?"

She nodded.

"You don't think it might be a little callous to ask them such questions just now?"

"Well, it would be fresh in their minds, you know. They wouldn't have time to process it, so whatever they say will be raw, real. Just what I need to get a feel for the subject. I mean, this is the first actual case study I've been involved with." She shrugged, "I don't mean to sound insensitive, but I'd be a fool to pass up this opportunity for some hands-on experience to flesh out my dissertation."

"You're talking about using people's pain for your own benefit."

"Not just mine. What I have to say could go a long way to understanding public fascination with violent death and how the media manipulates that to boost audience and circulation. Besides, it would help Alex with his research too. You know he's writing a novel."

"So I've heard. Aren't you concerned that your work may overlap? What if he uses your evidence, or vice versa?"

"It's not the same at all. I'm doing a scholarly paper on media, he's doing this terrific investigation of the psychotic mind. The stuff he's come up with is really great, he's got such insight. It's going to be a bestseller when he's done."

"I didn't realize he had that much written."

"He's only got the framework. I've been keying in his introductory chapters; he's hopeless with technology. You know he even writes with a fountain pen? I didn't think you could buy those any more." She smiled fondly.

"You know Alex pretty well," I suggested, thinking of the byplay between Ani and her friend Lisa in my office the other day.

She flushed. "He's been really helpful. He was my supervisor when I first came here and he steered me into Media Studies. I owe him a lot. He even thinks he might be able to get one of the Toronto papers to look at some of the material I've written on Sophia."

"I don't think John Demetris would appreciate information about his family in the paper." That must be the understatement of the year, I thought. "I don't think this is the best time to approach him. Mrs. Demetris is ill, for one thing. And they haven't even had the funeral yet."

"Alex said something about a cousin?"

"Alex talks too much."

When she fidgetted, the chair's springs squealed. "He's just trying to help. This project is perfect for me, a way to achieve a decent body of work. I've done a lot of writing, and I think I'm pretty good at it, once I get going. But it's all so dry, so detached. I need to get into the real meat of the matter, the real people involved. And in the end, my work might help her daughter."

"What do you mean?"

"When she's grown up, don't you think she'll want to know everything there is to know about her mother?"

"I suppose." I swivelled my chair around to look at my patch of grey sky. "I tell you what. I'll introduce you to the two detectives I know who're working on the case." I scribbled Finlay's and Quinn's names on a pad along with an introductory note, tore it off, and handed it to her. "They can call me to confirm that you're a student and that I know you. And after they've got the killer and after Sophia's been buried, I'll give you her cousin's phone number. Okay?"

"That's great." When Ani stood, she kicked the garbage pail which toppled, spilling flowers and petals across the floor. "Sorry."

"Don't worry about it."

She helped me scoop up the mess. "Maybe we could have coffee and talk about the case sometime?" she asked. "You must have some ideas about it, a suspect or two?"

"I'm trying not to think about it, I've got so much else to do. But I'd like to see what you come up with."

"Sure thing. Thanks for your help. Bye." Ani grinned and strode out the door, letting it swing wide open behind her.

I got up to close it and realized from the ache in my back how long I'd been sitting still. It was time to take a break. I picked up the library books and grabbed my coat and umbrella. When I pulled the door shut, I turned the knob to make sure the lock had engaged. I didn't want any more surprises when I returned.

I hurried along the paved paths that linked the various teaching buildings and the two residences to the library, a cement monolith that resembled a bunker with its slit windows and flat roof. I ran with my head down, umbrella tilted against the wind which drove the rain in stinging sheets and ruffled the standing water in puddles that dotted the lawns. Although I met no one outdoors, the lobby of the library was full of chattering students, smoking cigarettes on break, waiting for a pay phone to be free, punching numbers into the bank machine located next to the small tuck shop that seemed to sell only chocolate bars and ballpoint pens. The first floor of the library was equally busy, with long line-ups at the computer terminals. In my more cynical moments, I imagined that this was where all the research that students did took place: they searched the screen for every book title on their essay subject, inserted them into the bibliography, but never bothered to find, much less read, the books themselves. I shook away the thought. I'd only marked a few first term, first-year essays so far; it wasn't fair to make such a general condemnation of the rest of my students.

The student working behind the desk smiled as I dumped my books into the return chute. I recognized him as one of my fourth-year students, in the same poetry seminar that Ani was auditing. Of course, I couldn't remember his name.

"You're working today?" he asked. "I thought all the profs took off for Florida as soon as the break began."

"Fat chance. I've got a pile of essays that seems to get higher the more I mark. Yours is in there somewhere."

"Deathly prose," he grinned, and pushed his heavy spectacles up his nose.

"Is that a pun?" I pushed through the turnstiles into the reference section. Since I was here, I might as well take a few minutes to browse through the stacks, to see what might catch my fancy. I'd developed a passion for between-the-wars British fiction and was slowly working my way through the collection on the topic, on the lookout for the obscure country-house mysteries that were so popular then. No one else seemed much interested in the period, so I usually could find one or two hidden gems.

"Are you going up to the stacks?" the boy called to me.

"Thinking of it."

"They're doing some maintenance work on the fourth floor. Something to do with asbestos removal, we think, but they're not telling us what. If we knew what was really floating around in the air, we might refuse to come into the building. They put in that whole new air circulation system last semester and it's made no difference at all, especially on the fourth floor. You wouldn't believe how many shelvers get sick working in there. No one's up there today; the new bookcases aren't very stable ordinarily and with all the pounding this past week and the dust, it's dangerous."

I glanced upwards. "Are the workers here today?"

"No. At least I haven't heard any racket. You should've heard the noise earlier this week; no one could study. Maybe the administration finally woke up to the fact that this is called study week and that people need quiet to work on their papers."

I looked around at the knots of young people, most of them engaged in conversations that required a maximum of hand gestures and a minimum of notes. "I only want to check out a few references. I won't be long."

"Well, don't breathe too deeply and take care."

I climbed the winding open staircase which rose the full height of the building under an immense skylight which today drummed with rain. Each landing was circled with floor-to-ceiling windows punctuated by a thick black firedoor. I looked in as I passed. A few easy chairs were lined along the windows to take advantage of the available light and to give their occupants a view of the activity in the foyer below. Most of the chairs were empty and the rows of stacks I could see were deserted. I pushed open the heavy door on the fourth floor and entered the familiar world of dust and dusk: the long rows of high shelves creating avenues of shadows spotted by dim lights whose glow was swallowed by the dark grey carpeting, the green and brown spines of thousands of books shoved into orderly ranks. I wandered down one aisle after another, pulling a book out here and there to flip through its pages, dwelling on a paragraph or smiling at a piece of witty dialogue. Once I thought I heard the doors open, but when I reached the end of the row and looked back, I saw no one. Footsteps made no sound. I yawned again and again, my automatic reaction to being in the stacks. Around one bank of shelves, down at the far end of the room, I saw a wall of opaque plastic blocking off a work area. I couldn't believe that, if asbestos were a problem up here, anyone would be allowed up to wander at will as I was doing. Perhaps the workmen were electricians finally doing something about the lights. That end of the floor seemed to be in total darkness, what light the day had unable to penetrate the grimy glass of the narrow windows or the heavy polyethylene barriers. I squatted down to check out the Du Maurier titles.

I'm not sure what alerted me to the danger: a slither, a crack, a rumble that wasn't the freight elevator or cleaning equipment. I jumped up. The shelves were trembling, the floor vibrating with some kind of seismic movement. I began to run down the aisle as books from the higher shelves loosened and fell, a heavy rain. Someone grabbed me, pulled me into the safety of the stairwell.

"Ani!" I pulled away from her grasp. "What are you doing?"

"Look," she said, pointing.

The shelves toppled like dominoes, one leaning, leaning, leaning over the aisles into the next, the books dropping, pages fluttering as they fell.

"You could've been squashed," Ani said. "Good thing I was on my way up to the video lab when I saw them begin to go. Are you okay?"

I sat down on the steps, my knees suddenly weak. A group of students in the foyer below were staring up, a few beginning to race up the stairs as the accumulated crashes grew louder, more rhythmic. "What's happening? What's happening?" broke out all around us.

Bud Levin appeared. I couldn't see where he had come from. He glanced through where the dust was beginning to settle with the last of the crashing shelves, then turned to wave off the crowding sightseers.

"Go on. Back to work. There's nothing to see here." They grumbled, but began to filter down the stairs. He knelt down beside me. "Professor Cairns, isn't it? Are you all right? What happened in there?"

Before I could answer Ani babbled out her story. The desk clerk, who must have been acting as some sort of interim manager in the weekend absence of the professional librarians, joined us, his face white.

"I warned you," he said, reproachfully. "God, it's a good thing none of the shelvers were working on that floor today. We knew there was danger up here, we said that the floor should be closed until the renovation was finished, but do you think the administration would listen to us? Oh no, we're just students, what do we know?"

Levin ignored him. "Was there anyone else in there?" He had his hand on my arm and shook it slightly, as if waking a sleeping child.

"I thought I might have heard someone come in, but I didn't see anyone. I wasn't there very long."

Ani shook her head rapidly. "I didn't see anyone else. Honest." Her eyes glistened with tears and I realized that she was as shocked as I by what had almost happened.

Two more security guards, one talking into a portable radio, dashed in the library doors and mounted the steps at a run. Levin stood to greet them.

"It's over now," he said. "We'd better check, make sure no one's …" he paused, taking in the open-mouthed girl, the paling face of the clerk.

I pulled myself to my feet. "I'm going back to my office. I have work to do. You know where it is, in the Arts Building. I'll be there until five. Perhaps you can come and tell me what caused all this."

"Those shelving units were way too high, and top heavy," the desk clerk said, his voice loud and vindictive. "All that pounding all week must have loosened something and maybe just the pressure of you walking around, picking books … All it would take is one good shove in the right spot, and over they went."

"I doubt it happened on purpose," Levin growled, "and you'd be wise not to say anything else unless you have proof. There's been enough trouble on this campus for one week. Go back downstairs and ring the closing bell. I think we should clear the building until we get this all straightened out."

The boy opened his mouth to object but one look at the grim set of Levin's face decided him. He hurried back down the stairs.

One of the guards took a white mask from his belt and looped it over his face. He gulped several times, then plunged into the gloom. Through the windows looking out on the stairwell, we could see him circling the room, skirting the spilled books and poking with the powerful beam of a large flashlight into the caves under the downed shelves. There were not as many fallen over as I had assumed from the sound: only the section in which I'd been browsing. I shivered again.

"Are you sure you're all right?" Levin let go of my arm. "Why don't you wait downstairs and I'll escort you to your car. You should go home after this."

I shook my head. "It was an accident. But I think you're right. I'll just pick up my essays and go home. If you don't need me ..."

"I know where to reach you," he said.

The security guard came out of the room, coughing. "No sign of anyone. Nothing but dust in there."

A bell began to chime rhythmically. Dissatisfied, a murmur rose from the students gathered down below, staring up at us. I heard someone say, "asbestos dust," and "danger." The trickle of movement towards the door became a flood.

"Is there asbestos removal going on?" I asked.

"I don't know about that."

I noticed that Levin too had a mask hanging from his belt. He caught my glance at it and grimaced in warning.

"I'll go, then," I said. I had to hold on to the railing all the way down. Ani followed me until we reached the foyer, deserted now of all but a couple of staff members who were methodically turning off computer terminals and lights. She pushed past me and ran out the door. I caught it on the back swing and stepped out into clean air. I stood there on the steps for long minutes, my face raised to the rain.

THIRTEEN

"Asbestos?" Will poured more wine into my glass.

I huddled in the rocking chair, the afghan tucked in tight around me, shivering more from delayed shock than from the cold. Since coming home, I'd had a long hot bath fragrant with scented oil and nearly a whole bottle of wine to myself. I should have been feeling mellow. Instead, my ears still rang with the crash of tumbling books, toppling shelves.

"Levin didn't actually deny it. And he and the other security guards put on face masks before they went through the door."

"But surely, if workmen were removing asbestos, the library would be shut down? It's a closed air building like all the others, isn't it? Once the dust got into the circulation system, it would be everywhere."

"There would be a lot of flak if the administration tried to close the library right now. It's Study Week, remember? A lot of people are working on research papers or preparing for exams. I mean, this is a university: the library is its heart."

"Even so, given the dangers of asbestos, I can't believe any administration would be so cynical as to allow people to wander at will while removal was going on. They'd be liable for all kinds of damage suits."

"If it's asbestos removal that's going on." I sipped the wine, an Australian chardonnay. "I never realized what a rumour mill a campus is. No one seems to know the truth about anything that goes on, and stories get wilder with every telling. Seems to me it would be far better to simply explain what the workmen are doing so that people could make up their own minds about the degree of danger. They're so afraid of criticism that everything becomes a big secret, and that encourages suspicion about motives. For all I know, the workmen could be changing lightbulbs."

"But the shelves did fall," Will pointed out.

"They sure did." I drew my knees up on the seat and wrapped my arms around them, setting the chair into a gentle rock. "I don't understand it. I was just browsing; I wasn't leaning on the shelves, or stamping my feet."

"Could be coincidence. If the first shelf was top heavy, it could have been slowly leaning over until the critical moment came. You just happened to be there."

"I thought I heard someone else come into the stacks. Maybe whoever it was pushed them over by accident. Or on purpose."

"And you complain about other people jumping to conclusions!" Will stood up. "Look, let's have dinner and forget about all this for tonight. Okay?"

Sunday was our day for laundry and housecleaning chores. In the late afternoon, a weak sun filtered through the clouds. We took Sadie down to the river for a walk through the brush along the shore where she chased imaginary rabbits. Geese racketed overhead, arrowing south. Where the river widened into a stretch of still water barely ruffled by the current, a flock of ducks paddled. It was almost like being in the country, as long as we didn't look across the water to the rooftops and church spires of downtown, or pay attention to the whizz of traffic along the other bank.

The change in the weather brought a number of people out to the park, most of them walking dogs or children. Sadie encountered one pal after another, Will and I nodding to their owners. One puppy was determined to play. It was a such a little thing, a short-haired white terrier with black ears and a black ring around its tail, that it seemed to be an entirely different species from our lumbering mutt. It yipped and circled Sadie, bouncing and turning in mid-air, rushing forwards and then tumbling back out of her reach. She soon got bored with the game and lay down to roll in a pile of leaves. The little dog watched her, its head cocked to one side.

"Pi - ip! Pip, Pip, Pip. Here, Pip." A faint call alerted the pup. It looked up for a moment and wagged its stump of tail, but didn't budge from its examination of Sadie, her long legs flapping as she wriggled on her back.

"There you are. " A big woman in a mauve and black jogging suit came out of the thicket of trees behind us. A braided leather leash dangled from one hand. She bent down to clip it to the pup's collar but it took off, racing in mad circles, barking delightedly as Will and I joined the chase. Sadie sat up, and watched, her tongue hanging.

I caught the pup. It wiggled excitedly, licking my face and hands. When its owner came over to claim it, I recognized her.

"Professor Ladurie. What are you doing here?"

Norma Ladurie peered at me. "Oh, Rosalie Cairns. I didn't recognize you. Thanks for the help with this little beast — she's a monster, she is, takes off the moment my back is turned." She hugged the pup who licked her chin with its slip of tongue.

I introduced her to Will. "This is my husband, Will Cairns. And, Will, this is Norma Ladurie, principal of Jamieson Hall."

They shook hands. Sadie ambled over to greet her as well. Norma looked at her in some dismay, clutching the pup so that it squeaked with discomfort.

I took hold of Sadie's collar before she could get too close. "This is Sadie. She's big, but very gentle. She won't hurt your pup."

Norma put Pip down. The puppy began to leap about, half-strangling on its collar. It tired, all of a sudden, and flopped down, its head on its mistress's shoe.

"I just had to get away from campus," Norma confessed. "It's been a terrible week. That poor girl! You knew her, of course."

I nodded.

"And the wee baby? It's all right?"

"She's still in hospital," Will said. "But the CAS has found a family for her. She'll be going to a new home soon. One where she's really wanted."

"Why didn't you tell me before?" I demanded.

He shrugged. "Didn't get a chance. Jack phoned just before you got home yesterday. I meant to tell you, but you were so upset about the library."

"What happened?" Norma's right fist curled protectively over her heart.

I told her my story, ending with, "So are they taking asbestos out of the library?"

"Where do these stories come from?" Norma sighed. "That's not the problem at all. There's something wrong with the air filters on that floor. Well, you've been up there, you know how stuffy it can be. So they have to be replaced. Hugh Ascott is very annoyed."

"Who's he?" Will asked.

"Vice-president of finance. The board's hatchet man for cutting costs."

"So what's the big deal about changing the air filters?" I asked. "Why is it so secret?"

"The new air conditioning system went in only last year at great expense and with a great deal of inconvenience to the library. And now it has to have this major overhaul. Hugh is concerned about how the support staff will take the news of this added expense, given that he's had to insist on across-the-board pay cuts or lay-offs in order to balance the budget; the board won't stand for another increase in the deficit this year. The contract negotiations are going on right now, you know. But rumours about asbestos – that's the last thing we need!"

"I hadn't heard about pay cuts," I said.

"Oh, it won't affect you – you're faculty and you've got the union. Support staff just has an association; they can't strike."

"But that's unfair," I protested. "They shouldn't have to pay for the administration's mistakes."

"It's the way things look, not the way things are," Norma explained. "The contractor has to pay part of the cost of replacement, so the work isn't costing the university all that much. The cuts are more to do with changing priorities, technological advances. With e-mail and computers, we don't need as many secretaries, for instance. But," she continued, "I don't want to talk about all this, if you don't mind. I've been in meetings all weekend, including this morning when I should have been at Mass. I don't mind telling you, I'm sick to death of the whole lot of them." She bit her lip. "I'm sorry. I didn't mean to say that."

"That's all right. It will be a relief when the police get the killer and we can get back to normal."

"If there is anything like normal on a university campus." Norma's lips quirked in a smile.

Thunder rumbled. Sadie's ears went flat, her tail curled between her legs. She whined.

"What a big coward you are," I said to her. "She hates thunderstorms. We'd better get home before she thoroughly disgraces herself. And us."

Norma tugged at the leash in her hand. Pip rose unsteadily, yawning. "I'll see you at the memorial service for Ms. Demetris, of course? And you will keep this conversation confidential? I know I talk too much sometimes."

"Don't worry." I patted her arm. "Mum's the word."

Monday was a perfect fall morning: crisp, blue sky, warm sun, not a cloud to be seen – the perfect beginning of study week. I dawdled over breakfast and the morning paper, and took Sadie for another long walk before biking to campus, luxuriating in the freedom from schedule. A whole week without classes or student appointments and only eight essays left to mark: I could finish them today and then be free to do my own work.

The yellow ribbon was gone from the alley mouth; the pile of flowers and posters had been hauled away. A starling hopped about the lawn in the quad; a blue jay squawked overhead. I chained my bike to a post under the awning over the Arts Tower door, and stood there looking over the campus towards the river, savouring the day. I glanced down the walkway to the library: people were going in and out, seemingly unconcerned. Business was back to usual.

But my corridor in the Arts Tower was unusually silent. The secretary's office was locked. I looked at my watch: nearly noon. Either Irene had taken a day off, for the first time in history, or she had gone off to an early lunch. There were no sounds from any of the other offices either: evidently my colleagues were taking the "break" part of the week seriously.

A phone rang over and over: my phone. I rushed to answer it, dropping my knapsack on the floor in my haste to open the door. Of course, it went silent the moment I had my hand on the receiver. I picked it up anyway, listened to the buzz of disconnection for a moment, then hung up. If it was important, the caller would call back.

I fetched my papers and sat down to the last session of marking. Something felt different, although everything – computer, printer, stacks of books, piles of paper – seemed to be in their usual places. Will often complained about the untidiness of my work spaces and it's true that there wasn't much order evident in the accumulation of files and books that covered my desk. But there was a method of sorts, and I could usually find what I needed with a minimum of searching. I swivelled my chair around to check the shelves and window behind me.

The roses had been removed from the wastepaper basket where I'd thrown them on Saturday and lined up along the sill. Withered petals littered the floor. Three fresh flowers had been added to the bunch.

My good mood evaporated in an instant. This intrusion had gone too far. I fingered the keys which I still held in one hand and stared at the wall separating my office from Alex's. Since the partition had been put up to make the two offices out of one; since the job had been done in a hurry; since Karen had insinuated that Alex's interest in me was more than collegial – I wondered if the key to my door might just fit his. And vice versa.

Before I had a chance to try out my theory, the phone rang again. I picked it up immediately.

"Rosalie?" The voice quivered, thick with tears. It was Lucy Easton, the department chair.

"Lucy, what's the matter? Are your kids all right?"

"It's not them. I'm sorry to bother you, but could you put a notice on the department office door that it will be closed today?"

"Is Irene sick?" She had certainly seemed unwell for the past few days.

"No," Lucy caught her breath in a sob. "She's dead."

I gasped, the phone suddenly slippery in my hand.

"Are you still there?" she asked.

"Yes. What happened?"

"Oh, it's too awful. The poor woman, if only she'd confided in me."

"Tell me, Lucy."

"She killed herself, that's all I know. I've got to go to a meeting with the administration in five minutes; the police will be there. But, Rosie, the worst part is: she was the one who did it, who killed Sophia."

"I don't believe it."

"There was a note. She did it for Frank, to stop the petition."

"I still don't believe it. The petition wasn't enough reason to kill someone. Actions like that come and go; everyone would have forgotten about it by this time next year. Surely she would have realized that."

"You'd think so," Lucy agreed. "But, obviously, she wasn't herself. She must have been in the middle of some kind of breakdown, and I never noticed. How can I forgive myself?"

"It's not your fault," I protested.

"I worked with her every day. I spoke to her about the petition, about how it would affect the students. I don't know, maybe something I said …"

"Stop it," I commanded. "If Irene did this, which I seriously doubt, it had nothing to do with you. If anyone, Frank Stanich is to blame. He used Irene, and not just for typing and filing. She was really in love with him."

"I know. I guess everyone knows. Frank is so obviously on the make I don't know why women keep falling for him. He's so selfish, so self-centred." She paused. "His wife called me. Apparently, the police took him into the station for questioning after they found the note."

"Who found her?"

"Her own mother! She's under doctor's care now. Apparently they always went to church together and when Irene didn't show up, her mother went to her house to fetch her. She had a key and let herself in." Lucy began to cry. "It's all so awful. I can't take much more of this."

"Well, it seems to be over now. *If* Irene confessed to killing Sophia."

Lucy got her voice under control. "You're right. I'm going to have to insist that Frank be relieved from teaching his course this term, maybe that he step down. Whatever influence he had with Irene, he should have realized how unstable she was. And if he knew that she'd done it, he should have said something to the police so that she could have been arrested before she did this to herself." A click on the line interrupted her. "That's another call coming in," she said. "I have to go. Put the notice up, will you? I'll be in later this afternoon. Let's have coffee then."

"Sure thing."

"And Rosie, don't breathe a word of this to anyone, will you? The police have asked us to keep the news confidential until they're finished with their investigation. The administration will be issuing a joint news release with them tonight."

"All right. You take care."

"Yeah." Lucy laughed a little unsteadily and then hung up for her other call.

I used a black marker pen to print a simple *Office Closed Today* message and trudged down the hall to tape it to Irene's door. I stood there for a moment, head bowed, remembering the argument I'd overheard on Saturday. Whatever Irene had done, Frank was equally to blame. I decided to call Finlay and tell him about it. He couldn't use hearsay as evidence, but it might help to lay the case for some sort of action against the Media Studies chair.

I still had my keys in my pocket. I paused outside Alex's door, looking up and down the hall. The only sounds were my own breathing and the faint huff of the air circulation system. I pressed my ear to the panel: silence.

It's not really breaking in, I told myself. I found the right key and pushed it into the lock. It fit. Before I turned it, I looked around again. Why was I so nervous? This was just an experiment to see if our office doors would open with the same key. If not, at least I could stop suspecting Alex of unwanted attention. If so: well, that would give me something to think about.

The key turned. The door opened.

Unlike my room, Alex's was neat, almost obsessively so. He had a better view than I; his office was that much closer to the corner of the building that he could see past Jamieson Hall to a glimpse of the hills on the far side of the river, scarlet with sumach, a colour reflected in the blooms of the roses in a cut glass vase on the windowsill: six of them, identical, I'd swear, to the ones in my own room. Was Alex also the recipient of the mysterious florist's attentions? Or were my suspicions about him correct?

I surveyed the room, my hand still on the door handle. The books on the shelves that filled all available wall space were lined up according to spine size and colour. Two wire baskets on opposite desk corners and aligned with its edges each held a couple of files and a thin sheaf of papers clipped together. Between them, along the outer rim of the desk, were a pen set on a marble stand, a pencil sharpener, a blue jar filled with coloured pens and pencils, a stapler, and a clear acrylic box of paperclips. Sticking out of the green metal wastebasket shoved into a corner was the long rectangle of a florist's box, a sharp white exclamation I echoed in shocked recognition.

I slammed the door shut, not caring if the lock engaged, and flounced back to my own desk. I tried calling Will, but got only his answering machine. "It's Alex," I said. "I found the evidence in his office." I hung up, then immediately redialled. "I'm talking about the roses. I'm going to have it out with him as soon as I see him."

I called Karen, forgetting that for her this was a work week and she would be in class teaching six-year-olds how to read. Lucy's line was busy; Alex's apartment phone rang unanswered. I swept the flowers into my garbage pail, squashing them down. Not content with that and sickened by their reek, I put the can in the hall outside his door. Only then did I begin to calm down. Whatever game Alex was up to with these flowers, the sight of them discarded on his threshold would prove that I couldn't be fooled any more.

"Of all the nerve," I said out loud and smiled to hear in my voice an echo of my mother's. "Just who does he think he is?"

"Who?" As if conjured by my curse, Alex's head appeared around the edge of my half-open door.

"You," I snapped.

He eased into the room. "What do you mean?"

"Don't act the innocent. I know you've been coming into my office and leaving roses for me. What's the idea?"

"Can't you accept a little honest flattery?"

"What's so honest about sneaking into someone's office behind her back? And lying about it?"

"I never said ..."

"You were in here the first day I found one, and all you said was that I must have a secret admirer."

"And you do."

"Give me a break. Besides, I don't like people coming into my office without permission."

"You figured out about the keys, huh?" He grinned and twirled his own key ring around one finger, the metal ringing merrily as the keys slid against each other.

"It's no joke. You were trespassing."

He held up both hands, palm out. "I'm sorry, I'm sorry. If I realized you'd get so upset, I never would have done it. I figured you'd like a little mystery in your life. And it's not like I hurt anything, or touched anything."

"I just don't like it." I swivelled so that my back was to him, then jumped when his hand touched my shoulder. "Don't touch me."

"Okay, okay. I said I'm sorry. I truly am. Can't we forget about it and still be friends?"

He looked so hang-dog that I couldn't help but give way. "All right. But this is the end of this, right? There won't be any more flowers? And you won't come in here unless I invite you?"

He nodded his head in agreement with each question.

"I have work to do." I pointed to the essays. "Did you have something specific you wanted to talk to me about? Or did you just come to see if I'd figured out about the roses yet?"

"I really am sorry." Alex apologized again, this time his voice serious. "But why I came by was," and his voice lightened, "to tell you I was right after all."

I raised an eyebrow.

"About Irene Smith. Haven't you heard?"

"Lucy Easton told me. I'm not sure I believe it."

"What do you mean? She left a note of confession. How can you doubt that?"

"It just doesn't seem the sort of thing she'd do."

"She'd do anything for love, apparently. I bet the cops are giving old Frank a roasting he'll never forget. He won't get out of this one easily. It's one thing to have students revolting about an insensitive course outline; it's quite another to instigate a murder."

"That's going a bit far. Do you think he actually told her to do it? If she did it," I added.

"Sure. He probably said something like, *My life would be so much better if that girl was out of the way,* and she took him literally. I can just see her note: *It was I who killed Sophia Demetris in the alley with a knife.* Just like that game, what's it called, Clue. Then she got into a nice hot bath and slit her wrists. Case closed." He rubbed his hands together.

"But this isn't a game. This is real people we're talking about."

"But you have to agree that I figured it out: method, motive, and opportunity. I'll have a bestseller yet!"

"How do you know so much about it? Lucy said the police were keeping it quiet until after their investigation finished."

"I ran into Bud Levin on the way in here. He told me."

"I would have thought he'd be at the big meeting that Lucy was going to: all the senior administrative types and the police."

Alex snapped his fingers. "Good thing you mentioned that. That's why I'm here to see you. Well, not the only reason why," he mimed a kiss.

"Cut it out, Alex. That's not funny. I don't appreciate it."

"Jeez, don't be so sensitive. Anyway, we've been summoned from on high."

"What are you talking about?" I couldn't keep my irritation with his manner out of my voice.

He grimaced. "What's your problem, Rosie? Okay, maybe I did go a bit overboard putting the roses in your room, but I thought they would spice life up for you, what with all the marking and worry about your student who got killed. I mean, she would have been my supervisee if I wasn't commuting to the city so much."

"I said I forgive you and that's the end of it. No more flowers, and no more talk about them. Agreed?"

"Agreed." He sighed. "But I'm serious about the summons. We've been asked to attend the big meeting of the administrative poohbahs up at Rock Lake. At Harding-Jervase's place. I hear it's fantastic, a cedar-and-glass house built right up on the cliff beside crown land. I've always wanted to see it."

"Will worked on it. Giles had him practically gut the place and begin over again."

"Did he?" Alex grinned, a bit sourly. "It must be perfect then."

I frowned. "Why do they want us at the meeting?"

He shrugged. "I guess because of our connections with Sophia. And maybe because Irene was supposed to be our secretary too. Although I never got a chance to use her much; she was always too preoccupied with department business to bother with my little jobs."

I slapped my palm to my forehead. "I forgot. I was going to call George Finlay."

"The cop? Why?"

"I heard Irene and Frank having an argument on Saturday afternoon. It might help their case to know about it."

"You can tell him up at the lake. He'll be there. Come on, we've got to get going or we'll be late."

I stood up reluctantly. "Why is the meeting up at the lake anyway? Why isn't it being held at President Comaine's house?"

"It's all hush hush, deep cover, Camp David sort of thing. They don't want any of the media who're around to nose out that something's up. It's not that far, half-an-hour or so is all."

"I should call Will," I leaned to pick up the phone. Alex put his hand on mine, holding it down.

"You have to check in with him every time you go anywhere? Now that I call married."

I flushed.

"Besides," Alex went on, "we'll only be a couple of hours. I'll drive you right home to your very doorstep. How would that be?"

I slipped my hand out from under his palm. It was hot and dry, trembling as if with a fever. His eyes were bright too. For the first time I noticed how dark they were, almost black, the iris a thin golden corona. He blinked and I looked away, embarrassed to be caught staring.

"Let's go then."

I noticed as I turned from locking my door to follow Alex to the stairs, that my pail of flowers was no longer in the hall. He'd taken the hint and removed them. I sighed, relieved that all the mysteries that had been plaguing me this week were over.

FOURTEEN

Alex led the way to the far parking lot where he unlocked the door of a green jeep so covered in dust that the rims of rust and the various scratches and dents that pocked its body could scarcely be seen. It was hard to believe that the same man who was so fanatically neat about his office would drive a vehicle that looked scarcely roadworthy.

"Don't you think it's time you started thinking about a new car? Or a wash for this one?"

I folded myself into the front seat. I could feel springs even through the padding of its yellowed sheepskin cover.

In spite of its appearance, the car started immediately and rattled quickly into high gear when Alex turned off the university driveway on to the highway heading north.

"I wouldn't trade in this beauty for anything." He patted the dash. "Besides, living where I do in the city, I'd be nuts to get a new vehicle. I'll drive her till she drops."

"As long as she doesn't drop while I'm in it." I gritted my teeth against the rattling.

A quick survey revealed that the car had neither radio nor tape deck. Alex noticed me looking. He grinned and yelled above the whine of the engine, "We wouldn't be able to hear anything anyway. I'm afraid she's a bit noisy."

I nodded, grimly, and stared out the window as the straggle of bungalows that trailed the highway on the outskirts of town gave way to a solid line of bush intercut here and there by rocky spurs. It was cold in the car too. Evidently, its heater had already given up the ghost.

Alex slowed to turn off on to a paved county road. With one hand on the wheel, he reached into the back seat for a red file folder.

"Why don't you read this on the way?" he suggested. "It'll take your mind off the drive."

"What is it?" I fingered the neatly typed pages, no more than half-a-dozen held together by a red paperclip.

"Read it. Read it. I want to know what you think."

Steps into Darkness by Alexander L. Warren: "Your novel?"

"Just the bare beginnings. You don't mind, do you?"

"Are you sure you want me to look at it now? Wouldn't it be better to wait until you've got a first draft done?"

"I really need the input. I want to be sure that it sounds believable."

I removed the paperclip. Alex kept glancing from my face to the road.

"What do you think about the title?" he suddenly asked.

I read it again. "It's okay. It doesn't really say much though, does it? Shouldn't you have 'murder' or 'death' or something like that in the title so that readers will know what it's about?"

"It's not just a whodunit," Alex objected. "It's more of a psychological profile thing. And what about my name? Do you think I should use a pseudonym? Or just the initials: A.L. Warren? That would de-gender the author, maybe get the feminist crowd hooked. What do you think?"

I laughed. "You're asking the wrong person, Alex. You are who you are. What's wrong with Alex Warren?"

"Doesn't sound serious enough." He caught my grin before I could smother it, and managed a laugh. "Maybe when you've read it the title will make more sense."

I held the paper to the light. Already the sun seemed to be on the decline.

1: HIT AND RUN

Ariane Ramos whistled, not just because she was happy (although she was that) but because she thought it was something a man would do, a man who could walk across this deserted parking lot in the near dark of an August evening without looking over his shoulder. She glanced up at a sodium light as she passed by one of the poles that dotted the tarmac. It flickered a sickly yellow, too dim to attract moths. Higher still, the first stars were beginning to appear in the black matte of a sky still cloudless after three weeks of drought. Ariane was glad she'd finally decided to cut her hair; she loved the cool breath of what wind there was on the back of her neck, the lightness of a scalp free of the rope of braids that her mother had always insisted she wear. Cutting her hair was the latest in the series of steps she'd taken to liberate herself from the expectations of a home in which her parents had talked of grandchildren from the day she herself was born.

Besides, seen from a distance, she believed the short hair made her look less vulnerable than she felt. All her mother's dire predictions about the fate of a girl on her own bubbled up beneath her song. She shook open her denim jacket, thankful for the fan of air on her bare arms. In spite of the heat, she wore the jacket along with jeans and leather boots, all part of the costume she felt was necessary when she knew she would be working late. This end of the campus, separated by the bulk of residences and science labs from the library, student centre and bus stop, was nearly deserted in summer. She knew she should have left with the rest of the gang an hour ago, but she didn't like their spurious camaraderie, the careful listing of complaints about faculty advisors, the gossip that was harmless only on the surface. Now that she and Bobby were no longer dating, she found it too uncomfortable to go drinking with their mutual friends; someone was sure to start talking about Susan who'd moved into Bobby's bed scarcely a week after she herself had left it. Besides, access to the mainframe was so hard to get. And the results of her last series of tests were so promising. One more session and that would be it: her thesis would be in the bag. She grinned, interrupting her song. "So there, Mother," she said out loud. "I am going to be a scientist after all: Dr. Ramos, Ph.D. Even you will have to admit I was right."

A twig cracked with the sudden explosion of a shot. Ariane stopped in mid-stride, her bookbag sliding off her shoulder. She shifted the keys in her right fist so that the sharp shafts poked out between her fingers. She listened. A breeze rustled through the overgrown hedge of cedars that bordered the lot. Something splashed in the river, a carp perhaps or even a beaver. The other bank was a park, left in a near-wilderness state, a dense *black shadow that loomed over the water. She waited, listening: nothing but the faint susurrations of wind and water. She tossed her head, hiked her bag higher, and began to whistle again. She walked with long strides, her boots hitting the pavement with solid, confident steps.*

She heard a car turn into the lot behind her. She hoped it was the security guard, or someone who hadn't realized the road ended here, someone who needed a place to turn around to get back to town or the highway; someone, at any rate, who would ignore her. She kept on marching towards her car, visible now in the shadow under one of the few big maples spared by construction of the science buildings and parking lots. When she arrived early that afternoon, it had seemed a godsend that one of the only shady spots in the lot was free. Now she wished she'd had the foresight to park closer to the footpath to the lab.

She turned as, behind her, a car's transmission ratcheted into higher gear. Why aren't the headlights on? she wondered.

"Look out," she almost yelled, but there wasn't time. There wasn't time for anything but the shock of impact, the stunning fall. I told you so, she thought she heard her mother say, the words fading into the rush of wind and water, the slick of tires hissing in reverse.

My mouth was dry. I licked my lips, looking away from the document and out the window. The trees had closed in even more, a solid line of woods on either side of the road. Every once in a while a clearing offered a glimpse of the lake, a cold blue glare. Thinking about the landscape was far preferable to acknowledging what I held in my hands.

"Well?" Alex glanced at me. "What do you think?"

"It's very graphic. Wasn't Ariane Ramos the graduate student who was killed last summer?"

"Okay, I confess: I'm using true stories here – with a little artistic licence to fill in the blanks!" He grinned. "Don't worry though, I'm well aware of libel chill; I'll change all the names to something else when I'm done."

"But all this stuff about her boyfriend and her mother – you invented all that?"

"Not exactly. My research assistant helped me with that."

"Ani Lyons?"

"None other. She has a friend who was a friend of the deceased. I got her to ask some questions." He frowned at me. "Don't look at me like that, Rosie."

"Like what?" I glanced down again at the manuscript in my hand, rereading a few of the lines. I'd been in that parking lot at night. I knew how deserted it could be. I shivered.

"All purse-lipped and disapproving. It's just a beginning, you know."

"Then maybe I shouldn't be reading it yet." I began to close the file, but Alex's right hand shot out and gripped my wrist. "Ouch. That hurts," I exclaimed.

"Sorry." He loosened his hold, but didn't let go. "I really need you to read it all, Rosie. It's important to me. I want to see if I've been able to get it right, how the women characters think, their feelings and stuff. I'm not too worried about the male characters." He paused. "To tell the truth, I haven't written much from the male point of view yet. You'll see. Anyway, I want to make sure that there's no question in the reader's mind that these are real people, which is pretty difficult when they're only figments of the imagination."

I stared down at his hand until he let go of my wrist, then rubbed at the white marks his fingers had left on my skin. "You don't have to be so rough about it."

"I said I was sorry," he snapped, then softened his tone. "It's just that I'm so anxious about it. This book means the world to me. Well, tenure anyway." He laughed again and I bit back a smile. He caught it out of the corner of his eye. "See, I knew you'd understand. You know about these things, what work writing is, how writers have to struggle to get their facts straight, the characters exactly right, so that what happens is believable. How the writer has to grab hold of experience with both hands and wrestle it into words. It's like sweating blood. You have to take advantage of every moment, every story that you read or hear. Otherwise, it's all empty verbiage, journalism or, as I like to tell my students who keep diaries, *journals-ism*: self-indulgent, poetical crap. You know the old saying: *write what you know*."

"Norman Mailer didn't murder anyone to make *The Executioner's Song* seem real. And what about writers like Dame Agatha herself: you think she actually stumbled over all the bodies she wrote about?"

"You can't call that sort of book real literature," Alex scoffed. "And as for Mailer, he was in the army, he saw death close at hand."

"But surely that's not the same thing?"

Alex's smile was tense. "Look, will you just read the rest of the manuscript? Is that too much to ask, without getting into such specious arguments?"

I looked out the window. The day was beginning to grey into early evening. We were in deep woods now with no sign of lake or cottages. "Where are we?"

"Almost there. Look, just read the book, okay? And be honest with me. I want to know what you really think."

I sighed and flipped open the file, thumbing through the pages to find my place.

2: ACCIDENTAL DROWNING

For Carol Austin, running was both exercise and escape. At home, her route was a circuit of suburban blocks she shared with other silent, single runners. Here, on the campus where her profession was holding its annual conference, she had hoped that John would run with her. He would have liked the series of paved paths that wound past the grey stone residences and glass and concrete teaching buildings. Even more, he would enjoy these trails of wood chips and pine needles that threaded the park on the other side of the river and accessible by a bridge used only by traffic entering and leaving the campus. A chickadee kept pace with her, flitting through the cedars, chattering away, scolding or warning, she didn't know which. Her own breath was loud in her ears.

This wasn't what she intended, this solitary run at dawn, the shadows under the trees grudgingly melting before the onslaught of one more day of heat. For five summers, she'd made her plans so carefully, arranging for her sister and brother-in-law to take care of the twins and convincing Derek to take Brian on a canoe trip in Algonquin Park. "Two men in the woods," she'd said the first time, not completely joking. "You can bond in the wild." It was a tradition now, one that they anticipated almost as eagerly as she looked forward to her own adventure.

And then there was Father. Derek's father, really, but somehow she'd ended up taking care of him. Derek and his sisters assumed that she, a social worker, would know how to deal with a man in the preliminary stages of senility. It was easier treating strangers than listening to old Mac rave on about his children's plots to deprive him of his savings and freedom. She visited him every day, did his laundry, cleaned his house, and cooked his dinner before rushing home to her own family. It was never enough. When she told him she was going away for the weekend and that her friend Nell Green would look in on him in her stead, he accused her of all kinds of sins, infidelity to Derek high on the list.

But this year, there was no fear of that. Or hope, she amended. She burst out of the woods into a clearing. Sunlight glared on rippling green water. A fish jumped and fell back in a widening pool of waves. Two ducks, spying her, swam over to investigate the possibility of food. She slid down the steep slope of the bank but stopped her fall by grabbing hold of a cedar sapling that leaned precariously close to the surface. The bottom dropped so quickly she couldn't see whether it was sand, mud, or rock. She grimaced, and stepped back a pace. Because she'd never learned to swim, she feared the swiftness of the current that swept towards the dams further downstream. Derek had given up trying to persuade her to take lessons. The idea of putting her head underwater, of being unable to see where she was going or what was coming after her ... she shivered, and wiped the sweat off her face with the back of one hand.

Downstream, she could see the arch of the bridge spanning the river. Last night, lying alone on the single bed in her residence room, naked under a starched sheet, she had heard her fellow conferees celebrate the full moon by swimming there, in spite of the notices about the dangerous undertow. She felt as if they were laughing at her, because she had admitted she couldn't swim, because she was so obviously miserable. She deserved their scorn and pity. To be forty years old and the victim of romance: there weren't tears enough to wash away the shame.

She straightened, arching her back, feeling the tug of muscle along her thighs. Yesterday, she'd been so shamelessly eager, expecting John to turn up any minute, looking for her as she looked everywhere for him. She endured the opening night cocktail party as long as possible before approaching a woman she knew was one of his colleagues, a woman whom she suspected knew about their annual fling.

There was no mistaking the glint of understanding in her eyes. "John Longman," she had said. "But didn't anyone tell you? He's been suspended, until after the trial."

"What trial?" Carol demanded. "What are you talking about?"

"I guess it didn't make the papers where you are." The woman took a slow sip of her drink. "He's been charged with molesting minors. Three girls so far have accused him, but they say there are more."

"Girls?" Carol repeated. She placed her glass in the centre of a coaster, inched the coaster to the centre of the bar.

"One was only twelve when it started," the woman put her hand on Carol's arm. "Are you all right? You're very pale."

"Just tired," Carol muttered. "It's been a long day."

The ducks grew bored waiting for her to notice them and paddled away. She leaned back into the tree's embrace, face to the sun, eyes closed. There was no use being angry or disgusted any longer. What hurt most was that he hadn't contacted her, hadn't given her a chance to judge his confession or denial. She ran through the platitudes that she would have used to solace someone else in her position and the sheer uselessness of the rhetoric made her smile at last. It was time to go back. She could pretend that she was needed at home. It wasn't really a lie; she was sure that old Mac would welcome her at least.

Another runner appeared where the path left the woods. Carol tensed for a second, then relaxed.

"You're not thinking about swimming here, are you?" The other was panting slightly as if not used to running, although the jogging shoes were as stained and broken down as Carol's own.

"I don't swim," Carol attempted a laugh. "Never learned how. Silly, isn't it? Especially in weather like this."

"It's dangerous this close to the edge. You could trip."

She shrugged. "I'm leaving in a second. Have to finish my run."

"You're with the conference this weekend?"

"That's right." She let go of the tree trunk, and stretched, arms high above her head, back arched.

The shove was so sudden, so unexpected she didn't realize at first what had happened. Arms windmilling, she toppled towards the river. The toe of one sneaker caught for a moment on a rock, then pulled it loose to follow her in.

She sank, panicking all the way, her mouth open in a scream that bubbled the water, forcing it deeper into her throat. She managed somehow to kick herself up towards the light, breaking through to the surface a few feet out from shore. She could see her killer watching, intent.

She coughed, her arms and legs flapping madly at the current.

"Help me," she screamed once before water again filled her mouth. She sank for the second time. She couldn't touch bottom, there was nothing solid for her to feel, to push against. The undertow played with her, spinning her head over heels, around and down. The last air bubbled out of her lungs, her legs relaxed their feeble kicking. It was dark down there in the river. Dark and cold to the bone.

I stared out the window, rubbing goose bumps from my arms.

"Well?" Alex challenged.

"It's good," I said.

"I can hear a 'but' in your voice," he answered. His lips thinned, his fists clenched on the wheel. "What's the problem?"

"You're using that other campus death, that social worker who drowned."

"So? What's the difference between using her or the Ramos kid? Same principle. When I'm through the writing, no one will guess where the material comes from. I'm going to set the novel in New York, remember? She'll fall in the East River or the Hudson."

"She was pushed." I shivered. "God, that description's so real." Alex was a far better writer than I'd given him credit for. How Canadian that was, to be unable to believe in the talent of one's friends.

"Hey, that's great. It really works!"

"I guess." I caught his frown and hurried on, "I'm not saying it isn't good. I'm just saying it makes me a little uncomfortable, using real people and real situations."

"Just finish reading, okay?" Alex glared out the window.

"It's getting late." I peered out the windscreen to see if I recognized the road from my visit with Will last spring. "Are you sure we're not lost?"

"I know exactly where I'm going." The jeep lurched over a bump, and Alex swore as he shifted gears. "Damn road."

I glanced down at the remaining pages. They seemed to be in point form, a sketch of ideas for the development of the plot, a plot which was not yet clear. The descriptive passages I'd read had a certain power and he'd done a fairly good job with setting up the victims. It was the killer who was missing. "I don't know if I can read this. Why don't I leave it until we get home?"

"You can't do that to me," Alex parodied a child's whine. "You've got to finish it, now you've started it. Please? Pretty please? With sugar on top?"

"Okay, okay."

3: NOTES
Age: *26 (or thereabouts. Must check records. Or the newspaper will have it. Right. Make a note to check the paper.)*

"This is in pretty rough shape. Are you sure you want me to read it?"

"We're almost there. You have time to finish it." The jeep bumped again as it turned into a dirt sideroad.

I grabbed the dash to try to steady myself. "You'll have to slow down then. I can hardly keep the pages steady."

The car slowed. I looked out into woods so overgrown and dotted with stands of cedar and pine as to be almost impenetrable. Yellow leaves swirled in the wind and lay in drifts along the side of the road. "Are you sure you know where we're going? I don't recognize any of this."

"I'm taking the more scenic route. The other road's too busy. Now read!"

I sighed and bent my head to the paper.

Weight: *100 pounds (at a guess. A lot less than me anyway. Smart idea to pick a small one, made it easy. Should this be in metric? Have to find a conversion table. In a cookbook maybe. Think of shopping: 1 kilo is 2.2 pounds. That makes – damn, where's the calculator. Make a note: buy batteries for the calculator.)*
Hair colour: *black. (Or is it dyed. So many dye their hair these days. Dye/die: word play. Can I use this?)*
Eye colour: *should have checked. Too late now. Black hair, probably brown eyes. I could say blue, that would be startling. And would indicate that the hair is dyed. Now, if the hair is dyed, that's evidence of concealment. Yes, this could lead somewhere. This is good!*

Background: *why do we run into each other on campus on this dark afternoon? Maybe there's a lover in the picture; yes, that's it. The wife of one of the professors, a lecturer. Married the day after graduation, now unhappy; met a graduate student; they're having an affair; the partner's found out, is nagging about having a baby: that's it, that'll do to begin with.*
Scene: *alley between the Arts Building and the back wall of the women's residence. What used to be the women's residence before the whole campus went co-ed. Disgusting, kids that age sharing bathrooms and showers. I mean, then they talk about sexual harassment. What do they expect? Girls in those short nighties they wear. Guys, first thing in the morning, of course they're hard, of course they want it. And there it is, just for the taking. Not like when I was an undergrad. Oh no, things were different then. House monitors and dons and such.*

Back to the point: visualize the scene: grey concrete walls on either side absorbing what little sunlight there is. Maybe a few leaves underfoot: golden, red, scarlet = blood, blood-red, yes. Damp cold. Still light enough that the short cut past the refuse bins and recycling canisters seems safe and no one's around, we both stop to check (can't see me, I'm crouched down behind the garbage, good thing I'm not very big). No windows in the high walls on either side, a delivery door halfway along padlocked shut. Feel more than hear the dull throb of music [they call it music. Jungle drums, I call it, rap or rock or whatever, the beat feeding the pump of blood, bodies moving in rhythms they call a dance but it looks to me like upright fucking] in the residence where roommates are getting ready for supper, having showers [with a friend? saving water like they used to say, hah!], the porter has closed the lodge, the custodians have finished for the day. Footsteps on the flags. Stops, looks back. Nothing. (I like this part. Draw it out.) Reaches the fire door at the back of the Arts Building — too late, it's locked, forgot in the hurry that it's always locked at 5:00? Turns to go back and — here I am!
Dialogue: *should there be some dialogue here? I think there were some words, a kind of mumble. People should speak up if they want to be heard. Even a scream wouldn't have done much good though, that alley swallows sounds. I checked. Doesn't matter. Besides, I had the plan, a pear in my hand held out as a gift to confuse the issue. Leans forward to take it, body bending towards me, off-balance, perfect. Right at the end though, I thought I heard "Mama" so I guess it's true what they say, that a dying person always calls out for Mother, though it's too late then. Oh boy.*

Action: *have to think about this. Would it be better to dwell on the details, how I stuffed the fruit in that [stupidly] open mouth; how the cheeks bulged and the eyes widened [why can't I remember their colour?]; pulp on the chin. Wrestled the body around so the back is against me [the delicious wriggle of the bum against my crotch; can't believe how hot I am; does this make me a pervert?]; one of my arms holding down both of the others; ignore the kicking feet, they can't touch ground.*

Now the sounds: chokes and snorts; "snick" of the blade as the knife pops open; tear of cloth; zip of flesh; squish of blood, again and again, a pattering like rain; feet scrabbling on my shins and the pavement as I dropped the body face down; the pear popping out; that word, almost a sigh, "Mama."

Do I need to describe smells: the rich aroma of pooling blood, that stink as the organs let go so that I had to force myself to wait until the fingers stopped twitching. It wouldn't do to leave too soon, in case there's a chance of survival. No. This only works when the act is completed.

How little time it takes to end a life.

Finish: *I shrug off the raincoat I'm wearing [green-and-yellow hardware store mackintosh, like a hundred others on campus, now the sleeves dyed — that word again — red with blood] and let it drop, a shroud, the small corpse barely visible under it. There's blood on my boots too, that's okay, they're standard issue too, bought in Toronto three weeks ago at one of those warehouse outlets and three sizes larger than my own feet so that my running shoes fit in quite neatly. I step back three or four paces away from the mess and shake each one loose, letting them fly wherever. They land with a soft squash, one right against the thigh. Then the gloves, yellow rubber, for keeping skin unsullied by rude household tasks. I peel them off, turning them inside out as I go and drop them in the sports bag I left ready and open at the mouth of the alley when I took my chance and followed [such luck that I happened to be passing just then on the way to the parking lot. Be prepared. The boots and coat wrapped around the knife and gloves in the bag I always carry. It took only a minute to dress. The campus deserted. That throb of drums. Of blood.] The knife goes in the bag too. I've thought a long time about what to do with them, I've read they've got a way to get fingerprints from rubber now. They'll not get mine. I'll go for a run tonight, like I do every night, and no one will notice me pause on the bridge above the dam. No one will see the parcel go over or hear the splash* as the rock-heavy canvas bag hits water. If anyone asks, I'll say I'm throwing stones. People do. It's deep there and the water runs fast. And I've got another sports bag just like this one at home so that I can carry it with me tomorrow and no one will know it's different. Some people complain about the uniformity of products, the lack of choice available no matter what store you go into. One black and red sports bag exactly matches another. Camouflage. Alibi. A lack of evidence. Everything my way.

Timing: 5:30. I step briskly out of the alley without looking back and head directly for the parking lot. I can see a small crowd gathering at the bus stop; they're peering down the road, not looking my way. Just in case, I stop, I snap my fingers, put my hand to my head, and turn back to the Arts Building. The fire door would have locked shut behind me [you can get out, but can't get back in, everyone knows that]. I circle around to the front door, nod at the students who are trickling out of lecture halls and seminar rooms, chatting in the halls, stopping me with a question about the weather, I don't mind, I joke about my flushed face, I swing my sports bag, I've been out running. The offices and reading room are upstairs, I don't need an excuse to wait around, I can say I'm working late if I have to though I'm too excited to work on anything but these notes, getting down the first impressions. I'll flesh it out later. Giggle. Another word play. What a clever person I am ... Hands-on practice: so much more fulfilling than I imagined, so much more **real** than faking accidents, than the arm's length power of a bullet.

    How long before someone finds her?
    How long before the game begins?

FIFTEEN

"Stop the car." My voice shook.

"What? You finished?"

"Stop the car," I repeated. "I think I'm going to be sick."

"Come on, Rosie, the road's not that rough." He let up on the gas a little and the car slowed down. "We're nearly there."

I had one hand over my mouth, while the other scrabbled for the handle. It wouldn't budge. It must have one of those child-lock devices that meant the door could only be opened from the outside.

"Let me out of here," I slammed my fist against the door.

The car shuddered and the engine coughed two or three times before subsiding in a series of strangled ticks.

"What's the problem? Don't you like my story?"

"It's real, isn't it?" I strained as far away from him as the seatbelt would let me get. "You killed Sophia. And the other two."

Alex laughed out loud. "You really believe it, then? It works."

"So it's not true? It's just fiction?" I clung to a small hope.

"Just the parts I didn't make up." He laughed again.

"I don't like this, Alex." I stared out the window: bush all around, thick bush, mostly cedar. I'd been too engrossed in reading to notice that the road had degenerated into a rutted track on the crown of a steep embankment: one of the fire trails that criss-crossed crown land or an abandoned rail line. "Where are we? I thought we were going to Giles' place."

"Later. After you tell me what you think of my work. And after one other step I want to discuss with you."

"What do you mean: step?"

"It's my protagonist. I haven't got him fully worked out yet."

"So I noticed." I tried to find some way to open the window, but the crank had been wrenched off. I fingered the seat belt, trying to loosen the strap without him noticing what I was doing. Being trapped in the car with him was bad enough, but I could at least make myself as free for movement as possible.

He bridled. "That's not a very nice thing to say, Rosie. These are just drafts, steps into the action, so to speak. My hero, you see – can I use the word 'hero'? It's how I think of him."

I nodded. The seatbelt was undone. Now, I needed some sort of weapon for defence. Even while I felt with my foot along the floor and with my right hand under the seat along the door, I told myself how ridiculous I was being. Alex was a colleague and this, although in admittedly unusual circumstances, was just a variation on the many conversations we'd had in the past six weeks about writing and fiction.

"Are you listening?" Alex snapped. "What are you up to?"

"Nothing." I froze. My foot had found something, round and hard, that had rolled deeper under the dash at the first touch. I was trying to edge it back towards me. "Your hero, you were saying?"

Alex glared at me for a moment, then picked up the file from my lap and flipped gently through the pages before closing it. He stroked the cover while he talked. "I'm having some difficulty with him. I've got his motivation down pat: he has this thing about death, a fascination about the way life goes out of a body. I figure that when he was a kid he saw his mother on her deathbed. More than that, he was having a nap with his Mama, she always had a nap in the afternoon, she had a weak heart, and though she knew she shouldn't, she liked to drink, it helped to pass the time when Father was out of town and she was left to take care of the little boy all by herself. She'd give him just a little too, to help him settle down and she'd make him get into bed with her even though he didn't like the way she smelled and she wouldn't let him snuggle with her but put pillows in between them, a soft implacable barrier." He stopped. "Do you like that phrase: implacable barrier?"

"It's all right." I had the object now under my sole. It was about a foot long, one end slightly larger than the other. A flashlight. I wondered how I could get it into my hand without him noticing.

"You don't think it's too poetic?"

"It's fine," I repeated.

He leaned over suddenly and retrieved the flashlight from under my foot. "I wondered where that had got to." He flipped the switch but nothing happened. "Batteries. They always give out when you need them." He flipped it into the back seat. "Now, pay attention, Rosie. I was telling you about this kid. So one day his mother dies right there beside him. He hears the death rattle, he smells the stink when her bowels let go. And then he's stuck there with her for hours, not able to wake her up."

"That's a terrible story."

"A story like all the others," he sighed. "Banal, if it's not told right. And you notice I leave out the Father? Quite deliberately, you understand. All he could do was yell at the boy for not calling an ambulance. I mean, we're talking about a very little boy, here, five years old, and a very dysfunctional family."

"You're right about that," I said, leaning hard against the door in the faint hope that the pressure of my weight would spring the lock. It didn't.

"Are you really interested in this?" Alex leaned towards me again, his eyes narrowed, his hands in fists.

"Of course I am," I babbled, forcing myself to smile, to appear relaxed. "What happens to him? The little boy?"

Alex stared at me for a moment, then settled back into his seat. When he spoke again, his voice had the lilt of someone repeating a familiar story. "He wants to experience death again, but he's been civilized, afraid to trust his animal instincts. He wants to hunt, but he doesn't know how. So he takes it step by step: animals first, mice he traps, and then stray cats, even a dog. He gets caught with that one, and gets sent to a special school to learn how to control these impulses, and for a long time he does, he goes to university, he gets a job, he even gets married and has a couple of kids. Then, somehow, it all starts to go wrong. And he realizes he's got to get back to the hunt, to when he was happy. But he's still a little bit afraid of getting caught so he begins with a hit and run, a drowning. Accidents."

"You followed me to the library." I interrupted. "You pushed the stacks over."

"Couldn't resist. Though I'm glad you got out in time; made this part of the plan feasible. Anyway, back to the story: each step brings him just that much closer …"

"I don't want to hear any more." I rattled the useless door handle. "Let me out right now."

He reached over and fingered a strand of my hair that lay loose on the headrest.

I shuddered. "Don't touch me."

He grimaced and dropped his hand. "Problem is, you see, none of those really satisfies him. He doesn't get to choose his subjects, he has to take advantage of whatever opportunities present themselves. And he doesn't want to be caught, so that when he does get a chance to do some close work, a knifing, he has to set someone else up as a murderer. I haven't written that part yet, but what it'll be is a suicide: he lays a trail pointing his finger at – oh, let's say Irene Smith. She's unstable, she's got a motive. All he has to do is go to her house pretending to have a message from Frank, get her to invite him in for a drink. He's got some chloroform from the science labs, it's not hard if you know where to look. He knocks her out, strips her – that's not a pleasant part, she's terribly old and not very pretty – and puts her in a hot bath. He uses the same knife he used on the girl in the alley to slit her wrists. He even leaves it there for the police to find." He ran out of breath, and grinned at me. "What do you think? Sound plausible?

"I don't want to hear any more." I turned my back on him. "Take me home."

"I didn't bring you all the way out here just to turn around and go home."

"What did you bring me here for? Where are we?"

He unbuckled his seatbelt and slid closer to me, his leg nudging mine. He grabbed my shoulder and pulled me around to face him.

"I still haven't been able to get it right. My hero hasn't, I mean. See, he doesn't like Irene, he doesn't find her attractive. And she's so drugged, that it's hard to tell when the life goes out of her. You see what I mean? You see why I need your help?"

"No. I don't like this game any more, Alex. I don't want to play."

"It's not a question of play." He had both hands on my shoulders now.

I ducked my head as he bent over to kiss me. There was a crack as his chin met my skull. He gasped and let go.

"That wasn't very nice." He rubbed his chin.

"I want out. Right now. I'll scream if you come near me again."

"And who do you think will hear you: the birds and the bees? I need your help, Rosie, for the last step: he's got to kill someone he loves, in the act of love, with his bare hands." He held up his hands.

"Why me?" I hated to hear the whimper in my voice, but couldn't suppress it.

"I suppose I could have used Ani, but she's so transparent. You're a much better character." He lunged at me, his mouth a wet slobber on my face.

"Get off." I elbowed his throat, my knees struggling to pry him off me. One of his hands grabbed my right breast, the other scrabbled at the band of my jeans. What I couldn't do alone, the combined weight of our bodies accomplished: the door sprang open and we tumbled out in a flurry of limbs. We rolled over and over, but he ended up on top, straddling my legs, holding my right hand flat to the ground. My left arm was caught behind my back.

He slapped me hard, an open-handed blow that stopped my struggle for a moment. He took advantage of my shock by ripping open my shirt.

"This part doesn't have to hurt," he panted. He reached down between my legs and pinched hard.

I screamed, wriggling to free my arm and to dislodge him. He hit me again, this time across the breasts. The pain took my breath away.

"Rough or easy, doesn't matter to me." He let go of me to unzip his pants.

I brought up my left leg in a deep bend and kneed him hard in the groin. He shrieked and doubled over, clutching himself. I slid out from under him and without a second look plunged down the slope of the embankment, ignoring the sting of nettles, the pull of spiked vines. Cedars grew thick to the ground on the far side of a ditch whose surface was a carpet of leaves. I went straight through, gasping as icy water soaked me to the knees. Dry cattail stalks clattered as I threw myself through them. Mud sucked at my shoes. The intertwined cedar branches made an impenetrable barrier; I dropped down to my belly and wriggled my way under them, heading away from the road.

"Rosie!" His voice was a mournful cry. "It didn't have to be this way. I didn't mean to hurt you, I got carried away. Come on, Rosie, what's the point in this? Let's forgive and forget and I'll take you home."

He didn't bother waiting for me to answer but floundered down the bank, splashed through the swamp. I dug heels and elbows into the dirt, and crawled, head bent, through the tangle of bare branches that whipped my face no matter how I tried to protect it.

I don't know how long the chase continued through the tangle of trees before Alex called out to me, his voice raw and panting, but too close to give me much hope or comfort.

"Rosie, be reasonable. You can't get away, you might as well give up. The temperature's going down below freezing tonight and it's supposed to snow. If we keep on like this, we'll both be lost, and what's the use of that?"

I lay still so that no rustle of branches or deadfall would give away my position. My face and bared breasts burned from his slaps and the prick of vine and needles. I smelled the sweet pungency of rotting vegetation and my own cold fear. I was surprised he couldn't hear the pounding of my heart.

"I was only joking, you know," he tried again. "I'm a writer; those stories were just fictions. I made them up." A branch snapped loudly and he cursed. I hoped it caught him full in the face.

"No one will believe I wrote those stories or that I let you read them. I'd have to be crazy to do that, and people know me at the university, they trust me there. All I have to do is erase my discs, then there's no proof. I've got no motive, no weapon, I've got alibis ... You don't have a prayer of bringing charges against me or making them stick." He paused for a minute. We both listened to a chickadee scolding us from the tree tops. Alex couldn't stop talking. "Look, this is ridiculous, we're grown-ups, too old to play games. Come on out and let's be friends again. I promise I won't touch you. I've said I'm sorry and I mean it. I didn't want it to be like this between us. Ever since we met, I've wanted you, you must have sensed it. Please, Rosie, I'm apologizing to you. Can't you forgive me?"

I bit my lip and buried my face deeper into the dirt, trying to stifle tears and the little moans of fear that scratched at my throat.

"If that's the way you want it ..." Alex began crashing through the bush, coming closer. I got up on my hands and knees and scuttled faster. There seemed to be less undergrowth now, the forest floor a thin cover of leaves over granite pitted and cracked with deep cuts and caves too small to offer me shelter. I kept my head down and wriggled on until a sudden crash and scream stopped me. I lay still, cheek on a mossy stone, and listened.

"I hope you're happy now," Alex cried out. "I've broken my bloody ankle. Or sprained it. Damn." Another crash as he must have fallen. "I can hardly stand up. It's all your fault. You've got to come and help me."

I said nothing. He continued to curse and thrash about for a few more minutes. Under cover of the noise he made, I chanced getting to my feet and running forward. After only a few paces, I slowed down, afraid that I too might catch my foot in one of the hidden crevices. It felt good to be up on my feet, no longer cowering, although I was still too afraid to stop. I pushed my way between saplings and kept going, gravity helping to pull me down a steep slope further and further away from the road and Alex.

"Rosie?" Alex called. "Can you hear me? Enough of this playing around, okay? Come back and give me a hand. I can hardly walk, I don't know if I can make it back to the car. Please?" He waited, but I said nothing. I leaned my forehead against the rough bark of a big pine whose sweeping branches seemed to reach out to hold me.

"All right then, I'm leaving, you stupid cow," Alex shouted to cover up the pain in his voice. "But don't think you're going to get away with this. You'll never find your way out of these woods without a car. And there are wolves out here, too. Just think of that, think how they'll be out hunting once the moon is up. If you'll just come and help me, I'll take you straight home, I promise."

Yeah, right, I said to myself. I wasn't afraid of wolves. At least, I didn't think I was. Wolves weren't supposed to attack humans. Unless they're hungry, a small voice inside my head insisted. Unless they're really feral dogs, then they'll go after you. I shivered, but didn't move. Better to be lost, but still whole, than to find out what waited for me at his hands.

There was another long pause before Alex finally gave up and stumbled off, cursing and groaning. I hoped every step he took was an agony to him. I almost grinned thinking of him trying to scale the embankment to the car with one useless ankle. The noises he made faded into near silence. Far overhead a small plane buzzed through the sky. I looked around: nothing but trees, rocks, trees.

After a long silence, the car door slammed, a crash of metal that set birds squawking in the trees. The engine coughed into life and ground through a series of changes as Alex forced the jeep through a tight three-point turn. He idled for a moment, perhaps hoping I might give up at the last moment. Fat chance of that. The motor roared once more as he shoved into gear and then diminished as he headed out the way he'd brought me here.

Still I waited, my muscles tense, ready for another desperate crawl if he should come back. Only as the minutes stretched and the birds resumed their usual quarrels did I begin to relax. I curled up, hugging myself, giving into tears. I didn't cry for long. I was cold; not only had crossing the ditch soaked me past my knees but in my terror I'd wet myself. My blouse was ripped along the button band; only two buttons were still in place. I undid them and wrapped the two sides as far around as they'd go, tucking the ends into my waistband. The long sweater I wore over the blouse was meant more for style than warmth, with a v-neck and wide sleeves. I belted it as tightly as I could, but it still gaped open. I crouched in my hiding place, my arms wrapped around my knees, waiting.

My only hope was to get back on to the embankment and follow Alex's car tracks out. That crack he made about wolves must mean that he had taken me into the Crown Game Preserve, thousands of acres of untracked bush with no farms or cottages in any direction. What had I been thinking about to go with him in the first place? Why hadn't I paid more attention to the road, realizing that we'd turned into a fire trail and were no longer on a regular concession? *You stupid, gullible woman. You deserve this, for trusting him. You should have known ...* I dropped my face into my hands. No one deserved this.

A small wind had found its way through the trees and nipped at my neck, my wet ankles. Still I waited. I believed that Alex was capable of parking just out of earshot and returning on foot, hoping to catch me. I swallowed convulsively, so thirsty that I had no room for hunger. I didn't think I could bring myself to drink the ditch water. How far away was the lake? Had we passed over any bridges, any streams?

I looked at my watch, but the tumble down the hill had cracked the glass and stopped it. It was mid-afternoon when Alex came into my office; it must be near suppertime now. Had Will realized yet that I was missing? Would my phone message about the roses make sense to him? And would he guess that Alex had something to do with my disappearance? Would he be able to see through Alex's lies and force him to come and find me?

A wolf howled, a long drawn out ululation that raised the hair on the back of my neck. It sounded nothing like a dog, that primeval call to the hunt. I put my hands over my ears but could not shut out the sound which was answered and echoed by other members of the pack. "They don't hunt humans," I said out loud, but the words were small comfort. Lost in the dark, I was prey to teeth and claws and the fear that shouted at me now to get up and run, in any direction, as long as I could.

I couldn't worry about Alex any longer. I thought that by now he must have headed home so that he could claim ignorance of my whereabouts. He'd need an alibi; the longer he waited in the woods for me to come out, the harder it would be for him to prove he had nothing to do with my disappearance.

The light was waning quickly. If I was to find the embankment and the trail, I'd have to retrace my own path, if I could find it. I got back down on my hands and knees and, facing the direction I thought I'd come from I began to search for signs of my passage through the cedars. It wasn't too difficult. I'd had to follow the line of least resistance to my bulk and left broken branches above me and grooves in the matted leaves and needles on the ground where my knees and hands had scrabbled for purchase. I hurried back as quickly as I could, telling myself that I was following my own route, not a random trail made by some other animal. I came out into the open at the ditch much sooner than I expected. I retreated quickly back under the shelter of the cedars and listened. A trio of crows cawed as they flapped to their nests overhead. That was all.

My passage across the ditch was marked by a break in its mat of leaves. I looked up and down the bank; the ditch didn't seem to get any narrower. I gritted my teeth and plunged back through the icy water, gasping as mud sucked at my shoes and weeds pulled at my ankles. The embankment was a steep slope of massed vines over pebble, marred now where Alex and I had clambered down. I followed his trail back up, finding purchase on larger rocks but unable to avoid the stinging slap of nettles as I pulled my way up past them. At the top, I lay flat, gasping for breath.

A gleam of white drew my eyes: a piece of paper. It must be one of Alex's papers, his novel, his confession. I sat up, steadying myself, then got to my feet. I felt dizzy, but didn't fall even when I bent over to pick it up. It was too dark to read, but the even lines of type confirmed that it was his plot. I folded it carefully and stuck it in the back pocket of my jeans.

Wolf howl.

Fresh tire tracks were clearly visible in the ruts of the trail. I began to follow them, running at first, until a stitch lanced through my side, bringing me to a sudden halt, bent over, gasping. The thin shadows of bare-branched trees were thickening with dusk.

Years ago, in Girl Guides, we'd practiced "Scout's pace": twenty steps running, twenty steps walking, a pace our leaders told us that Indian scouts used to travel many miles, regardless of how tired they were. I counted out loud to give myself a rhythm, but soon had to save my breath. I knew I should let my arms swing, but I was too cold for that. I kept my hands on my elbows tucked into my chest, and my chin down over my bare throat. Soon I noticed how difficult it was to see the tire marks; I needed all my attention to watch out for the roots and deadfall that would trip me. Once I fell, and I wasn't sure I'd be able to get up again.

At least the wolves had stopped howling. My feet thudded on the hard-packed dirt, my breath whistled. The track I was on ended at a T-junction; the road curved out of sight in both directions, eerily silver in the starlight. To my left it seemed in slightly better condition, as if what traffic did come this way – hikers and hunters – had worn down the gravelled surface. I turned that way, stepping out right into the middle where I paused to listen for traffic, a dog, any sign of human life. I put my head back and looked up to the sky.

Lights shimmered across the arc of the horizon in green, pink, and white waves that surged and faded to a music I could almost feel singing in my blood. Their dance crackled and pulsed in curtains of colours that wove into and around each other, almost disappearing in one spot only to burst out in a fanfare of energy in another.

I would have stood there, entranced, for much longer but out here, on the wider road, the wind found me too. I shivered and began to jog again, my head tilted to catch the show overhead, a distraction from the cramp of thirst and the strain on my leg muscles.

The road divided again, and this time, without really thinking about it, I followed the oiled surface. I couldn't run any longer, but stumbled along, my arms held out for balance. I was so thirsty that I picked a pebble off the verge, rubbed it on my sleeve and sucked on it, remembering some story I'd read long ago about the survival tricks of native scouts in the wilderness. It only made my thirst worse.

So engrossed was I with the effort to keep moving upright and forward that I almost passed the farm gate before I saw the light. I stopped, swaying, in the middle of the road. Barking began: the high-pitched warning of a small dog, nothing as big or fearsome as a wolf. I pushed open the gate and stumbled up the drive. Above me, the lights rolled in one long wave, and went out.

With a clank of chains, the dog rushed at me from the darkness under a hedge of lilacs, leafless but still thick enough to hide the box shape of its kennel. I jumped back and hit something with my foot, something that clapped shut with the clank of steel teeth. I peered into the shadow, trying to ignore the dog which, hopping on its hind legs, was choking itself in its passion to reach me.

Light poured onto the drive from an open doorway.

"Shaddup," an old voice commanded. "Who's out there?"

Blinded by the glare, I looked down at my feet. My stumble away from the dog had triggered a leg-hold trap – one more step and it would have closed on my shin. I swallowed bile.

"Who are you?" the voice demanded. "Don't you try nothing. I got a gun."

"Please." I raised my hands. "I need a phone."

"Is that a girl? All alone out there?" An old woman tottered down the steps towards me. I fell into her arms, into the warmth of yeast and ivory snow, the fresh bread scent of old flannel lovingly and often washed. Her grey hair was tied back in a long braid that hung over the shoulder of her sprigged nightgown. Under it she was layered in so many clothes I felt as if I were being hugged by a pillow.

The man following her down the steps looked as if he too had just gotten out of bed, his thin white hair sticking out over large red ears, his eyes blinking continuously in harmony with a tic that twitched at the corner of his mouth. He'd dressed in a hurry: one suspender hung loose, the other held up a pair of worn corduroy pants over a striped nightshirt. He picked up a long stick from the grass and used it to whip the dog into grovelling whines.

"Don't," I said, but the woman hushed me.

"We think it's got rabies," she said. "It don't matter."

Her husband left the whimpering animal and stumped over to us. "Where's your car? I didn't hear no car."

"I don't have one," I said, struggling to keep from crying. "I was lost in the woods." I shrugged off the woman's comforting arm. "I need to use your phone. It's an emergency."

"Emergency." The old man spat a thick wad of something into the grass. "You get yourself into an *emergency*, you just get yourself out of it."

"Don't pay no attention to him," his wife said. She put her arm around me again. I let her lead me towards the door. "You come in and sit down a spell. You look like you could use something to eat. Dougal, you find yourself some manners, now." The old man grunted, but said nothing as he followed us into the kitchen. Lit only by an oil lamp centred in the middle of a worn wood table, the room was dominated by a huge white ceramic woodstove on which a kettle gently steamed. The room smelled of bread rising. My stomach growled.

"I need a phone," I said again. I looked around: other than the table with its two high-backed chairs and a rocking chair close by the stove, the room held only a hutch containing an odd assortment of plates and glasses and a green hand pump attached to the side of a wide tin sink. There were no pictures, no phone, no radio, not even a clock.

"We ain't got a phone, do we, Daphne?" Dougal grinned and spat a wad of brown juice into an open ring on the stove. The fire hissed. "Only can get a party line out here and we don't want no one listening in on our business. All them nosy parkers up and down the line." He snorted.

"A car, then? Is there a store nearby, someplace with a phone you can take me to?"

"Ain't got a car neither. Not one that works, anyhow. Unless you got a tank of gas out on the road there with you?"

"I told you I'm alone, on foot," I snapped. "What's wrong with you? Can't you see I need help here? There's a man out there killing people and he's got to be stopped. I have to get a phone, I have to call the police." My voice rose.

"There, there, don't take on so," Daphne put her hands on my shoulders and pushed me gently down into the rocking chair. "Let me get you a cup of tea."

I stood right back up, though my legs were trembling. "I don't want tea. If you can't help me, you can at least tell me how to find someone who will. There must be other people on this road, people with phones and cars."

"That's right, dear." Daphne poured steaming water into a cup and dropped in a handful of loose leaves. "Dougal, you go on down the road to the Prince's place. You tell Ed Prince to get himself up here with that fancy new jeep of his, take this lady into town. Get a move on, now."

The old man spat again. "Crazy time of night to be going out," he complained.

Daphne put her hands on her hips and stared him down. "I don't want to have to tell you twice," she threatened.

"Goddamn women," Dougal muttered. He shrugged into a stiff black jacket and pulled a cap out of its pocket which he jammed down over his hair, picked up his gun, and stamped out the door.

"How far does he have to go?" I asked. "Maybe I should go with him."

"Don't be silly. It's nearly a mile down to the crossroads and you don't look like you could make it to the end of the drive. Don't worry none. Dougal's not as old or slow as he looks, he'll be back in a jiffy.

You want something to go with this tea, now? I got bread, some cheese."

"No thanks." The thin china cup was warm in my hands, the tea a deep red colour.

"Sumach tea," Daphne said. "Good for what ails you. Now just wait a minute, here." She pushed open a door and disappeared into what might have been the only other room in the house, returning a moment later with a red wool blanket, a faded green sweater and black polyester pants. "You'll want to have a wash. And these clothes'll fit you, I think. They don't maybe look much, but they're clean."

Without waiting for me to answer, she fetched a tin bowl from a hook above the sink and filled it with water from the kettle. She handed me a thick bar of yellow soap and a soft blue washcloth. "I'll just go get a towel," she said. "You'll feel better once you get some of that dirt off you."

She was right. Although the soap stung the myriad scratches and scrapes on my chest, arms and face, the hot water soothed my bruises. The small act of cleaning off the mud helped to calm my fears, quiet my racing pulse. I stripped off my filthy clothes and pulled on the sweater and pants. "I'll need a belt," I said to Daphne. She looked at me and giggled.

"You are a sight," she said. I winked back tears. "There, now, don't take on. I meant it kindly." She rooted through a box of odds and ends under the table. "Here's a length of rope'll do you. Just tie that on round you and then wrap yourself up in that blanket. I got some new tea steeping here." She picked up my jeans and blouse, her nose wrinkling. "I don't imagine you want these any more, they look pretty far gone. I'll just go put them out in the 'cinerator, won't be but a moment."

As I was knotting the rope around my waist, the dog began howling again in the yard. "Shut up," Daphne yelled. She opened the door. "That's Ed Prince's jeep coming. I told you Dougal'd fetch 'em for you."

I was already out on the porch waiting for the car to stop. Dougal got out first, a woman nearly pushing him flat in her hurry to greet me. "You're Professor Cairns, aren't you?" she called out. "I just knew you had to be when Dougal here came along with some story of finding a woman in the woods. It's all over the radio, you being missing and all. Are you all right?"

Before I could answer, Daphne did. "She's had a wash and a cup of tea. Needs her own home and her own bed, she does. This is Sarah Prince, my neighbour. And that's her husband Ed in the jeep."

Sarah pumped my hand. "I'm so glad you're all right. Your husband's been on the radio and the cops too, asking for news of you." She tilted her head back to give me a long look. "That's not the clothes you were wearing?"

"I give her some of mine," Daphne said. "She'll be fine."

"Did you call the police?" I demanded.

Sarah put her arm around me, urging me down the steps. "Now you know, we'll do that as soon as we get you home. We just wanted to check …"

"Didn't believe me," Dougal chortled. "Think I'm addled. I know a thing or two, I do."

"I have to talk to the police," I said.

"Sure, sure."

"Thing is," said the driver of the car, a man who had never gotten out of his seat, but who leaned out the window, a cigarette drooping from one corner of his mouth, "would be faster to drive her down to town ourselves, rather than wait for the cops to get up here. What say?"

"Please," I begged.

"Hop in, then. You want me to drop you off at the house, Sarah?"

"We'll just tell the kids where we're going, make sure the little ones are in bed. Oh, this is so exciting." She opened the rear door. "You bed down back here. I got a quilt there, just in case. I said to Ed, we'd better bring a blanket."

I paused, halfway into the car. "Thank you, Daphne, for the clothes and the tea."

Daphne flapped her hand. "Now then, don't be getting all foolish. You come back and visit, you hear?"

"Huh," Dougal grunted. He stomped into the house.

Ed turned the car and headed down the lane. I looked back. Daphne stood in the light from the still open door, waving her hand in farewell.

SIXTEEN

I lay full-length on the back seat, the quilt wrapped tight around me. Even when the car stopped for a moment at their house and Ed got out to speak to his children, I didn't move. I was tired to the bone, more tired than I'd ever imagined it was possible for a person to be. Sarah tried to start a conversation, asking how I ended up lost in the woods. I couldn't answer.

"Leave her alone, Sarah. The woman's exhausted." Ed fumbled with the radio. Jazz filled the car, the aching wail of a saxophone. I let myself drift on its melodies.

The opening of the car door jolted me awake.

"Are you all right, Rosie?" Will nearly flung himself inside, his hands reaching for me. I grabbed hold of him, snuffling in the warm wood scent his clothes always carried.

"What happened, Mrs. Cairns?" Finlay was right behind, leaning in over the front seat. I could hear Sarah Prince chattering away to someone on the sidewalk, explaining where and how they had found me.

"Have you got Alex?" I said. I pushed away from Will, though I kept his hand in mine.

"Alex Warren? No."

"He's the one who did it," I said. "He killed all of them, the girl in the parking lot, and the woman in the river. Sophia and Irene. He tried to kill me too." I fished with my free hand in my pocket for the paper. "This should tell you some of it. He made me read it all." I shuddered.

Flashbulbs popped in the rear window and several voices started shouting out questions.

"Why don't we go inside?" Quinn suggested. She reached past Will to take the paper.

"Alex is out looking for you," Will said.

"I bet he is." I blinked in the glare of camera lights. Quinn was trying to persuade the reporters to leave me alone. I clutched the quilt like a giant shawl tighter around me, and stumbled up the steps into the building.

"Professor Cairns," Ani's voice rose above the others. "Are you all right?"

I tried to see her in the crowd, but couldn't. I simply nodded and let Will lead me into the relative peace of the station.

The one page I'd brought back was the description of the scene in the alley prior to Sophia's murder. Combined with my story of the attempted rape and threatened murder, it was enough to arrest Alex.

Will wanted me to come home while Finlay was out with the prowl cars but I was too keyed up to leave. Quinn wanted me to go the hospital, but I refused that too. I wouldn't be able to relax until I knew for sure that Alex was in custody.

The problem was, they couldn't find him. He'd appeared at President Comaine's office late for the meeting, but claimed to have had car trouble, something everyone who saw his vehicle could believe. When Will started calling round looking for me, he volunteered to join the search.

We waited nearly two hours before Finlay returned. He stamped back into the office, his face twisted with frustration. "Damn reporters," he growled. "It was all over the news that you were rescued. Warren must have heard it, and taken off. We've got an all-points out for him, but it may take some time. If he's headed south …" He shrugged.

"You should talk to Ani Lyons," I suggested. "She's his teaching assistant. She might have some idea where he's headed."

"The girl reporter?" Quinn asked.

I nodded, and she left the room.

"Can we go now, Rosie?" Will said. "There's no point in waiting here any longer."

"Mrs. Cairns," Finlay called as we reached the door. "I'm glad you're all right. Now don't take this the wrong way, but see if you can keep out of trouble for a little while, okay?"

I grinned, a little weakly, and let Will take me home.

The search for Alex Warren and the story of my escape made good copy for the news media. Sarah Prince was only too happy to be interviewed and photographed with her children posed around her. The Faircloughs were another story. When the camera crews found their way to their farm, it was locked tight, the dog dead on its chain. Ed Prince, who'd led the way to his neighbour's farm, was filmed standing in the yard.

"They don't care much for company," he drawled. "They're probably just back in the woods somewhere, got the gun trained on us right now." He waved and shouted, "Hiya Dougal. How's it going?"

It made great television.

The campus returned to what passed for normal. After the Demetris memorial and my recovery, a scandal broke out over the way the administration contracted the job that led to the "sick building" problem in the library. Clearly, someone had slipped up on checking the qualifications of the company with the lowest bid – a bid so low, some claimed, that they should have realized something was amiss and not let money outweigh safety. While that story simmered, erupting in outbursts over salary and job cutbacks, no one took much notice when Frank Stanich resigned "for reasons of health" from the chair of the Media Studies program. After Irene's death, as Alex had predicted, he couldn't stay in a position of authority any longer.

Ani Lyons got a job on one of the city newspapers and dropped out of the graduate program. I finished my thesis and defended it. In June's Convocation, I became Dr. Cairns. Not that it did me much good: Isaac Pleasant returned from the south of France with a thick manuscript and a deep tan. I spent the summer at the cottage, revising my thesis into a book for publication by a small academic press.

Jack Lansdown dropped by Will's shop to assure him that Mara was happy in her new home on a farm south of town. None of us heard from Sophia's cousin Rita Petrie or the Locks. Although Quinn argued for pressing charges of incest, without the one witness who could convict him, John Demetris was never forced to face up to what he'd done. I saw Mary-Ellen Demetris's obituary in the Toronto weekend paper; she survived her daughter by only six weeks.

In September, an American publisher trumpetted the publication of *One Step, Two Steps: The Education of a Killer*, by Ani Lyons. Called "a non-fiction novelization," the story chronicled a man's descent into madness and murder, a man who wanted to capture the ultimate meaning of life by witnessing death. He began with cats and rodents, and managed to hide his hobby until the break-up of his marriage provoked a mid-life crisis which induced him to experiment with human subjects. Part of the fuss created over the book centred on the fact that the young author had signed all royalties over to the children of two of the Trillium victims, Mara née Demetris, and Carol Austen's sons.

In excerpts printed in *Saturday Night* and *Vanity Fair*, I recognized passages that could only have come from Alex's red file. I tried contacting Ani through her publisher, but she didn't reply to any of my letters.

I took a copy of the book to show George Finlay. "What do you think?" I asked him. "Did she get this from Alex?"

He didn't reply, but leaned back in his chair, drumming his fingers on the cover. "I've already read this. Ms. Lyons brought me the manuscript."

"You never told me."

"No reason to think she'd ever get it published, a first book by an unknown writer. She wanted to know if it was ethical to use the material he'd left with her. Well, who's to say where it came from? It was on a disc, no signature, no handwriting, no identification except her word, and yours, that Warren wrote it. I told her that, as long as he didn't benefit from the book, I didn't see why it wasn't hers to do with as she wanted."

"But all this detail," I protested. "There's even a rape killing in the woods, just like what he tried to do to me. How could she know about all that if she didn't get it from him? I certainly never talked to her about it."

"She says she made it up from what did appear in the papers. She got those farmers – what was their name? Prince? – to take her out to the site where it happened. And then she exaggerated quite a bit. In the book, he kills you."

I shivered. "That's not funny."

Finlay agreed, "I know. But there's nothing much we can do about it. She's got the right to write what she wants."

"It doesn't seem fair."

He shrugged. "She's promised me if he ever contacts her, she'll let me know. There's no limitations on warrants for murder. He'll make a mistake and we'll get him. You'll see."

I had to be content with that.

One Step, Two Steps was wildly successful, going through three printings in its first season, adopted by several book clubs, and translated into six languages. Hollywood optioned the screenplay and hired Ani to write it.

So Alex Warren, wherever he was, had his bestseller in the end.